Ghost Platoon

JOHN C CAMPBELL

DEDICATION

I dedicate this book to any brave soul who not only sees an injustice but has the courage to do something about it.

ACKNOWLEDGMENTS

Acknowledgement to my wife for countless hours editing my characters who were often in two places at once! I would also like to acknowledge my editors Beth Butler and Ellen Brock

CHAPTER 1

April 13, 2012, Camp Rock, Southwest Afghanistan

"I ought to call you Diesel," Colonel Pitts said. The desert cat made goofy faces, stretching her neck and pressing her chin into his thick fingers. He closed his eyes, sleep tempting him. "All right, angel, let me stretch my legs and get some coffee." He cupped the gracile creature's chest and set her four paws on the dusty planks. She scampered under his desk, crawling into her hiding spot. Colonel Pitts gripped his cane and rose from the La-Z-Boy recliner. The first step hurt. "Damn hip!" The pain was from an anti-aircraft round. He recalled the 1969 mission over Hanoi. THRAAAK! The round hit the F-4's belly, passing through the ballistic tub, splintering his femur. He limped, leaning on the wooden cane as he walked to the long folding table at the back of the domed metal building. The tabletop was covered with a blue silk cloth from one of the Pashtun vendors at the bazaar. An old coffee maker, cups and condiments were scattered over the top. He poured the steaming liquid into the small foam cup and placed the pot back on its burner. He savored the aroma of the Colombian coffee and took a sip, the pleasant flavor

1

coating his tongue. "Ah, that's more like it," he said, moving easier now, ambling back without the cane. He set the cup on the improvised end table of stacked ammo boxes and eased back into the cloth recliner. Cleopatra trotted up, jumping back into his lap. Her crossed blue eyes stared at him inquisitively. He stroked her delicate head. "Today is our day, dear. Everything has finally come together." He scratched her favorite place under the chin. "By tomorrow I will be rich." He reached for the cup. BOOM! He flinched, spilling the scalding liquid down his crotch. Pain shot from his leg as Cleopatra launched off his lap, skittering under the desk. BOOM, BOOM, BOOM. A string of the massive detonations emanated from east of Camp Rock. His gut wrenched. Major Roberts is twenty miles to the east, right where those are coming from. He hopped up, hurrying to his desk and grabbing the black box. "Alpha Zulu, this is Zero-nine. State your situation, over." He paused. "Alpha Zulu, come in." Please pick up…let me know the shipment is okay. "Alpha Zulu, this is Zero-Nine come in, over." The hairs on the nape of his neck rose. "Major, are you okay? If you can't talk, key your radio." Motherfucker! Somebody's after my goddamn heroin. He threw the cane down and walked to the electronic display. A satellite message had been sent from that area but no radio messages. Those stupid sumbitches better not have used a satellite phone. He kicked open the flimsy door, hobbling down the cinderblock steps to the flat desert. He put his hand over his brow and peered to the east, his stomach roiling with nausea. Far out on the horizon, a single tendril of black smoke curled in the air. He followed the pigtail pattern to a black speck. WOP, WOP, WOP. It was the familiar resonance of the Cobra. As it came closer, the profile of the damaged helicopter came into focus. Colonel Pitts's mouth fell open. "That can't be!" He put his fingers in his ears as the wounded gunship flew over. The tail rotor and six feet of the rear boom were obscured by billowing black smoke. The Cobra disappeared behind the large aircraft hangar that stood between his office and the airstrip. Crackle. It was the radio in the office. Major Roberts! He ignored the pain in his hip, trotting back up the two steps. He took a deep breath and grabbed the radio. "I'm here. Go ahead, Major."

"We've been fucking ambushed! Only a few of us are still alive and I'm hurt. We're heading back in two Humvees. Get the medics ready!"

"I heard the explosions here at the base, but they've stopped."

"Ten-four, when we made it back to the Humvees, I tripped the GPS jammer and their mortars stopped."

"Mortars? Who attacked you?"

"I have no idea, but they're armed to the teeth. I don't know where they came from. We cleared the pass but when we came back through with the goods, they killed us."

Colonel Pitts's eyelids fluttered as the adrenaline hit. "What about the packages? You still have them, right?"

"I'm sorry, boss, but they're scattered all over the floor of that pass along with what's left of my men. I'm lucky to be alive, had my helmet blown off, even lost my goddamn Yankees cap."

Colonel Pitts doubled over. "Major Roberts, that's millions of dollars' worth of heroin and you're worried about a fucking ball cap? You have to turn around and go back!"

"With what?! I have nothing left to counterattack with!" Major Roberts hung up.

Colonel Pitts wobbled on his feet, reaching out for the desk edge. Goddamn these fucking pussies! They have a red carpet to walk in on, and they still fuck it up. He kicked the metal door open and stumbled down the steps. His legs were wooden, his gait unsteady, and the chilly desert air unwelcome. He shivered, dizziness and fear setting in as he walked out to catch sight of the returning Humvees. He buttoned his peacoat as he moved clear of the visual obstruction of a small stone jailhouse and focused on the chain-link perimeter fence on the eastern edge of the camp. He followed it along the desert floor until it veered ninety degrees to the left all the way to the northern gate. Three dirt roads converged near the entrance. He strained his eyes. Nothing. I double-checked that no ISAF forces were in the vicinity and General Syed keeps a tight grip on his side of the border. He's not going to let anyone fuck with the shipments on his side. They must have come from our side! His thoughts went to his partner. Major Roberts was a wolf, cunning, brutal and efficient. How had he overlooked the attackers? A crushing pain, like an elephant standing on his chest, doubled him over. The angina was getting worse, now radiating to his arms and neck. He crammed his hand in his pants pocket, sliding the tips of his fingers along the bottom seam to the small glass vial. He pulled it free, his thick fingers fumbling with the tiny steel top. He tapped two of the small white nitroglycerin tablets out into his hand then popped them under his tongue. The pain subsided as the drug relaxed the smooth muscle of his coronary arteries. He pushed the vial back into his pocket, turning back to the north gate. A large rooster tail of dust approached. A Humvee sped through the checkpoint, engine wailing as the vehicle hurtled toward him. The machine carved gouges in the gravel as it slid to a stop in front of the office. Colonel Pitts limped over, waving the dust away as he examined the men being offloaded. Major Roberts wasn't among the three wounded. A bloodied young soldier sat, hugging his legs, gripped in rigors. Colonel Pitts removed his own peacoat and wrapped it around the boyish private. "Where's your commander, soldier?"

The young man looked up, only a tiny rim of green visible around the pupils. He turned his head, eyes rolling toward the east. "He's behind us."

Colonel Pitts squeezed his shoulder. "It's okay. You're safe now. What did you see, son?"

The soldier's eyes bounced around. "We couldn't see them. It was horrible. There was no one to fight." His face was streaked with runners of salt. "They must have been hidden up in the face of the pass. It was impossible to tell where the fire was coming from and the blast waves in that narrow canyon .... I don't know how we made it out."

WHAAAA. The wailing sound of an engine outside of the base drew Colonel Pitts's attention. A huge cloud of dust trailed the second Humvee as it bounced through the northern gate. The truck slid up, showering him with dust and gravel. Colonel Pitts held his breath, eyes searching the truck until they fell on Major Roberts. He was a tall, muscular man at the tail end of his youth. His handsomeness was sullied by a thick scar running diagonally across his face. It stretched from the forehead, across his right eye, nose, and lips to the undersurface of his chin. Major Robert's weary brown eyes met his. "I'm sorry. I gave it everything I had."

Colonel Pitts rubbed the back of his neck. "We have to do something quick. If General Smith at Camp Leatherneck comes poking around that pass, we're finished." Colonel Pitts softened his tone. "Are you going to be okay?"

"Yeah, I'll be fine."

Colonel Pitts turned and walked toward the structure. "Come into my office." He walked up the stairs, holding the door open. Major Roberts limped in and sat on a small couch by the door. Colonel Pitts crossed his arms, staring down at him. "Well? What do you have to say for yourself?"

The scar twisted like a snake with the movement of his mouth. "I took a piece of shrapnel to the hip, and my ears are bleeding."

Colonel Pitts rolled his eyes. "Major, what I really want to know is how you, of all people, would allow some no-name bandits to steal our retirement. Jesus Christ, you had your crew, sixty Afghans, and an attack helicopter, and you still managed to let some no-name lowlifes take our retirement and fuck our future in the ass!" He jabbed a thumb into his sternum. "Look at me! I'm a crippled old man. I can't do this myself. You're the enforcer. That's the deal!" His inner brows rose. "How in the flying fuck could you let them sneak up on you?"

Major Roberts began in his Tennessee drawl. "I, I …," He shrugged his shoulders. "I have no fucking idea. I've been thinking about it nonstop. I cleared the pass before the couriers went through, just like we always have. The Cobra went in with the thermal optics, and I followed with the men. Four of us went up the east face, the other four up the west side. We looked through every nook and cranny we could find. What we couldn't search, we tossed grenades into. It took us two hours to get to the border, then we worked our way back down. We joined the caravan on the Afghan side and led them in. I had no idea anything was wrong until we got a kilometer in." His eyes narrowed. "We came across four tribesmen burning a campfire. They turned on us and engaged us with RPGs and machine guns. We took those fuckers out with grenades." SMACK! He drove a closed fist into his hand. "Like that, the whole world opened up on us. We were sitting ducks in that canyon. There was no cover and those blast waves tore through like a ripsaw. Some of the men tried to climb out but it was too steep." He put his fist to his mouth and coughed. "Dust was so thick I couldn't do much of anything. We might as well have been at the end of an airstrike or an artillery barrage. I was lucky to even make it back out. When I got to the Humvee, I tripped the GPS jammers." He snapped his fingers. "Like that … silence. I caught a glimpse of one of them as we were running for the open desert." He ran his hands over his head. "He wore a sci-fi-like helmet that came down low on the back of the neck with a large visor covering most of his upper face. I've never seen anything like it. Their guns sounded like 81mm mortars, but the rounds were too powerful. They may have been 120 mms."

Colonel Pitts's eyebrows scrunched together. "What the fuck happened to the gunship?"

Major Roberts licked his lips. "The pilot must have seen one of their positions. They caught him in a narrow channel with some heavy machine guns hidden in a high cave. Tracer rounds chewed the shit out of the ass end of it." He put his arms around himself and shivered. "Those bastards must have been there when we scouted the pass. They were watching me the whole fucking time."

Goosebumps rippled across Colonel Pitts's skin. "I monitored every frequency on every communication device within a hundred miles. There wasn't a peep of any NATO activity. Hold on!" He raised a finger, eyes twinkling. "I picked up a satellite transmission before you turned on the jammers. I thought it was you. The coordinates match the mouth of pass." He sniffed the air, nostrils flaring. "That's where they're holed up!"

Major Roberts rubbed his chin. "Who would be dumb enough to broadcast their position like that? Could it be Mullah Mehsud? He hates you for charging him to move his goods through that godforsaken little crack."

Colonel Pitts scoffed. "That's quite a step up for that serpent. Besides, Mullah Mehsud knows what would happen if he were to tangle with General Syed." He chewed his lip. "It's someone who knows more about this land than we do." He locked eyes with Major Roberts. "Six of you made it back?"

Major Roberts frowned. "Six – out of all of those men."

Colonel Pitts ran his hands over his bald head. "People dying. This is bad, real bad. When General Smith finds out, he's going to come back here again to settle his score with me. When he finds the drugs with dead personnel from Camp Rock ...," He made a motion of shooting a pistol at his own head. "There's too much evidence leading back to us." He paced back and forth. "Either we get back in there and sterilize that pass or General Smith finally gets to bend me over and fuck me in the ass."

Major Roberts's eyes grew enormous. "Sterilize the pass?

CHAPTER 2

"How are we going to sterilize that pass?!" Major Roberts exclaimed. "What am I going to go back with? I have three, maybe four men that can still fight. I'd need heavy weapons and a battalion of men to flush those guys out. Besides, we don't know exactly where they are. There's no guarantee that satellite signal was them."

"Jesus Christ! Don't be so goddamn dense. Who else could it be?"

"You don't understand, Colonel. They're dug in. You could bomb the whole damn pass and never muss their hair. They've also got heavy fuckin' weapons and they know how to use them. If we go back in there, they'll kill every goddamn one of us!"

Colonel Pitts bit his upper lip. "Hmmm." He picked up the phone and dialed the hangar. "Louie, listen to me and listen good. Contact General Syed. Tell him our chopper is damaged and we're going to need him to authorize another flatbed truck to come over the border. When you've done that, get the BLU-96 on the Harrier! Yes! The big one, put it on the Harrier. Damn it, Louie, let me worry about that. Just do what you're told. Have that jet ready in twenty minutes!" A macabre grin came over his face as he regarded Major Roberts. "I told you that monster would come in handy someday."

"You can't be serious! That's a two thousand-pound thermobaric warhead. Every seismic sensor in the Eastern Hemisphere will detect it. General Smith will be up our ass in no time."

"Who cares? It will incinerate everything in that narrow crevice." Colonel Pitts's pupils dilated. "I remember when the Russians introduced those things in the sixties. They kill with pressure waves that are intensified in hollow spaces. Hollow spaces like the human chest cavity. It shreds the lungs, but the best part is the brain remains intact. They say it is an agonizing death, lasting four to five minutes until they suffocate. I want these thieves to feel that panic. I want them to suffer."

Major Roberts's eyes widened. "I left the Humvee with the jammer parked next to the pass, and I never turned the jammer off! They'll never know you're coming."

Colonel Pitts mimicked a plane with his right hand. "I'll fly close to the mountain and climb along the base of the Chagai Hills. I'll be able to keep the Harrier under the radar's floor. I'll pop up right over those fuckers and drop the BLU-96 then fall back behind the mountain. I'll be nothing more than a blip on Camp Leatherneck's radar."

"General Smith will have investigators here in no time."

Colonel Pitts shrugged. "So what? They'll be coming on our terms, won't they? They'll snoop around and cross-check the inventory. They will see that we haven't been resupplied with a thermobaric warhead since the two we used last year." He wiped his hands together. "No evidence, no problem. But I have to be quick!" He pointed at Major Roberts. "You get close to the pass. After the explosion, get in there and comb the area. You'll have about two hours. Get your men and meet me at the airstrip. When I get airborne, hightail it toward the pass. By the time you get there, I'll be at Camp Rock, loading the Harrier onto the transport. If everything goes well, that truck will be in Pakistan before you get back."

Colonel Pitts struggled into his flight suit then plodded out the door and down the steps to the airstrip. As he rounded the corner, several men were already scurrying around the Harrier. He walked over and climbed gingerly up the steps, eventually settling into the tiny cockpit. The glass canopy closed as the crew pulled away the staircase. He flipped a fat black toggle switch on the dash, the turbine's whine soon growing to a roar. A wicked grin spread across his face as he mashed the play button on his MP3. "Sympathy for the Devil" rang out. Movement to his left drew his eye to the tarmac. It was Major Roberts and three others, waiting in a Humvee.

***

Major Roberts sat with the three soldiers, watching Colonel Pitts. "That is the craziest son of a bitch I've ever known."

Colonel Pitts pulled the visor of his helmet down and flashed a thumbs-up. The roar of the turbine's exhaust gas through the nozzle grew deafening. "Here we go, boys." Major Roberts backed up as the jump jet lifted off the ground. The Harrier struggled with the weight of the BLU-96, its wings dipping back and forth as it fought for altitude. In less than a minute, the jet dipped its nose and disappeared toward the Chagai Hills.

Major Roberts thought of Colonel Pitts. The old man was cashing out, and his own tour was almost over. Even if we lose this entire shipment, my share has to be at least ten million. He thought of Barbie, his one true love. She'd become an obsession as of late. They were to be married straight out of college, but he had scared her away with his roughness. She left him for a wealthy anesthesiologist, whom she had recently divorced. I'll go back and sweep her off her feet. Everything will be perfect. He allowed an indulgent smile as he eased the Humvee into drive, accelerating east, back toward the pass. He slowed the vehicle as the rising terrain gave way from deep sand to boulders and scrubs of woody brush. He stopped the Humvee about a mile from the pass and put it in park. Within seconds an enormous flash of light filled the windshield, followed by a thick mushroom cloud of fire, dust and smoke, rising high into the atmosphere. The blast wave bent scrub bushes and threw dust and stones as it sped toward him. "Brace yourselves!" He ducked low in the seat and covered his head. CRACK! The Humvee was pushed backward, the windshield spidering but holding. He rolled his window down and watched the column of fire rise into the sky. Seconds later a blast of hot air rolled over the left side of his face. He coaxed his Humvee closer to the mouth of the pass, pulling up next to the one he had left behind with the jammers. The windowless vehicle's paint was missing, all four tires flat and burning.

"SHIIIIITTTT!" exclaimed the man behind him.

"Everybody out of the truck," Major Roberts ordered. He led the trio to the opening of the pass, struggling to recognize once-familiar landmarks. "It's got to be fifty feet wider, but all this rubble is blocking the way in." He started to crawl over the unstable boulders, but the acrid fumes of the bomb's chemicals burned his nose and throat. He pulled his shirt up over his mouth, motioning to the man next to him. "Go get the masks. Move it!" As he waited for the equipment, he gawked at the devastation the bomb had wrought. The granite walls of the canyon were scorched black and stone rubble was strewn as far up the channel as he could see. It appeared as if a giant avalanche of rock and gravel had raced down, settling at the bottom where he stood. He took the mask from the returning soldier, securing it snugly over his face. The satellite transmission came from up there somewhere. Major Roberts turned to the man closer to him. "You come with me. We'll search the eastern side." Then he pointed to the western face. "You two head that way. Let's find those fucking rats in their hole." Major Roberts made his way through the unsteady terrain, coming across an occasional piece of fabric, flesh or bone but none of the yellow heroin bundles he sought. He focused on the butt of an assault rifle under some rubble. He wiggled the rifle free from the heavy stones and brushed it off. As he held it up, his eyes tightened. "That's odd. It's a U.S.-issue Colt M4."

"I found another one!" the man with him shouted, holding an M4 up over his head. High above him, something glinted in the sun. Major Roberts climbed until the shiny object lay at his feet. He crouched down, knees popping as he pulled out his Ka-Bar. He slid the tip of the blade under a metallic watch band, lifting it free of the gravel. A severed hand was still attached to the silvery watch. He pried the Bulova off the wrist, stepping back with a look of distaste as the limb landed with a thud at his feet. I will consider this a consolation piece for my Yankees cap. He placed the watch in his pocket as he scanned the rock face, looking for an entrance. A thick granite slab a few feet above him caught his attention. It appeared to have shifted, revealing a space. "There's the cave!" He hoisted himself up then wriggled on his belly underneath the slab and into a dark, cavernous space. "This must have been where they were hiding," he whispered. He held his hand out to the man behind. "Give me your flashlight." He took the small metal torch and turned it on, but the space was empty. He crept through the maze of tunnels and small caves. Supplies lay scattered everywhere but there was no sign of the heroin. As he turned and began down another dark tunnel, a human form materialized. "Arrgh!" he gasped, stumbling backward as he fired. The man lay motionless, already dead. His still smoldering flesh filled the space with the smell of burnt hamburger. The body was charred beyond recognition, its hands clenched around its throat. Major Roberts thought of Colonel Pitts's lecture. "Poor bastard."

He shone the light around the space. At least eight more charred and smoldering forms lay around in similar states. He returned to the main cave. "Grab the M4s and let's go. There's nothing here."

As they exited the pass and walked out into the desert, a large dog stumbled along the desert floor. Most of the beast's hair was burnt off, revealing patches of pink skin.

"What do you make of it, boss?"

"Don't care. Shut up and head for the Humvee."

CHAPTER 3

April 13, 2012, Nimroz Afghanistan

Commander Adair chomped the soggy cigar, brown liquid running down his chin. He dragged the back of his hand across his mouth, scanning the refuge for Joseph Roddick. There were Montacayo and the others, still panting from the battle, but the reporter was gone. "Where is that fuckin' weasel?" Adair pushed the cigar to the corner of his mouth. "Goddammit, Montacayo! What the fuck did I tell you about him?"

Montacayo glanced around. The sturdy American Indian pointed to an empty blanket lying against the back of the cave. "He was right there a minute ago." Montacayo hung his head. "My bad, sir. That asshole is like Harry Houdini."

"If I catch him on that Satcom, I'm going to fuck him up," Adair said. He leaned the M4 against the granite then crouched and listened. Silence. Slipping on the thermal goggles, he moved out of the main cave into the spoke like layout of tunnels radiating from the main cavern. Adair tiptoed toward Roddick's tiny alcove in the back of one of the passageways. He snuck closer, rolling his weight on the sides of his boots. Adair stopped short of the small grotto's entrance, holding his breath as he inched closer. He flipped the goggles up and turned his head as he leaned forward. Tap, tap, tap. He swung into view, stomping his boot as he slapped the wall.

Joseph Roddick jolted upright, yanking a blanket over something rectangular in his lap. He placed his hand over his mouth, stifling a yawn. "Hey, what's up?"

Adair's face burned as he charged in and grabbed the base of Roddick's ponytail, wrapping it around his thick hand. With one arm, he lifted Roddick off the ground, the man's feet dangling in the air. Roddick's fingernails dug into his forearm. "Goddammit, Adair, that hurts! Let go of me! Oh my God, I hate you – all of you fucking Neanderthals!"

I could crush his skull against the rock! Adair lifted him higher, compressing Roddick's head against the uneven stone. "You traitor. You signed an agreement! No satellite uplinks. That was the deal!" Adair let the man fall to his knees, still torqueing the ponytail. "You exposed our coordinates, you fool. They know where we are!" He pushed the wiry man hard to the stone floor, raising his boot. "I ought to break your neck."

Roddick put his hands up. "Commander, I understand you're angry, but I swear on my grandmother's grave I wasn't transmitting. I was just entering a data log! Come on, I give you my word."

"Your word? Fuck your word!" He held out his hand. "Give it to me!"

Roddick's eyes darted around the cave. His hand trembled as he pulled the object from the blanket and held it up. "Please be careful. My whole life is on that hard drive." Adair jerked the device from Roddick's grasp. He opened the notebook and leaned against the wall, scouring the computer files and data logs. Hundreds of logs had been sent – all by Satcom. The last one was before the satellite and GPS were jammed. Adair's legs buckled. "I knew it. You serpent! You've been transmitting since we arrived at Camp Leatherneck. You sent one hundred and six transmissions, the last one three minutes ago." Adair hurled the laptop to the ground and stomped it to pieces. He grabbed and twisted the reporter's pencil-sized ponytail again. "Come with me," he bellowed as he pulled Roddick down the tunnel. The small man struggled in vain as Adair manhandled him. Adair approached the dim light of the main cave. As he entered, he yanked Roddick to his feet and mule-kicked him in the small of the back. The reporter's arms windmilled backward as he slid face-first onto the jagged cave floor.

Roddick jumped up, brandishing his middle finger. "Fuck you, you stupid son of a bitch! I've been a war correspondent in Afghanistan for five years." Roddick shook his fist. "Not once have I seen anyone killed over a satellite uplink!"

Montacayo looked at the reporter. "You've been on the fucking satellite?"

Adair watched the reporter lift his chin, upper lip rising as he flipped off Montacayo.

Adair took a quick step forward, snapping his lower leg into Roddick's groin as if trying for a game-winning 50-yard field goal. Joseph Roddick popped three feet into the air, landing in a motionless heap at Montacayo's feet. Adair spat the cigar on the floor. "Cuff his wrists to his ankles. That son of bitch stays hogtied 'til we get out of here!"

Montacayo cuffed the unconscious man then approached the opening of the cave. He shook his head, his eyes darting around. "Sweet Jesus, I can't believe this is happening."

"He's been transmitting this whole time. If they haven't figured it out by now, they probably won't this time.

"We just wiped out their whole goddamn team. What if they send in an airstrike?"

"Relax, Montacayo. ORION may be out, but we

still have the IEDs hard-wired into the pass and three men outside on the .50-calibers. We'll be fine." He picked a piece of cigar from his teeth. "Besides, as well as we're dug in, it would take a nuke to get to us in here."

Montacayo's brows rose, eyes wide. "Who did we just kill? Who has attack helicopters around here? The team that led the caravan in was well-trained. Special Ops, I'd say. But they weren't ours. Where did they come from?"

Adair picked up his M4. "I don't know but we've stumbled into something we don't want any part of. Maybe it's the Pakistanis. They've got hundreds of Cobras." He dug out a cigar from his shirt pocket as he walked closer to the concealed entrance. Leaning forward, he peered through the eight-inch slit. The ant like Pashtuns scurried around the rocky canyon floor, gathering the bound yellow bundles lying among the rocks and dirt, strapping them quickly and efficiently to twenty shell-shocked donkeys. "We're losing our guides," Adair mused.

Montacayo's eyes narrowed. "Opportunistic little bastards. They were never to leave us, under any circumstances! Now they're taking off to make a drug deal." He walked over and brought up his rifle. "We oughta shoot everyone one of them skinnies. How many do you think we can drop from here?"

Salar, the leader of the Pashtun tribesmen, shouted encouragement to the sinewy men. Without haste the men and beasts proceeded, organizing into a caravan as they moved south up the narrow gorge toward Pakistan. Adair pushed the barrel of the M4 down. "They've served their purpose getting us here. Besides, they left behind the dog, and he's the best early warning system we have now." The beast sat like a sphinx, guarding the front of the cave.

Montacayo's brow furrowed. "This is some creepy shit, John. It's too damn quiet out there."

Adair donned his helmet and looked up at the screens on his visor. "All the UAV cameras are still blank."

He tapped his microphone. "Anything?"

"Hell no, it's fuckin' dead." Montacayo turned toward the tiger-striped dog the Pashtuns had abandoned. "He didn't want to follow them. Why do you supposed he stayed with us?"

Adair moved the unlit cigar to the other side of his mouth. "After Hamed was killed, we're the only ones that fed or watered him." He made a dismissive sweep with his hand. "I've never seen the Pashtuns offer him a damn thing. They'd kick him around if they weren't afraid of him."

Montacayo leaned toward the animal. "How is he going to detect anything if he's holed up here with us?" He scratched his chin. "No ears. No tail. I don't like the way he stares at me."

Adair chuckled. "Sher Dil is a tournament dog. Ears and tails are a liability. Just makes him look mean. He's the least of our worries. You just keep monitoring for that GPS signal. Even if it doesn't come up, the Pashtuns will soon be out of the range of those jammers. They'll use their satellite phones to call Colonel Kelley." Adair looked at the brushed aluminum face of his Bulova watch. "We'll be safe at Camp Rose by nightfall."

Montacayo's voice trembled. "I'm sure they intercepted Roddick's transmission. Maybe we should get outta here and move up the canyon?"

Sher Dil got up and crept toward the opening of the cave. His nose twitched, a deep growl rumbling through the hollow chamber. Sher Dil's gaze locked onto Adair. The animal whined, its eyes pleading.

"He's telling us to get out of here. Let's move up the canyon and hide," Montacayo said.

"No, if he can sense them, they're too close. We could get caught out there." He looked at Sher Dil. "Thanks for the warning, but we're not going anywhere, dog."

The animal stood tall, staring at him for several

moments before turning and crawling under the slab, beginning his descent down the steep face of the gorge. Adair watched the muscular form bound from rock to rock until it stood a hundred feet below. Sher Dil glanced up one last time then trotted out of sight.

CHAPTER 4

April 20, 2012, Pittsburgh County Prison

Robert Flynn lay on the uncomfortable cot dreaming of what could have been had he not been such a fool. He closed his eyes and thought of the judge's words for the thousandth time. Like a drum, their tormenting rhythm played in his head. "You are being charged with double homicide." How was I so sloppy? I could've gotten away, but I just stood there and watched them die. Disjointed thoughts bombarded his mind. What about ORION and Izzy? What if he can't find another leader to take the team in? They could all be killed, and I'd be to blame. If I could just find a way out of here, I could lead them. He stared at the ceiling, images of college and the Marines flashing by. And what about Mom's lymphoma? Now we can't afford treatment. He rolled onto his side and tucked his chin into his knees, his mind drifting to his father. He would have been so disappointed.

An excruciatingly loud electric buzz engulfed the cellblock, rattling the walls as the steel door opened. The tormenting thoughts vanished as the boots of the prison guard dragged down the corridor toward him. The obese guard stopped outside the cell, his characteristic stench wafting in. Flynn opened an eye for a split second. Cal Smitty had his hands on his knees, peering down at him with interest.

"I saw that!" Cal snapped.

"Smitty, why you gotta torment me?" Flynn said as he propped himself up on an elbow.

"I swear I'm not. This time it's for real." Smitty's eyes widened. "Someone important is here to see you. The warden wants me to bring him down right away. Says the man is a United States senator?"

Flynn bolted upright. "Senator? What's he want with me?"

"Dunno. I was wondering the same myself."

"Hummph." Flynn threw back the small blanket and rolled his legs off, his bare feet touching the cold, gritty floor.

Smitty righted himself and plodded back down the hall. "I'll fetch him," he said over his shoulder. The enormous metal door opened, then rattled the space again as it clanged shut behind him. Moments later Cal Smitty emerged, walking like the Royal Guard, his shoulders back, the waddle replaced by a dignified march. He led in a handsome, silver-haired man who looked to be somewhere in his early sixties. He wore a dark silk suit layered with a white oxford finished with a red tie and a handkerchief. The two men stopped in front of Flynn's cell.

"Thank you," the gentleman said to Smitty. Smitty stood between them for an awkward moment before murmuring something unintelligible as he returned to his normal posture and shuffled away with his head down.

The well-heeled man smiled. "My name is Senator Bill Ryan, from Pennsylvania. I'm here on behalf of Samuel Khan." He extended his hand through the bars.

Senator Ryan? Never heard of him. Flynn stood up and shook his hand. "Robert Flynn, sir."

Senator Ryan's smile faded. "I am aware that you

were supposed to lead Samuel Khan's first mission into Nimroz – to test ORION."

Flynn tilted his head. "ORION? The mission? That's supposed to be classified. No disrespect but I don't feel comfortable discussing this with someone I don't know."

"I can appreciate that, but I've been friends with Samuel Khan for many years. He has allowed me a sizeable investment in ORION."

"Good for you, but I no longer have anything to do with it." Flynn peered around at the concrete walls. "I'm off to bigger and better things."

"Samuel told me how you got here, but he says you're a good man." Senator Ryan had a chagrined expression. "I know about those men killing your dog and you killing them." He turned, pacing in front of the bars. "My wife and I have eight dogs, all rescues." His eyes narrowed. "If someone hurt them for fun, I would want to hurt them too, but you went too far, son."

"That puppy was the only thing in my life that was innocent," Flynn said. His mind drifted back to Helmand and to his service dog. He winced at the unanticipated pit in his stomach as the memories flashed back. "Anything that I love is fated for death. That's the second special one I've lost."

"Second one?" prodded Senator Ryan.

"The first was my service dog." Flynn's brows rose. "That was the really special one. There'll never be another like him. His name was Mac. He was my combat dog when I served in Helmand."

"I hope I'm not out of line for asking, Robert, but what kind of dog was he? Your service dog, that is?"

Warmth filled him as Mac's smiling face, tongue hanging to one side, flashed into his mind. "He was a Belgian Shepherd, more like my mother than a service dog, always worrying about me. He never barked, even if the enemy was close, and kept a constant watch over us. I don't know if Mac ever slept. He was too busy slinking around the perimeter of the camp. That dog understood what was going on. He really did." A painful lump grew in his throat. He rubbed his hands through his hair, his expression grim. "He got ill so quick, some kind of aggressive virus – vaccine-resistant distemper or something. We were on one of those eternal foot patrols, two days from our forward operating base. By the beginning of the second day, he couldn't walk and was having trouble breathing. I couldn't sit there and watch him suffocate." Flynn covered his face with his hands. "So, I injected him with all the morphine we had in the kit. Before he stopped breathing, he stared into my eyes. We shared something in that instant that I've never experienced with another living being. He wagged his tail as if to tell me, 'It's all right.'" A single tear rolled from each eye. "Even then he was protecting me."

Senator Ryan recoiled, his eyes welling with tears. "Good Lord, I'm sorry for bringing it up."

Flynn tried to speak but his larynx was locked. He wiped his face and took a deep breath, allowing himself to feel the pain. "It was better that way. Military brass at the time were forcing the handlers to abandon their dogs without provisions at the airports. I wouldn't have left Mac to starve. I would have had to look him in the eyes and shoot him. I couldn't live with that. Good ol' Mac, even he couldn't get me out of the trouble that I'm in now."

Senator Ryan leaned back on his wingtips. "I can."

"What?"

"I can get you out of here."

Flynn stood up and wrapped his fingers around the cold steel bars. "Senator, you do know the charges against me?"

"Double homicide," Senator Ryan said. He stared at the floor, as if summoning some courage before looking up. "Robert, that's not why I'm here though. I'm here because Samuel could not be." He stood stoically, closing his eyes momentarily before he spoke. "Six days ago, the whole team that you were supposed to lead in was killed in the pass."

Flynn's knees buckled. He searched Senator Ryan's eyes. "Izzy Khan?"

"No, no. Ishmael is fine. He's been in Pittsburgh at S&K Industries working on ORION's electronic upgrades."

"Peter Montacayo?"

The older man's inner brows rose. "I'm sorry, Robert."

Flynn's core ached. He shook his head from side to side. "That can't be. I … we, spent an enormous amount of time researching that location. Nimroz Province is far to the west. Only bandits and smugglers hang around out there. They should have been able to annihilate anything in their path. Tell me, how did they die?"

"A huge airstrike. We had a search team in the pass less than four hours later, but they found only utter destruction. By the lack of a crater and the accelerants found all over the rocks, it must have been a thermobaric blast." His eyes tightened. "That type of weaponry is exclusive. In that area, only an American or Pakistani source could avail such armament. All we have is radar in the area showing an unusual blip around the time of the airstrike."

"Helicopter?"

"No, whatever it was, it was much too fast. We have eyewitnesses that said it was a jet that bombed that pass. It could have been a jump jet. The problem is no Harriers are known to be in that part of the country."

"Who's investigating?"

"General Smith from Camp Leatherneck, and the CIA."

"What do you know about the witnesses?"

"Earlier in the day, your friends used ORION to

annihilate a band of smugglers pushing through the pass with two tons of heroin. The Afghan guides Samuel Khan hired to watch the team abandoned them and took the heroin across the border to sell in Pakistan. They were on their way back when they saw the strike. They thought it was a nuclear blast."

"What the fuck? How could this be?" Flynn glared at the hard floor as if his anguish would crack it.

"Thank God you and Izzy weren't with them. I take it you are close to Izzy?"

"He's like a brother. I was his company commander during his first tour in Afghanistan. That's how I got to know him."

"Which is why I'm here. Samuel's sending in Izzy with another team, and you're going to protect him."

CHAPTER 5

Flynn reached for one of the bars to steady himself, his vision tunneling. "When and where?"

"The same area."

Millions of thoughts jammed Flynn's brain. "The same area?"

Senator Ryan put a hand out. "It may sound absurd but hear me out. The upgrades to ORION are complete, and the flaws have been corrected. You also know some of the guys going in. I know it's not much to go on, but what do you think?"

"What if we get attacked by a jump jet with a thermobaric warhead strapped to it?"

"Colonel Kelley will provide air support."

"Isn't that the same asshole that was supposed to cover the first team?"

Senator Ryan frowned. "He's not an asshole. As a matter of fact, he's a damn good man and one of the few allies we have." He glanced around, lowering his voice. "Keep this under your hat." He grinned, his lips drawing back like the Cheshire Cat's. "At great risk to myself, I have procured two shoulder-fired anti-aircraft missiles. That could be my undoing so...." He put his finger to his lips.

"That's all well and good, but I gotta be honest. I get the sense you're more worried about your investment than our boys."

The senator's face reddened, his clenched fists coming up with impressive ferocity. "How dare you make assumptions as to my motives? My own son is a Marine and, goddammit, I want him to have the best!" A large vein bulged on his forehead. "Just remember, I'm here to help YOU! You can't beat this double homicide rap without me."

Flynn pushed off the bars, turning back and walking to his bunk. He sat on the edge of the mattress. "Say what you gotta say."

Senator Ryan's pupils dilated. "Double homicide. That's what I gotta say so don't act so damned tough! You killed those thugs with your bare hands, and you had better believe that without me your life is over. Do you hear me? Good Lord, son, what the hell got into you that night?"

"It's a long story."

"I live for long stories."

Flynn rubbed his hands over his face. "I had been back from my last tour for a couple of months before they started killing our animals—first in the neighborhood behind my mother's house, then on our street."

Senator Ryan tilted his head. "The animal killings?"

"Those sadists were crucifying people's pets then taunting the owners afterwards. One night late, I got a taste of it when I let our golden retriever out to pee. Minutes later a noise like a car wreck came from outside. A red pickup had crashed through the mailbox and into the front yard. I got out the door in time to see June-Bug taking her last breath. They left a Bowie knife in her chest and took off for the interstate. I didn't get the plate number and didn't have time to grab my gun, so I jumped in my truck."

"You chased them down and murdered them."

"I was running on instinct. The same instinct that allows me to survive on the battlefield and keep my men alive."

Senator Ryan's upper lip curled. "Yeah, your gift, that's what Izzy calls it. He thinks that you can do no wrong, like you are Superman. I hope for his sake that you are worthy as he believes you are."

"Out in the field, I have to make split-second decisions and I'm damned good at it. That's what I did here."

Senator Ryan tilted his head. "Maybe. But Robert, you have to realize that often what we see as our greatest attribute is actually our ultimate weakness. You made the decision not to call the police but to follow them instead. In the process, you killed two men and threw your own life away. I wouldn't call that good instincts."

"I didn't want to kill anybody."

Senator Ryan shrugged. "Doesn't matter. I saw the evidence. There is not a jury out there that's going to take your side. If you were in Texas, they'd inject your ass."

"Evidence? What evidence?" Flynn stood up and moved to the bars. Senator Ryan stepped back, just out of his reach.

"The film from the high-resolution security camera across the street from where you ran those men off the road. It captured the whole thing. You are a violent man, Mr. Flynn. What were you thinking?"

Flynn scoffed. "Are you so naïve as to think that at that point I had a choice? What I thought was irrelevant. I wanted to fight but those men got out of that truck to kill me." He jammed his thumb into his chest. "It was a mistake to run them off the road and get out of my truck, but after that it was self-defense."

"Why did you get out of your vehicle in the first place? That will be the district attorney's first question."

"They boxed me in against a light pole. A parked car is a coffin when two men are out to kill you. Who cares that they are dead? They brought it upon themselves. I figure I have a decent shot at acquittal."

Senator Ryan put his index finger and thumb close together. "Not a tiny chance. The jury will see the same thing I did, a physically superior man attacking the driver and ruthlessly snapping his neck."

Flynn stood up and turned around. He pulled up his prison smock, running his fingers across three beet red scars on his back. "I got stabbed three times in the back by the second."

"Then you took his knife and killed him. The red blood squirting from his neck covered the whole damn street. Pity the camera was high definition. The footage will sicken the average juror."

Flynn recalled the blade piercing his back over and over before he grabbed the man's wrist. He had spun around, clamping his teeth onto the attacker's nose as he wrestled the knife from his grasp. He remembered the feel of the steel piercing the thug's skin, blade snapping off as it buried deep into his vertebrae. The metallic smell of the man's blood and the horror on his face was burned into his memory.

Senator Ryan looked at the floor, silent for a moment. "Mr. Flynn, there's something else. We have a competitor, someone powerful within the Pentagon that doesn't want ORION to succeed. I'm convinced that it's some bigwig in the Central Intelligence Agency. It's frustrating. I sit on the Defense Policy Board at the Pentagon that coordinates purchasing with private vendors." He touched his own chest. "I decide what the military buys and what they don't, and I can't even get ORION on the table for discussion." His eyes narrowed. "I know it has to do with Switchblade."

"Switchblade?"

Senator Ryan spread his arms like wings. "It's a

small airplane developed by the CIA with a wingspan of about five feet with a first-person POV camera similar to ORION's quadcopters. However, instead of being used as a reconnaissance and targeting platform, it actually carries a small warhead, directly attacking the target. It is inferior to our system because no redundancies are built into it, not to mention it only has twelve percent of the blast force of ORION's 81mm mortar, much less the 120mm round. It's a decent idea, but once it attacks, you lose your bird's-eye view of the battlefield. It is the only weapon system that remotely competes with ORION." Senator Ryan rubbed his fingers together. "Much better profit margins than the one thousand-dollar tailfin kits on ORION's mortars. Switchblade costs a half-million dollars apiece, and the field agents have used five hundred million dollars' worth since last year. I figure ORION is a direct threat to their cash cow."

Flynn's hands grew sweaty. "CIA? You said only an American or Pakistani force could field a thermobaric weapon. Do you think the CIA …"

"Killed our team? No, of course not. That is not the case, I can assure you. I've proven it to myself."

"Have you?"

Senator Ryan frowned. "They are greedy, but they have a creed. They aren't murderers for their own sake. Some of the finest, most decent people I know work at the CIA."

"Yeah, if you say so."

"Switchblade isn't all of it. We've got a more acute problem. The Central Afghani government has been kicking private military contractors out of the country. This may be the last chance we ever get."

Flynn eyed the man. "So if I lead the team back into Nimroz and test ORION, I'm off the hook?"

Senator Ryan nodded. "If you get back alive."

"Will I get paid?"

"The same as the rest."

Flynn took a deep breath, scrutinizing the man. "I hope you are who you say you are." He extended his arm through the bars and shook Senator Ryan's hand. "So now that we're on the same team, how are you busting me out? Nail file? Explosives?"

Senator Ryan winked. "It's a matter of national security. You let me worry about that."

CHAPTER 6

Flynn craned his neck out of his mom's front door. Betty was nowhere in sight, only two squirrels frolicking in the wet grass disturbed the morning calm. He cracked the door open and closed his eyes, listening. Wind rustled through the trees, but the block was otherwise quiet. He stole one last glance, opened the door and tiptoed into the heavy morning air, beelining it toward his truck. CRACK. A limb snapped behind him, his stomach sinking as he spun around. Betty had materialized out of a row of bushes and closed the distance like a bathrobed ninja, the stout woman managing to get mere feet from him in seconds. She held a ceramic mug, coffee spilling from it, in her left hand and a lit cigarette in the right.

She craned her neck toward him. "I heard about what happened," she said in a gravelly voice, acquired from a hundred pack years. "Those men were bad!" She poked her cigarette at him, her expression angry. "They deserved it. I support you, Bobby. We all do. I'm so sorry you got caught." She tilted her head to take an enormous drag, blowing it out the side of her mouth. "If there is anything I can do, please let me know." She leaned in, eyes burning. "Barbara Russell says your mother is dying of cancer. Is that true? What kind?"

"You are so kind to offer your help, Mrs. Hughes." Flynn pointed to his watch as he broke away toward the vehicle. "I'm sorry but I'm ten minutes late for a job interview."

"Who are you interviewing with? What job?"

Flynn blew her a kiss. "Wish me luck," he said as he pulled himself up and plopped into the lifted white Silverado. He shut the door, turned the key and slipped it into gear, waving to Mrs. Hughes. "Jeez, lady." The small block burbled as he cruised down Mockingbird Lane. The street was famous for the rows of magnificent oak trees lining each side. They towered like giant sentinels, protecting Victorian mansions replete with manicured lawns and lush, colorful gardens. I can't believe I'm getting a second chance. The positive sentiment vanished as Peter Montacayo's plump, round face popped into his head. Montacayo, my friend. He thought of basic training. "That was it, the first day I met you," he said aloud. He was back at Parris Island, the first week of basic, where he first encountered the full-blooded Apache. A smile flashed across his face. There they stood, sixty feet high atop the wooden structure, only safety ropes hanging from their waists. The abusive drill sergeant had been all over Montacayo on the climb up, getting into his face on the top platform. "Son, if you love the Marine Corps, you'll jump off this tower!" That was it. Montacayo was high in the air, hurtling over the edge. The wide-eyed instructor endured eight feet of rope burn, somehow stopping Montacayo's fall. Vintage Montacayo. I miss you, my friend. Who did this? Did you suffer? His jaw clenched. I'm going to find those sons of bitches. I promise, Pete. He slowed the truck and hit his clicker, turning into the west entrance of S&K. The elaborate metal gate opened, revealing a dark slate cobblestone road. Terraced rows lined with thousands of blooming tulips promised the renewal of life. He idled deeper into the estate. Tended lawns and gardens with exotic trees were crisscrossed by a web of pea gravel pathways peppered with fountains and benches. A parking lot came into view. He pulled into a shaded spot under a large overhanging oak branch and parked. The largest building, housing Izzy and Samuel's office and where most of the training facilities were located, was visible through the limbs. He turned off the ignition and got out, waking down the footpath to the main building. Of all the structures on the property, this was his favorite. Colossal limestone columns rose high into the air, supporting the impossible weight of three gothic arches that rose to the roofline. Castle-like oak doors with black cast-iron handles were centered under the middle arch. Flynn reached for the twisted iron, opening the balanced door. It swung effortlessly on its hinges, revealing a grand chamber. Beams of light from high stained-glass windows illuminated rough-hewn marble floors in a kaleidoscope of colors. The inside of the edifice was like a European Gothic cathedral. He turned to the right and walked down the familiar hall, the heels of his boots echoing. He approached the "War Room" and stepped through the open doors. Two men with jet-black hair and heavy beards looked up from a table in the back. Warmth spread through his body at the sight. It was Samuel and Ishmael Khan.

Izzy waved to him. "Well, if it isn't Robert Flynn. Come on in, friend." Izzy pointed to the ceiling. "Look, the mural is finally finished." The domed stone ceiling depicted a hand-painted scene of a chaotic and desperate naval battle between the Turks and Venetians in the ancient port of Venice. The Turkish vessels were outnumbered. The men were fighting to the death, their faces stoic as the Venetians poured into what was left of the Turkish navy. The War Room was like a time capsule of some long-ago place. Its soaring walls, paneled in black walnut, were adorned with tapestries and oil paintings of Genghis Khan's armies engaged in epic battle scenes.

"You know that our family is descended from him?" Izzy asked, pointing to one of the paintings.

"I think you may have told me a time or two," Flynn said as he walked on the decorative rugs and past the East Asian sculptures. Samuel and Izzy came into focus. God, they look gaunt. Their smiles did little to disguise the hollow look of sorrow and exhaustion. "I thought I would never see you guys again."

Izzy stood up and hugged him, slapping him on the back as he often did. "It's good to see you too!"

"Believe me, it's good to be seen." Flynn said, wincing. He pulled away and extended his hand to Samuel. "Mr. Khan, thank you for sending Senator Ryan to get me out of that hellhole. You have no idea what that means to me, sir."

Samuel shook Flynn's hand. "You're welcome, Robert." He motioned to the table. "Grab a chair and sit down," he said curtly.

"Sure." Flynn felt a bolt of alarm as he pulled out a chair out and sat down.

Samuel's gaze bore into him. "I was shocked when I heard of you killing those men. Shocked that you would do something so impetuous. I must know that I can trust you not to be impulsive. To think before you do anything and to utilize all resources before you make a decision."

Flynn's face, neck, and ears felt impossibly hot. "Yes sir, it's a team effort and I will be as cautious as possible."

Samuel continued to stare at him like a hawk. "It is essential that you watch Izzy. He will be burdened with the technical specifics of keeping the system operational."

Izzy nodded. "You have the intuition to get us back alive."

Flynn shrunk in his chair. "Thanks, but considering how I screwed up, I figured Brian Bollick would be your choice for commander. He was the most capable operative in the last group. I understand he didn't go in with the last team either. What happened?"

Izzy rubbed his eyes. "Bollick and that psychopath Jay Black finally came to blows. They cut a swath like a tornado through the barracks at the training grounds. It wasn't pretty."

Flynn leaned in. "Those monsters tangled? Tell me more."

Izzy held Jay Black's file in front of him. "You know how those two were always one- upping and jawing at each other. Yada fucking yada." Izzy shot a glance at Samuel. "Excuse the language, Dad." He looked back. "When the final rankings came out, Bollick edged out Black. Black's ego couldn't take it. I didn't see the altercation but Montacayo said it was gruesome."

Flynn crossed his arms. "Well?"

"Montacayo said they beat the shit out of each other for a while, but Jay Black got tired and Bollick got a hold of his arm." Izzy made the motion of breaking a stick. "Montacayo said it sounded like a giant piece of celery."

"Couldn't have happened to a nicer guy," Flynn said.

"No shit, but that wasn't the end of it. The next morning all the water to the training center had been shut off." Izzy smirked, sharing a knowing look with Samuel. "Best we can figure is that Black came back during the night and shut it off. Then he rigged the outhouses with flashbang grenades under the seats, with weight-sensitive triggers only Bollick was heavy enough to trip. Montacayo described an explosion, then smoke pouring out of one of the outhouses. Bollick supposedly fell out, pants around his ankles, covered in blood and shit, crying about his balls."

Flynn recoiled. "What a sadistic son of a bitch. Is Bollick okay?"

"Yeah, yeah, Bollick recovered intact but Black got away. Nobody knows where he went." Izzy scratched his beard. "What piqued my interest was the quality of those ad hoc fuses that Black built for those outhouse bombs." His eyes narrowed. "They were sophisticated, even for Father and myself. The fact he was able to throw them together frightened me. He must have had government training. I started thinking of how he was always vanishing or late to the sessions, and those weird questions he would ask. That's when I had the epiphany: He was a spy. I couldn't believe I didn't put it together sooner! I rushed back to S&K and found malware linked to his password in all our computers. That son of a bitch had even broken into both of our offices and accessed our personal mainframes. Black copied every one of our hard drives!"

Flynn felt his blood pressure rise. "Fucking lowlife."

"The local police put a warrant out for Black's arrest – attempted murder." Izzy scratched his temple. "But the SOB vanished. We called in the FBI, but they couldn't find a trace of him. Turns out, all of his military records were fabricated. There's no official record of our 'Jay Black' ever existing."

"He was after the targeting system," Flynn said.

Izzy crossed his arms, his face twisting into that familiar, triumphant smirk. "The bastard got nothing! I had our hard drives filled with bogus data." Izzy tapped his head. "I never leave an electronic trail, you know. I do most of my work with pencil and paper."

Samuel smiled, affectionately gripping Izzy's shoulder. "He takes after his father."

"Are there any new leads on the first team?"

Izzy held up his index finger. "One, and it's terrifying. The investigators from Camp Leatherneck found ethylene oxide, an oxygen catalyst. It was all over the pass where we lost our team."

"Yeah, a thermobaric warhead, Senator Ryan told me."

Samuel pulled out a laminate map, running his pen over the lower left corner. "The only collection of force we know of in that area is our two U.S. bases. The northern one here, seventy miles from the border, is our home base, Camp Rose." His pen traced southwest. "The only other, Camp Rock, is more of a border outpost than a base. It's in no-man's land. They cover a twenty-mile stretch of the southwestern border with Pakistan. It is equipped with two 155mm Howitzers with Excalibur GPS-guided shells, but they have no attack aircraft, just one old Huey for basic transportation." Samuel's brows drew close. "It's hard to imagine how U.S. forces could be involved." Samuel placed his index finger under a black line at the bottom of map. "That leaves Pakistan here south of the border. I'd say rogue Pakistani Special Forces officers smuggling heroin back into Pakistan. It's no mystery that the Pakistani ISI controls the lion's share of heroin once it crosses into Pakistan." Samuel's eyes were laden with worry. "The problem with that theory is that historically the Pakistani smugglers direct the drugs through short overland routes to Iran and Turkey. They move product out of Afghanistan but don't deliver through it to Pakistan because the Afghani steppes are full of outlaws. Besides, they don't want to risk getting caught by our ISAF forces. If it was the Pakistani ISI, chances are they are in collusion with someone in Afghanistan."

Flynn fidgeted in his chair. "No doubt the same someone who killed our team." The conversation with the senator at the jail flashed back. "Senator Ryan said no radar logs of any planes were detected flying into Nimroz, just a blip coming up off of the mountain and then back down. Whoever killed our squad is high-tech." Flynn swallowed hard. "And we're headed back to the same area?"

Izzy's jaw clenched. "Tons and tons of heroin are being trafficked through that area. The smugglers have made it ungovernable, and international troops haven't been able to do anything about it. If we go in and secure that part of the border with a twelve-man unit, it would be as unfathomable as King Leonidas and his three hundred Spartans at Thermopylae."

Samuel raised a finger. "There's another reason. Colonel Kelley was Senator Ryan's roommate at Annapolis and as gruff an SOB as Colonel Kelley is, he's the only one willing to risk his neck for our cause. He says the CIA commanders from eastern Afghanistan have personally called the western base commanders, all but ordering them not to associate with private military contractors representing ORION."

Flynn's breathing quickened. "The CIA doesn't want them associating—with us? What are we, terrorists?" He alternated glances between Samuel and Izzy. "What if it was the CIA that bombed that pass? I know you guys have entertained the thought."

Izzy grimaced, rubbing the back of his neck as he shared an uneasy stare with Samuel. "Flynn, we have to trust people more informed than us. Senator Ryan assures us that, though the CIA may consider ORION a threat to their device, they had nothing to do with it."

Flynn drummed his fingers on the table. "Switchblade. How could I forget?"

"Humph," Samuel rolled his eyes, a tired smile following. "God love him, Senator Ryan is a short-sighted man. He is fixated on that 'Switchblade' contraption, but the real threats ORION poses to the industry go far deeper than that suicidal drone."

Izzy lowered his voice. "When we couldn't get any contracts, we brought in consultants to help us figure out why. They said the eLORAN operating system alone is a paradigm shift in individual capability. Throw in the fact that ORION can serve as the targeting system for ballistic missiles and other heavy weapons and it is not hard to see that ORION threatens many multibillion-dollar weapons platforms." Izzy counted on his fingers. "Close air support such as attack helicopters, A-10 Warthogs, short-range bombers as well as artillery pieces and Multiple Launch Rocket Systems would take serious hits."

Samuel's emerald-colored eyes darted between Flynn and Izzy. "That's just the tip of the iceberg. The need for air, land, and naval transport for those obsolete systems is lessened. The members of the think tank were concerned for us. They suggested shadow banking groups, ones that pick presidents and senators, control not only our currency but how most of it is spent. Military procurement is the darling of all the cash-sucking drains, the ideal way to funnel trillions of taxpayer dollars into the bloated coffers of unaccountable weapon programs. They articulated that, though well-meaning, we were naïve and in waters we didn't comprehend. They appealed to us that if we were determined to proceed that we do it quietly and with great care. Nimroz Province fits that bill."

Flynn's eyes bugged. "Nice of you to finally share THAT with me." He hung his head like a man headed to his own execution. "How do I get myself into these situations?"

Izzy's face reddened. "Relax, Bobby. The CIA is not involved." He crossed his arms, leaning back in his chair. "Do you remember that first RC truck Dad sent to Helmand?"

"Don't change the topic."

"Flynn, I'm serious. Do you remember that little truck?"

Flynn let out a gush of air. "Of course, I remember. It started this whole thing."

"Well, I took that concept and ran with it, and I've never looked back, not until these men were killed." His eyes became misty. "I lost sight of a lot of things and a lot of people. If I had just waited for the eLORAN system to be completed before sending them in, they wouldn't have had their GPS system jammed. The robotic avatars with bigger mortars were almost ready as well. They could have fought their way out of anything." He hung his head. "But I couldn't wait."

Flynn shifted in the chair. "How could you have known advanced weapon systems were at play? I helped you with the logistics on Nimroz Province. Your own uncle did the ground reconnaissance. Only smugglers with machine guns and RPGs travel that mountain pass. It was the perfect proving ground."

Izzy held up several sheets of paper, dropping them back onto the table. "So we thought. The Afghan guides and a truncated satellite transmission from an embedded reporter named Joseph Roddick described a huge fight hours before the aerial attack. According to the reporter, an unmarked AH-1 Cobra attack helicopter led in a group of dark-clad commandos with bandannas on their arms. The drugs came in next. Roddick describes the battle as a large ambush our team sprung on the group. They wiped out the smugglers."

Flynn tilted his head. "Cobra attack helicopter? What happened to it?"

Izzy threw up his hands. "We don't know. Roddick never followed up on his initial transmission. By the time they tried to contact Colonel Kelley at Camp Rose, their communications had been jammed." Izzy rested his face into his hands. "We only brought eight partial bodies home to bury. The rest ..."

"So Roddick could send his data but the team couldn't reach Colonel Kelley? That doesn't make sense," Flynn said.

"Of course, it doesn't make sense to you because you understand that a satellite phone gives away your coordinates and you would never use one in that situation. Roddick sent the first part on the satellite phone and gave away their position. That was likely when all of their communications were jammed," Izzy said.

"Izzy, things are different this time. ORION is complete, not to mention the Stingers that Senator Ryan lifted. We'll go back in there – you and I – and we'll finish this. If we run into these killers again, we will pull off their masks and expose them for the murderers they are."

Izzy's fists clenched. "Damn straight! If there's any of them left alive after I finish with them." He patted the files in front of him. "First things first though. We have to put together a team." Izzy glanced at Samuel. "The failure of the first mission doesn't seem to affect the appetite for cash. Since Dad raised the pay, there's plenty of applicants."

Samuel's eyes tightened again as he regarded Flynn. "You are confident and strong. That confidence – it's the one thing about you, Bobby, the one thing that terrifies me. I spoke with one of your commanding officers in Helmand."

"Colonel Mercer?"

Samuel nodded, his face severe. "The colonel claims you're impulsive and stubborn and you don't trust others. He said you disobeyed an order to wait for air support and pulled your platoon into danger. Luckily, your instincts proved correct. It was the only reason you weren't court-martialed." He wagged his finger. "That independence is valuable, but I have to know that you will work with Colonel Kelley and any other resources at your disposal."

"I will, sir."

Samuel looked up. "I'm paying you to accomplish this mission, but more than that, I'm paying you to bring my son back alive. Be careful, Robert. This is going to be an extraordinarily dangerous mission." Samuel's phone rang. He pulled out the device, reading the caller ID. "Boys, I'm going to take this outside." Samuel stood up and made his way through the rows of chairs to the double doors and out of the War Room.

The stinging nettles of the unexpected criticism settled in as Samuel disappeared. Izzy peered at Flynn. "Hey, don't let it bother you too much. He's been under a lot of stress." He glanced toward the front of the room. "I've never seen him like this."

"It's okay," Flynn said as he reached for a file. "We have four men that know ORION backwards and forwards."

"You mean three?"

"You, myself, Brian Bollick, and Rex Laster."

Izzy crossed his arms.

"Did I say something?"

"Brian Bollick can be an unfocused hothead but he's brilliant. I'm not sold on Rex Laster."

Flynn's mouth fell open. "What are you talking about? He was one of the top five recruits and because of your personal beef with him, he got passed up for the first go-round. We can't pass him up this time; he's too good of an operator."

Izzy shook his head. "I don't want to be in the field with that guy. We don't like each other, and bottom line is I don't trust him. I don't like the way he behaves and I sure as hell don't appreciate his appearance. It's not normal. That red ZZ Top beard? Tribal tattoos crawling up his neck, covering half his damn face. Who does that?"

Flynn grinned. "I kinda like his tattoos."

"For god's sake, that freak was court-martialed for chewing part of a man's face off during a bar fight. Besides, I don't like the way those beady eyes burn into me. It's like he wants to frag me or something."

"Maybe he doesn't like you, big deal. He's a warrior."

Izzy scoffed. "Don't tell him that. He already thinks he's a reincarnated Viking."

"Damn it, Izzy, if he fights like one, who cares? We all draw inspiration from somewhere." Flynn picked up Laster's file, holding it in front of him. "Look, he may look like a freak and he may get into trouble outside of work but in combat, his commanders give him high praise. They said he is cunning and audacious but most of all that he is afraid of absolutely nothing. We could use that where we are headed."

Izzy clenched his jaw. "I see whose side you're on."

"Come on, Izzy, let's get to the bottom of this. Laster refuses to kiss your royal little bum, boss's son and all. That really chaps your ass, doesn't it?"

Izzy recoiled. "You can be a bastard sometimes." He leaned his head on his fist for a moment then reached for the files, pushing half of them across the small table toward Flynn. "Even if the freak gets a spot in our circus, that's still only four of us. We've got six more to go."

CHAPTER 7

Flynn peered around the War Room, sizing up the recruits. Some whispered, while others giggled like children, gaping at the grandiosity of the space. He rubbed his moist hands on his jeans. "I hate giving speeches."

Izzy cracked a toothy grin. "You'll do fine. I will admit, though, it's good to see you sweat."

"I don't like being the center of attention. Maybe you should be giving the introduction, Superfly."

Izzy blinked slowly. "Superfly? I like that, but really, I can't take all the glory. Recognition is important for the little guy as well. You go ahead."

Flynn cut his eyes. "Little guy, huh?" Suddenly, the room became quiet. Samuel Khan had walked in and was strolling right toward him.

"Senator Ryan called late last night with good news. Someone across the table at the Defense Policy Board approached him about ORION," said Samuel.

Izzy's eyes widened. "It's about damn time."

Samuel put his hands out. "Keep it down. I don't have all the details, but Senator Ryan said something horrible is happening in eastern Afghanistan. There are rumors at the Pentagon that airplanes filled with bodies of

U.S. servicemen are flying into D.C. every week." Samuel craned his neck as he scanned the room. "A woman named Hulsey, the liaison, is here now. I just met her."

Flynn followed Samuel's gaze to an attractive woman at the end of the room.

"That's her over there, admiring that Rodin." Samuel gawked at the woman like a schoolboy before noticing they were watching him. He cleared his throat as he brushed his lapels and straightened his tie. "I'll introduce you both after the orientation. Please be mindful and don't embarrass me—or yourselves." He shot Izzy an icy stare.

Izzy frowned. "Why are you looking at me? I am the consummate gentleman."

Samuel rolled his eyes. "Pfft. Tomorrow you two take her to breakfast, then on to the range for a demonstration. Show her whatever part of the system that she wants to see." Samuel turned and strolled away, past the seated applicants to the other side, taking a spot next to the woman.

Izzy covered his mouth with his hand. "I've seen plenty of good-looking gals in my life, but my god, she's the most beautiful woman I've ever seen. Even dad is losing it." He cast a concerned look at Flynn. "You're awful quiet. Are you okay?"

Flynn could barely hear him for the pounding sensation in his chest.

Izzy bumped him. "Dad wants us to impress her tomorrow. Better let me do the talking." Izzy winked, smiling as he ran his hands through his thick hair, nodding with confidence.

"Okay, amador, I had almost decided not to do it, but now—" A smirk covered Flynn's face. "You be screwed, cuz."

A suspicious scowl came over Izzy's face. "What do you mean, I be screwed?"

Flynn tossed his head back. "Buhahahaha! You'll

know it when everyone pees their pants laughing."

"What is it?!" Izzy's eyes shot to the projector, then to Ms. Hulsey. "A fucked-up picture?" Panic etched his face. "Flynn, please, not in front of her!" Izzy's emerald eyes became fierce. "I'm serious, Flynn. Don't make me look bad, not now."

Flynn glanced at his watch as he stood up. "I would love to discuss this further, friend, but it's time for this little guy to get some recognition." He stifled a laugh as he turned and walked toward the stage, sensing the recruits watching him as he took his place behind the podium. He pulled the microphone closer, wincing at the noise scratching through the PA. "Welcome to S&K. I'm Robert Flynn. Mr. Khan has entrusted me with command." He paused for a second. "Over the next six weeks only the finest men in this room will make the squad. As you all know, the previous team was killed less than a month ago. We have determined why it happened and have taken countermeasures to prevent it happening again but make no mistake: This mission is just as dangerous. Anyone having second thoughts should leave now." Flynn scanned the men for a few moments, but they all remained seated, faces stoic. "No one?" He felt a lightness in his chest. A commander could go his whole career and be lucky to have two or three exceptional soldiers. This room was full of them. He aimed the laser pointer at the ceiling. "I've arranged a small slideshow to supplement my lack of oratory skills, so bear with me." He nodded to the sound technician in the back of the room. "Dim the lights and lower the projector screen, please."

The room darkened, an electric motor buzzing as a huge white screen descended. Click. The first image popped up. It was a huge bodybuilder kissing his own bicep. Bemused murmurs rippled through the chamber. Flynn grinned. "I thought this image embodied the mentality of a soldier armed with ORION." He scanned the darkened space as if he could see all their faces. "You are sitting here today because you are intelligent, aggressive, and independent in the face of fire. We're going to need those instincts to survive long enough to prove that the concept of ORION is effective. If we succeed, the Pentagon will buy it and the foot patrols will finally have something concrete that they can protect themselves with." He hit the projector button, changing to a slide of a giant tan map. "This is southwest Afghanistan." He gripped his laser pointer, running the red dot over the map. "Nimroz Province is here, in the extreme southwest corner of the country. Most of us that have fought in Afghanistan have never seen southwest Afghanistan because not a lot happens there except drug smuggling." The red spot circled a long mountain range in the southwest, mostly in Pakistan. "These are the Chagai Hills, where we will take refuge while we prove our wares. The Chagai Hills are a medium-elevation mountain range that runs one hundred and fifty kilometers long and sixty-five kilometers wide." He circled the extreme northern end of the range. "Here you can see that only a tiny portion of the foothills lies in southwest Afghanistan. The rest of Nimroz Province, here to the north of the border, is flat desert." The red point moved north across the desert. "Our sponsor, Colonel Kelley, is here, at Camp Rose, seventy miles to the north." The red dot drifted back down to the northern edge of the mountain range. "The pass we'll hold is here. It is a geological bottleneck that runs perpendicular to the border into Pakistan and is the only unguarded ground route to get goods overland into Pakistan. We will assist Colonel Kelley by confiscating any contraband coming through, forcing smugglers east toward coalition assets." He flipped to a picture of a humanoid robot. "Let's get to our equipment. This is one of Izzy's avatars. Each member will have one. It is the size of a man but much stronger. It can carry six forty-pound 120 mm mortar rounds in this neatly designed ammunition clip on the back." He hit the projector button. Click. A picture of a gaunt, buck-toothed adolescent boy appeared. Pimples covered the unsure face, which was framed by greasy plastic glasses sitting cattywampus on his nose. "Speaking of Izzy Khan."

Laughter rolled through the room.

"This is before he learned to hide that one hundred and sixty-five IQ." Flynn bit his knuckles, trying not to laugh. Izzy had sunk into his seat, glaring at him. "Okay, back to business." A bird's-eye map of Iran, Pakistan, and Afghanistan popped up. He broadly circled southwestern Afghanistan. "Ninety percent of Afghanistan's opium and heroin flows through this corner of Afghanistan. If it doesn't go across the border crossings or through the pass to Pakistan, then it goes to Iran or Turkey. We don't know exactly why our first team was killed, but there is a good chance that disrupting the drug trade had something to do with it." He stole a quick breath. "Organized crime here is driven by the opium economy as well as the fact that the national government in Kabul has zero presence in Nimroz Province. The people in this area are as hard as nails. They are dependent on smuggling, and confiscating their livelihood will incite reactions, possibly from players on both sides of the border." Flynn observed the men's expressions. I wonder what's going through their minds. "That's one of the reasons the tour will be short. We plan to be in field as soon as the end of July and out by the start of September." The recruits remained stoic, only their bouncing feet betraying them. Flynn drew a line parallel to the long axis of the mountain range, itself perpendicular to the Afghanistan-Pakistan border. "The pass is along this line. It's an old smuggling route blasted out of the mountainside during the Soviet occupation."

Click. The first team's group picture popped onto the screen. "This is the previous team. These men ran into a force that jammed their GPS communication system.

We've taken measures to lessen that chance, but we can't set up the eLORAN grid until we get to the pass. That means we will be vulnerable to ambush all the way from Camp Leatherneck until that grid is up. That eighty-mile journey will likely be the most dangerous leg of the mission. We have intelligence that since we were there last, hundreds of smugglers have moved into the area with sophisticated electronics and weaponry. Odds are we will have to fight our way to the pass." The recruits didn't flinch. Look at 'em, all cool and laid back. "In Toyota pickup trucks." The recruits shifted in their seats. Oh, that got their attention. "The good news is Samuel Khan's brother, Salar Khan, is an Afghan national. Salar commands over fifty hardened Pashtun fighters who will shepherd us in." He turned off the projector, and the lights came back on. "You have all tested well on the simulator, but let's not kid ourselves. It's a glorified video game. Training on the range will begin tomorrow after your hardware is fitted and issued. I'll stick around for a moment to answer any immediate questions; otherwise, you're free to retire to your quarters. Good night, gentlemen."

The men filed out of the War Room to the wing of apartments built for contractors visiting S&K Industries. Samuel and Izzy stood at the back, speaking to Ms. Hulsey. Flynn walked toward them, buttoning his blue sport jacket as he approached.

The woman was tan, blonde and physically fit. She looked thirty-something with striking features. "Pardon me, Izzy," she said as she turned to Flynn, extending her hand. "Hello, I'm Kate Hulsey." Her long eyelashes accentuated brown, doe-like eyes.

I hope my hand isn't sweaty. Flynn shook her hand. He tried to sound smooth. "It's a pleasure. I'm Robert Flynn, the commander of the platoon."

Her hand gripped his with unusual firmness. "You gave a sobering presentation, commander. I don't know the specifics of ORION, but I am keen to learn all I can." She let go and turned to Samuel, placing her hand on his shoulder, the man's eyes fluttering as if he might faint. "Mr. Khan here said you and Izzy will walk me through ORION in the morning—show me the ropes, so to speak."

Izzy stepped in front of Flynn, squaring his shoulders. "I would be thrilled to show you my creation."

Flynn stepped back, observing Kate over Izzy's head.

Samuel's face turned red. He hip-checked Izzy, knocking him out of the way. "Ms. Hulsey, allow me to show you to your quarters." Samuel led her out of the grandiose area, his hand gently touching her elbow.

☐

CHAPTER 8

Flynn made his way to his quarters, thinking of her. She's too fantastic to be real. She must represent some powerful forces, but she acts so calm—and so sexy. The sentiment faded as he turned the corner into the "Leather Lounge," a collection of plush leather sofas and chairs centered in a gathering space between the halls of apartments. The tranquil setting had been hijacked by the applicants, who were goofing around. Flynn stopped, obscured from view, behind a large limestone column. He peeked around the hiding spot. Chen and Jefferson were seated away from the group, hands between their legs like two wallflowers already realizing they were of the same ilk and perhaps not part of the vanguard.

"I'm gonna make ya famous, boyee," someone said with a thick twang. That sounds like that skinny Texan. Flynn peeked around the column. Indeed, it was Robin Barnes. He was holding a Big Chief writing tablet in one hand and an oversized pencil in the other. He was sitting next to a thick-necked Hispanic man.

Barnes licked the end of the ridiculous pencil. "Mendez, what makes you tick?"

Mendez grimaced, looking around as if trying to

find a way out of the impromptu interview. His shoulders sagged as he turned toward Barnes. "I thought you gave up the writing gig, being that you suck at it." Mendez's mouth tightened into a thin-lipped smile, at once triumphant and condescending. "Have you even sold a single story?"

Barnes shrugged. "I need more interesting subject matter. Hanging out with you guys is perfect. I've got fascinating personalities, a dangerous mission and intrigue, all here in front of me."

Mendez crossed his arms. "Just don't write anything messed up about me this time. My mother read that repulsive letter you wrote to me. She still thinks I'm gay, you prick."

Barnes frowned, making a shooing motion at Mendez with his free hand. "I'm not out to make anybody look bad." He viewed the man with interest. "Okay, how old are you and where were you hatched?"

Mendez lifted his leg. RAPRAPRAPRAP. A loud fart reverberated off the thick leather, driving the inquisitive Texan back. "A little taste of home for ya," Mendez said, waving the fart toward Barnes.

Barnes cut his eyes. "Ugh. At least tell me what you know of our commander. You served with him before. What's he like?"

Flynn's ears perked up, straining to hear the response. Mendez was more comfortable talking about someone else, his posture relaxing as he melted into the sofa. "He's solid but suspicious till you earn his trust." Mendez spat snuff into a Styrofoam cup. "He's a clever bastard but a hard-ass if you're a fuck-up, so you'd better watch out." He shrugged. "Myself, I've never had a problem with him." Mendez rubbed his face then stood up. "I've had enough, Barnes. I'm headed to bed." He turned and ambled away, middle finger in the air.

Barnes frowned, turning to Rex Laster, who was arguing with a well-heeled man whom Flynn recognized as Stephen Rosenberg. Barnes walked over to the group, standing beside Rex Laster. "You two know each other?"

Laster kept his eyes pinned to Rosenberg. "All too well. Sobieski and I had to listen to this arrogant prick grumble for six months last year."

Jan Sobieski, a tall, skinny Slav born in Poland, groaned. "Uh-huh, six looong months." The Slav's brows rose high. "I must admit, though, he's good to have around—a veritable human genius this one."

Laster piled on. "Often wrong but never in doubt."

Rosenberg flipped a double bird. "Fuck both of you cave cunts!"

Laster rubbed his eyes. "Dish it out but can't take it?"

Barnes scribbled on his tablet. "Damn! You guys ALREADY hate each other. What's the story, Rosenberg?"

Rosenberg cast a contemptuous stare at Barnes. "Fuck you and your questions, you presumptuous little asshole. Prying into our business isn't going to earn you any brownie points, and it won't make up for your lack of verbal ability. You're tonguing the wrong hole, boy."

Barnes straightened and took a step back, scowling at Rosenberg. "Pfft. I stand corrected, Rosenberg. You truly are a prick." Barnes turned back to Laster, pointing at the man's Celtic tattoos. The art ran from Laster's left arm up the side of his neck and onto his face, framing his left eye. "What do the tats mean, bro?"

Laster glared at Barnes for a moment. "Bro? Seriously?" Laster rubbed his hands over his face. "Okay, if it'll make you go away. But get it through your head: We're not tight." His eyes moved to his left arm. "Each tattoo represents an event in my life, usually killing someone. A memento of the memory."

A loud smack rang out. Stephen Rosenberg was slapping his knee and pointing at Laster. "I'm telling you guys! This dude is one fucked-up red scare!" Laster flipped his middle finger up. Rosenberg shook his head. "It's all right, Laster. I'd be pissed off too if I looked like a freckled baboon's ass." Rosenberg threw his head back and cackled. "Man, I crack myself up."

Laster's lower jaw jutted out. "Oh, how I missed you, my friend." He made the motion of firing a handgun at Rosenberg's head.

Rosenberg now eagerly addressed Barnes, pointing to Laster and Sobieski. "Write this down in your preschool tablet. These two are mindless assholes. Laster cares only about fighting, and Sobieski only about food; otherwise, they're hollow vessels."

Barnes's brow puckered. "I've served with Sobieski, he's not so—"

A burst of sarcastic laughter rang out from Sobieski. "Hollow vessels? Who the fuck are you, Rosenberg? Moral Roberts?" Sobieski pointed his gangly finger at the man. "We didn't go to Princeton, but that doesn't make us inferior."

Rosenberg smiled, his eyes tightening. "It does, and you know it. Otherwise you wouldn't say it."

Rex Laster jumped up; fists tight as he kicked the ottoman away. "Rosenberg, you pretentious hemorrhoid, I'll beat your ass." Laster crouched, circling Rosenberg like a puma as Rosenberg assumed a boxer's stance.

Sobieski jumped between the two men, holding his arms out as if holding Laster back. "Stand back and watch for the blood spatter, boys. Time to see why we call him T. Rex!"

Barnes's head tilted to the side. He put the pencil to the tablet then peered at Sobieski with raised eyebrows. "T. Rex?"

Sobieski nodded. "He chews chunks out of motherfuckers. It's fucked up."

From across the room, Flynn could see the color fade from Rosenberg's face.

Barnes straightened as he moved closer to Rex

Laster. "Jesus Christ! You've sharpened your canines." Barnes glanced around at the others then turned back to the Viking. "You don't really eat people alive? It's not true, is it?" He regarded Laster with an uncertain childlike expression.

Laster cocked his head. "You want to find out, Tex?"

Barnes scooted out of Laster's reach with comedic timing, drawing snickers from some of the mercenaries.

Laster was visibly annoyed, shaking his head as if trying to get hold of his temper. "I don't fuckin' eat people. It's called kinamotay. It's a Filipino martial art which includes biting as a discipline."

Barnes leaned forward. "Shut the front door! Seriously? You practice chewing pieces off of human beings?"

Laster smirked. "Kinamotay is like jiu-jitsu but with biting instead of choking. It's a demoralizing maneuver. I go for the back of the neck, the ears, the latissimus muscle of the upper back, the nipples and the groin. The trick is that you have to practice not biting too much flesh at once." He rubbed his front row of teeth. "Using only my incisors, I can chew a five-pound roast to pieces in minutes."

Rosenberg jabbed his finger at the redheaded Celt. "I rest my case!" he said to no one in particular. "He belongs in a cage."

Barnes's head nodded like a bobble doll. "I'm impressed. That's psychopathic."

Laster sneered. "Just an interest." He tipped his chin at Rosenberg. "I reserve it for those who really hurt my feelings."

The skinny Texan slid farther away from Laster. "Remind me to shoot you if you ever get pissed at me." He shifted his focus, walking over to a large man.

Flynn put his fist to his mouth. Oh shit. He's

gonna go fuck with Bollick. Barnes looked like a kid as he plopped onto the sofa next to Bollick, the huge pencil ready to scribble. "You look more like a professional wrestler than a soldier. What's your story?"

Bollick mock-lunged at Barnes. "Raaaaaa! Fuck off. That's my story, worm."

Barnes fell on the ground as he tried to escape, laughter erupting from the others. Barnes simulated masturbation with his right hand. "Wankity-wank, Grumpy!"

Laster's voice echoed across the room. "Barnes, what's your story?"

The slender man gave an innocent smile. "I'm just a simple country boy from Texas trying to get a—"

Sobieski rushed over, wrapping up Barnes from behind and good-naturedly placing a hand over the Texan's mouth. "Oh, allow me since I had the pleasure of rooming with him." Sobieski wrinkled his nose like he smelled a fart. "He's a gross, uncouth son of a bitch, constantly adjusting his package. I think he's chasing off half the time."

Barnes looked sheepish. "I'm trying to quit," he mumbled from behind Sobieski's hand.

Sobieski blinked. "See what I mean? You can't say anything without some puerile retort." Sobieski's face contorted into amusement as he released Barnes and began to cackle. He spoke through snorting laughter, pointing at Robin Barnes. "One of the guys found his pocket pussy and hung it in the mess tent!"

"Pocket pussy?" What in the frosted fuck?!" Laster exclaimed, the room bursting into hilarity.

Sobieski's face was beet red. "No shit! A little pink latex thing with dark, big-ass lips and a clit!" He doubled over as if in pain. "That's not the best part. It had disgusting black hair glued all over it. By the look of it, Barnes pasted them on himself."

Barnes's chin dropped to his chest. "The bald one

made me feel unclean."

Laughter turned to cackling.

Barnes's brow furrowed. "You sons o' bitches are a bunch of damn hypocrites, like y'all don't spank it!"

Rosenberg stood up, arms in the air. "Most of us employ something different—female companionship. You should try it, hick."

Barnes shook his head in disagreement. "In the fucking field? Yeah, whatever, genius." He shrugged. "At least the pocket pussy doesn't tell me what to do and satisfaction is guaranteed." He laughed heartily. "I'm taking it with me if any of y'all need to borrow it." A shower of cups and leather cushions rained onto Barnes, driving him back to his room.

CHAPTER 9

Flynn sat at the breakfast table with Izzy and Kate. Gurgle, gurgle. He pressed his fist into his stomach and swallowed hard, tasting the acid reflux. Look natural and don't talk too fast. Kate looked up from her breakfast, her gaze fixing on his. Her eyes are so pretty, and her nose is perfect. You're staring at her. Say something. "Uh, Ms. Hulsey, I'm—"

"Ahem." Izzy cleared his throat. "Ms. Hulsey, how long do we have the honor of your company?"

Flynn shot a sideways glance at Izzy. Here comes the Izzy of Arabia routine.

"I have several hours until I need to get back," she said.

Izzy nodded. "Good, that's just enough time."

"What led you to develop ORION, Mr. Khan?"

"In the spring of 2010, I was on my first tour in Helmand Province. That's where I met Flynn. He was my commanding lieutenant. We were deep into a three-day patrol when we were ambushed. We had to hide behind a pile of rocks for forty-five minutes, waiting for air support. As we were getting picked apart, it became evident that if we had a little drone, we could use it to target the enemy.

We could shoot mortars while hidden behind the rocks, but we had no way to direct them in without seeing the insurgents." Izzy paused. "We lost eight out of twenty-four men that day. It was an awful experience and to make it worse, we were back on patrol the next day."

"Why?"

"We realized that to be effective, we had to project a larger presence than a single company. To convince them our numbers were greater, we had to stay on constant patrol, which exhausted the men." He shook his head. "That's obsolete now. We can kill without being seen while we establish plausible doubt in their psyches."

She reached for her coffee. "Plausible doubt?"

"That's right," Flynn interjected. "A platoon armed with ORION is like a submarine. It's the monster under the bed. ORION allows a small, hidden unit to dominate a geographical area with self-sufficiency and firepower never imagined in a foot platoon."

Kate changed position in her chair. "Okay ..."

Izzy leaned in. "The real brainstorming started when we heard about another unit using remote-controlled trucks for IED inspection. I talked to my father and he came up with several prototypes. We used them for reconnaissance and sniffing out improvised explosives. Before long, Flynn had us strapping Claymore mines and SLAM munitions on them and driving them into the enemy. When the quadcopters came out, we realized they were the holy grail we had been dreaming of. Father built a high-performance model with a high-definition camera and a GPS-based targeting system."

"Flynn? You had a hand in this too?"

"Hard to believe, right?"

Kate chuckled, casting a sideways glance at Izzy.

Izzy ignored them. "When I returned from Helmand, I studied the JDAM tailfin kit used to turn dumb bombs into satellite-guided bombs." He allowed a self-indulgent shrug. "I just applied the concept to mortars." Izzy rolled his arm and bowed. "Voila, ORION was born!" He straightened up and smoothed his shirt, speaking in a deeper tone. "We're in our eighth generation, using electronically enhanced encryption applied to the tower-based WWII-era long-range navigation system."

Kate's eyes narrowed. "Isn't that archaic technology? I remember them recently shutting down the last active LORAN station in Alaska."

"Yes, that's the beauty of it," Izzy said. "The land system was abandoned, and everyone went to global positioning satellites. Everyone. Father and I went the other direction and developed unassailable encryption codes that allowed us to electronically enhance the old, low- frequency technology."

Kate frowned. "eLORAN utilizes low frequencies. How is that revolutionary?"

Izzy put his thumb and index finger close together. "The powerful low frequencies are impossible to jam. Better yet, they're even below the noise-detection levels of GPS jammers. ORION's operating system is undetectable to modern anti-GPS electronics. The enemy won't have a clue we're out there."

Kate sat back, her eyes sharpening. "Surely there's a way to defeat your new system."

"There is, but it's difficult. Just like the old days, you have to locate and destroy the transmitters. Our strategy is to place a redundant grid of transmitters in an area we want to control. That way, even if multiple transmitters are destroyed, the network still provides accurate targeting and communication. The best part is when an enemy destroys one of our transmitters, we know exactly where they are."

"It sounds like an electronic spider web." Kate remained silent for a moment as if contemplating something. She put a handout. "Forgive me. This is off topic and I shouldn't be doing this, but I've been preoccupied with something I heard during the debriefing." Her ears turned red. "It has nothing to do with ORION, but I am a woman and sometimes these things matter to me."

One of Izzy's brows arched high. "Okay, what's on your mind?"

"Well, it's that dog. The one that Joseph Roddick wrote about. Do you know if it survived? It sounded like a member of the team."

"I'm not sure," Izzy said, stealing an uneasy glance at Flynn. "I heard it was injured. It could be dead for all I know."

Kate clutched herself. "Those Pashtuns should help the poor thing. Something could be done about it. A veterinarian would know what medicines to bring. If it's still alive," she said.

Flynn nodded. "I think that's a great idea, Ms. Hulsey. I'll go see a veterinarian. When we get to Nimroz Province, I'll make sure it gets the attention it deserves."

Kate took his hand and gave it a squeeze. "You're a doll."

Flynn looked at Izzy, beating back his jealous eyes. "You ready to head out?"

"Yeah," he said in a disgruntled tone as he pulled out his cellphone. "Miguel? … Yes, yes, bring the cars around." Izzy stood up, ushering Kate toward the exit. His manicured hand brushed the muscles of her low back, visible through the silk blouse. That son of a bitch is cockblocking me. Flynn followed ten feet behind the two to the rotunda. Sheeze, I'm already a third wheel. The banshee wail of the Ferrari Italia pierced the air, the exhaust popping in report as the eight cylinders wound down. The white beauty slid in, easing to a stop under the pavilion. A uniformed man opened the door and stepped out. Bang! Flynn jerked his head to the left at the explosion. A large cloud of black smoke followed the old jalopy of a van as it lurched in behind the Italia, coughing and dying. The smell of raw gasoline drifted in. It was the groundskeeper's trash vehicle. A sense of machismo grief filled him, his manhood wounded as Izzy led Kate to the sensuous Ferrari and opened the low-slung door. Her tight white jeans made her ass look as incredible as the vehicle she was sliding into. Izzy closed her door then turned, smiling at Flynn as he slipped on his aviators. Izzy walked around the car, holding his arms out wide. "Ahh, buddy, why the long face?" Izzy put his arms over his head, snapping his fingers as he twisted a perfect silhouette. "See ya at the range, sucker." He plopped into the supercar, revving the engine and dumping the clutch. An explosion of noise erupted under the portico. Flynn put his hands to his ears, engulfed in the acrid smoke pouring from the masterpiece as it wiggled away.

Cough, cough. Flynn waved his hand. "Dickhead." He trudged to the van and pulled on the door handle, but it wouldn't budge. "You gotta be kidding me!" He put his foot on the van and pulled. Thunk! The door popped loose, catapulting him backward. Oommph! The air burst from his lungs as he hit the concrete, door handle still in hand. He saw stars, looking around with embarrassment as he rubbed the sore bump growing on the back of his scalp. He gingerly pushed himself onto one knee then stood up and looked around. No one had witnessed his misfortune. Oh, Izzy, you sorry bastard. Flynn tossed the handle in and crawled into the stained seat. The stench of ground-in cigarettes marbled with stale alcohol and fresh vomit made his nostrils curl. He grabbed the door and pulled it shut, then turned the key. The van started with a shake, black smoke pouring from the back as he put it in gear and lurched forward.

An hour later he pulled the overheating vehicle off Highway 181 into the huge estate that served as S&K's gunnery range. He drove through the crunching gravel and parked alongside the Italia. He got out, slamming the door in defiance. It kicked back, pain exploding as the door dug into his shin. He flipped the vehicle off, indignantly limping toward Izzy and Kate. They stood chuckling under a palatial oak.

"How was the drive, Flynn?" Izzy asked.

Flynn felt his face flush. "How was the drive, Flynn?" he said in a high, mocking tone.

Kate stifled a laugh with her hand.

Izzy cut his eyes at Flynn then turned to Kate, pointing to a row of tables close by. "We've got the gear over here, Ms. Hulsey."

As they sauntered over, the agent scanned the gear, gazing over the helmets before settling on one of the snakelike robots. She picked one up, struggling to curl it. "What do we have here?"

Izzy took the slender robot out of her hands and dropped it on the ground. He reached for his glove and helmet and slipped them on, hitting the power button on the glove as he verbally cataloged the process. "Power on. Establishing communication link. Voila, we are live." The robotic snake slithered across Kate's feet.

She jumped away from it, covering her mouth with her hand. "It's so quiet! How fast can it go?"

Izzy scratched his chin. "Two miles per hour, which isn't that impressive but what is are these. Notice the modular segments arranged in series. They're constructed of 440 stainless steel and can take incredible abuse." He ran his finger over the inner ridges of another on the table. "By arranging the transmitters in series, we achieve signal amplification and even if it gets blown to bits, some of these transmitters will continue to function."

Kate bent over, running her fingers over the robotic snake. "If the transmitters in the grid are asymmetric, will it affect the accuracy of the targeting or communication systems?"

"No," Izzy said. "The snakebots or 'transmitters' use a pseudorandom code, known only to us, to authenticate tower and receiver position before each transmission. As long as they are close, it doesn't matter where each respective transmitter is."

Kate's eyes narrowed. "Why don't you just fly the transmitters in? Too heavy?"

Izzy nodded. "Uh-huh, and the quadcopters are too noisy at ground level. These snakes can't be heard from even three feet away. They will allow a unit to move in undetected under a protective umbrella, albeit a slow-moving umbrella."

Flynn collected a handful of pebbles, laying them out on the cafeteria-style table. "These pebbles represent the transmitters Izzy alluded to earlier. The operating system can only be rendered inoperable by destroying almost all of them, which would be near impossible. Anyone destroying or hacking a transmitter can be localized and engaged by the precision mortars."

Izzy broke back into the conversation. "Each man in the network has his own UAV and mortar tube, but one can target his mortars off of any of the UAVs. That's the lethality, the redundancy. Once a team with ORION is engaged, an enemy must knock all the UAVs from the air or kill every man with a mortar tube. Otherwise, pinpoint-accurate mortar strikes will continue."

Kate walked to one of the tables. She picked up an 81 mm mortar round. "This is what ORION is built around, the 81 mm mortar, correct?"

"Uh-huh," Izzy said. "The traditional 81 mm has four pounds of explosive, but ours hit a hell of a lot harder." He indulged in a satisfied smile. "We've increased the detonation energy threefold by using a new class of nitroamine explosive."

Kate stepped back and crossed her arms. "CL-20?"

Izzy's head jerked back. "You've heard of it?"

"I know India has adapted it to small warheads." She poked a finger at him. "You better not be colluding with them!"

Izzy put his hands up.

"Careful, Mr. Khan." She held his eyes for a moment then touched a bigger shell. "The 120 mm round, is it also CL-20?"

"Uh-huh, fifteen pounds per round. They hit with three times the energy of a TOW antitank missile. We have two types of warheads for the 120 mm. One is an anti-personnel round; the other utilizes a six-inch copper core capable of killing any tank in existence." He pointed to one with a blue stripe painted across the widest part of the mortar shell. "If one of those anti-personnel rounds detonated in the middle of a football field, it would kill everyone on the field and most in the stands. We use CL-20 for all of our explosive devices, including the remote-controlled rocks over there. They can be painted and moved at will with up to a fifty-kilogram warhead. With the CL-20 explosive, they pack the punch of a five-hundred-pound aerial bomb."

Kate whistled, "Good God! That's enormous firepower for a foot platoon. You guys are your own air force and artillery corps." She looked around. "Where are those robot avatars I've heard so much about?"

A flush spread across Izzy's face. "They're still at S&K." He pointed to his leg below his right knee. "Each robot has a 120 mm mortar tube mounted here into each of its lower legs. It can carry six rounds and will reload its own magazine as needed."

"What's their maximum rate of fire?"

"Twelve rounds per minute."

"How about moving targets?"

"No problem," Izzy said. "We can track multiple moving targets." He played with the movable fins attached to the back of the mortar round. "The round can correct one foot laterally for every twenty feet of vertical drop."

Kate looked at her wristwatch. "How about a demonstration?"

CHAPTER 10

Flynn cracked the bus window and placed his face in the cold morning air. The bus's right tires crashed into a deep pothole, a jarring double impact that tossed everyone except Bollick out of their seats. Flynn stole a sideways glance at the man seated in the adjacent row. Brian Bollick was introverted and radiated a toxic cloud of unfocused resentment. He was bigger than the rest of them and a hell of a lot more muscular. Flynn shook his head. No wonder people avoid you. His eyes narrowed as he thought about the man's vetting material. Court-martialed for slicing the throat of a Taliban commander? It's too fantastic to believe. He read the report back in his mind. HQ had suspected a Taliban chief was responsible for a brutal ambush that killed half of Bollick's patrol. Unfortunately, they had no hard evidence and the company commander refused to start a conflagration without proof. That's when he went over the edge. How could someone could be so cracked to walk through a fully manned Taliban compound in the dead of night and live through it?! Flynn closed his eyes, imagining he was Bollick. His heart thumped against his breastbone, abdomen tensing as he tiptoed into the high-walled compound, moving like a ghost around the sleeping fighters. He drew his blade and ducked into the musty chamber. Flynn opened his eyes, goose pimples erupting all over. Bollick was absent-mindedly staring out his window. He had to be crazy, but he was also diabolically clever. I hope he doesn't have a death wish. I have my hands full with Izzy as it is. Flynn put his fist to his mouth. "Ahem."

Bollick turned his head, his owl-like eyes locking onto him. "Hmmh?"

"Bollick, I need your assistance. Izzy is at the lab showing the woman from the Pentagon what the avatars can do. I need help demonstrating the hardware and getting this ball rolling. I thought you and Laster would be perfect."

Bollick straightened, brows rising. "Yeah, sure I'll fill in." His demeanor softened as he crossed his arms and cocked his head. "What you got in mind?"

"I want them firing rounds on the mortar tubes and above all they have to learn the intricacies of the quadcopters. You and Laster are faster than the rest. I want you two to set the bar high. Make it something they can't approach. It'll give the newbies something to shoot for."

Bollick smirked. "I'll do my best."

"Good. I knew I could count on you. I'm glad you're back, Brian. I hear you played semiprofessional baseball in Louisiana. Any chance I'm sitting next to a future big leaguer?"

"Pfft! Come on." Bollick crossed his arms, eyeing Flynn for deceit. "I used to think I could make it but, as usual, I screwed the pooch." He scratched his temple. "I gotta face it. I'm never going to be a Major League center fielder."

"Why?"

"I threw two runners out at home plate from the center-field fence."

"That's a bad thing?"

"I'm supposed to relay to the shortstop or one of the other infielders."

Flynn waved the comment away. "So what? You threw them out!"

A look of embarrassment came over him. "Yeah, but I missed two other throws, and it cost us a couple of games."

"Oh."

"It's funny. I said I'd never go back to Afghanistan but here I am, headed right back into the fray. Why are you going?"

Flynn considered the question. "Lots of reasons, I suppose. I guess partly because I owe Samuel, but I'd like to think it's for all those soldiers in the field that need something better. I just hope I can do it without getting us killed."

"I second the motion."

"How about you?"

Bollick became distant again, rubbing his arm as he turned to peer out the window. "I'm not reintegrating worth a shit. People and their social media, clawing for recognition and approval. I can't exist in a fishbowl of brainwashed sheeple." The hardness in his eyes returned. "But the real reason I'm going?" He ground his fist into his palm. "Whoever killed our first team, I know we'll run into them again." The man's eyes grew ghoulish. "When we do, I'm going to kill every goddamn one of 'em." Bollick shrugged, his expression lightening. "Besides, five million bones and no fucking foot patrols— shit, what a gig. I would never make that kind of coin as a half-ass center fielder."

The image of Bollick chunking a baseball over an entire field vanished as the bus slowed abruptly. Flynn braced himself on the seat in front of him, gasoline fumes wafting in as they pulled into the parking lot, squealing air brakes bringing them to a halt. He stood up, scanning the recruits as their eyes bored into him. "No more video games. It's time for live fire." He pointed out the windows. "We have educational stations set up for you to rotate through. Each station covers an integral facet of ORION that you must master. Your station chief will rotate through with your group." Flynn put his hand on his chest. "I will lead group one: Bollick, Barnes, Laster and Sobieski, come with me. Group two: Mendez, Chen, Jefferson and Rosenberg, go with Instructor Jordan. The remainder of you shadow Instructor Compton."

Flynn exited the bus into fresh air. Tendrils of warmth from the sun-soaked asphalt mixed with the fragrant cool air from the previous evening. "Let's go," he said, motioning for them to follow. He walked to the firing range. It consisted of a rolling meadow that extended out a mile before rising acutely into an enormous hill covered with green grass and pastel wildflowers. Clusters of manlike targets were arranged in groups of twenty as far as he could see.

"Here we are," Flynn said as he approached two old cafeteria-style tables covered with gear. At one end was a large belt-fed machine gun. On the other was ORION's lightweight composite mortar tube and baseplate. In the middle lay the RC truck and different sizes of mortar rounds. He motioned for the men to gather round as he retrieved a helmet with a bulletproof transparent aluminum visor. He put it on and cinched the chin strap. He next put on the protective jacket with the quadcopter's Kevlar holster sewn into the back of the armor. He slipped on the glove and pointed to the machine gun. "Here is S&K's modified Browning .50-caliber heavy machine gun. This beast will best be used as a concealed defensive weapon utilizing ORION's remote operating system." He swung his arm to the left, pointing to the other end of the table. "Over there is the beating heart of ORION, the 81 mm mortar system." He walked over and picked up one of the small mortar tubes. "The main physical hindrance with this is the adjustment wheels, which have to be turned for basic elevation and deflection. So, mind your thumbs." He set it down and walked to the next item on the table, the RC truck. Pride surged through him as he touched the big device, running his gloved hand over the indestructible knobby tires and the perfect carbon fiber suspension. "This is our prized Fatboy here." He patted the vehicle like it was a favorite child. "This is the ultimate Tonka truck, every piece of it engineered by S&K. It's got two types of warheads. SLAM charges—select light attack munition— to penetrate armor and an antipersonnel version. These Fatboys can carry a twenty-kilogram bomb at twenty-five miles per hour or a fifty-kilogram warhead at ten miles per hour." Flynn took a painted fiberglass shell and snapped it onto the truck, visually turning it into a harmless-looking rock. "These truck bombs are also packed with CL-20 so, for god's sake, don't be close to one when it detonates." He shook his head. "Needless to say, with this kind of power, we won't be setting any of these off in the U.S." Disappointed murmurs resonated from the group. He pointed to the boxes of helmets, vests, and gloves resting on the ground under the tables. "Your gear is labeled with your names. Find your stuff, put it on, and get on the line." The men located their gear and quickly had it on. They looked like storm troopers, with the helmets covering much of their faces. A protective bib extended from the back of the helmet to the back of the armored vest.

Flynn pulled out his stopwatch as he looked to Bollick and then to Laster. "Bollick, you and Laster get up here. Show these noobs how it's done. Laster, you're the speedster. You get on the mortar tube. Bollick, get ready with that UAV."

Bollick stepped to the line and crouched. "Ready."

"BANG! BANG!" Flynn said, observing Bollick react. The man reached back, yanking the UAV free, sending it skyward with a flick of the wrist. Buuuuzzz. The craft's whirring sound changed to a whine then became inaudible as it disappeared.

Flynn monitored Bollick's camera image on his own visor. Their human figures shrank into specks. Bollick decisively chose his target, the red cursor highlighting the bogey. "Fire!"

Laster's fingers deftly spun the wheels, adjusting for elevation and deflection. He grabbed the waist of the mortar round, dropping it down the tube as he ducked away. Kaboom!

Flynn watched the target, clicking the stopwatch as the target disappeared in a cloud of dirt. "Forty-seven seconds, a respectable time. Barnes and Sobieski, you guys get up there and see how you stack up."

Flynn watched their performance with interest. Soon, Barnes and Sobieski were within seconds of Bollick and Laster. Flynn beckoned them over, clapping like a Little League coach. "Great job, men. Time to move to the next station." He started across the grass, soon reaching another set of tables. Flynn turned to face them. "This is the M.A.I.L. station. M.A.I.L. stands for 'misdirection and invisibility equals life.' Misdirection and invisibility are important facets of ORION's enhanced survivability. Given the small numbers of our platoon, misdirection will be pivotal to our survival." Flynn tapped his temple. "The human brain is so clever that it can be made to fool itself. This is what magicians and pickpockets exploit. The mind believes what the eyes perceive, largely due to our lack of other developed senses. Think about a good dog. A man can easily be fooled whereas the dog cannot." Their faces looked blank. "Okay, I see I'm getting nowhere. Has anyone heard of Jasper Maskelyne?"

The four men offered only perplexed expressions and gestures. Flynn let out a deep sigh. "Oh, come on! Jasper Maskelyne was a British stage magician that saved the British seaport in Alexandria, Egypt, during the Second World War."

Barnes blurted out, "Wait a minute. He's that dude that built a fake city. Gave the Germans the Jedi mindfuck."

Flynn nodded. "Attaboy, Barnes. Yes, Maskelyne spent weeks concocting the elaborate con, placing thousands of rubber tanks, water lines and lights about seven miles down the coast from Alexandria. General Rommel was completely fooled, bombing the makeshift city every night while Alexandria lay safe in the darkness." Flynn glanced around at pieces of gear. "ORION uses similar tactics, namely these LED flashers and to a lesser extent, the tiny bomblets that mimic a mortar position." He grabbed one of the flashers. It looked like a child's toy of jacks with six metal legs, each with a loop for the quadcopter to hook to. A flashing reddish-orange light in the center mimicked bursts of machine gun fire. Flynn picked up one, running his thumb over one of the hooks. "These flashers will be set up by the quadcopters to draw fire away from us and to trick the enemy into exposing their location."

Brian Bollick walked to one of the tables, reaching for a cylindrical object the size of small jar of peanut butter. He pulled on it, but it held fast to the table. His brow furrowed. "Is this one of the magnetic thermite grenades I heard about?"

"It is."

Bollick pulled his hand away as if the grenade was hot. "What are its specifications against modern armored steel?"

Flynn looked up, recalling the data. "They burn at four thousand degrees Fahrenheit and will burn through any armored system in existence. Performance envelope is up to sixteen inches of AR500 plate armor."

Bollick admired the device, pulling on the small cord attached to it.

Flynn grabbed Bollick's arm. "Be careful! That triggers the thermite." Flynn reached back and pulled the UAV free. "You attach the string to your quad like this." He clipped the two together, the bomb hanging from the UAV. "Now just fly up unseen, attach it to any ferrous metal that you want to destroy, and haul ass." He pulled the string taut. "You accelerate the quadcopter away hard, which pulls out the pin." Flynn disconnected the two and put the device back on the table. He motioned to the adjacent tabletop filled with the LED flashers. "Okay, let's get to practicing."

CHAPTER 11

The short drive to his mother's house lasted forever. What would he tell her? Flynn pulled the vehicle along the curb. She was sitting on the porch of the red brick home, wringing her hands. He walked up the cracking sidewalk of his childhood dwelling, arms extended wide as she stood to greet him. He hugged her but she pulled away, examining his face with glistening blue-gray eyes. She stroked her crooked fingers through his short-cropped hair, her eyes darting around his face as if memorizing every detail. Another wave of guilt heaved through him. "Mom, relax, I'm going to be fine." Her posture slumped. "Mom, please, this is our big chance. The team is excellent, and the pay is astronomical—" He caught himself before mentioning the cost of the chemotherapy she needed. "The best thing is, when it's all over, I'll be free and clear of all this legal trouble."

She turned away and covered her mouth. "You're really going to do it, aren't you? You're leaving."

A frog built in his throat as he nodded. "Tomorrow as planned."

The sun on her face illuminated an expression of guilt. "I know you're doing this for me, but you don't have

77

to. I'll be fine." She squeezed his hand, a sliver of hope in her eyes. "You can still stay. Here, with me."

"Mom, I have to go."

She stamped her foot on the concrete. "I may never see you again. Don't you realize? You're everything I have. Why would you leave me now, at the end?"

Flynn mustered a tight-lipped smile. "What do you mean? It's not the end." He looked at the gold cross hanging from the tiny chain around her neck. "With treatment, the doctor said you have a good chance for remission." He put a hand on her shoulder. "You're going to have to look at my face for a long time to come."

She shook her head, a single tear spilling over. "Son, you can't bend the world to your will. You must realize you cannot control fate." She shook her finger. "But you can tempt it. Be careful, Robert."

Flynn cocked his head, his eyes severe. "No, Mom, I refuse to believe that I cannot influence our fate. I've been given a second chance and I must take it."

"Robert, son." She mustered a tired smile. "I am weary. That's why I want you to stay here with me." Her expression changed, face turning ashen. "I admit I have moments when I'm scared, not knowing what the end will be like, not able to take that last breath. Yes, that frightens me but dying alone, without you—that scares me more." Her eyes were bigger, sadder than ever before. She pulled a piece of paper from her pocket. "This is one of my favorite poems. I want you to read it every chance you get." She crammed the piece of paper into his hand and closed his fingers around it.

He put the paper in his pocket then drew her close, kissing the top of her head. "Mother, you can't give up. It's time for me to carry you for once."

She pulled away again. "Samuel Khan is sending you to the same place, isn't he? Do you really think he cares about you? You're just an expensive tool to get him what he wants."

Flynn groaned. "It doesn't matter. This is bigger than him, and it is bigger than me. I believe in what I'm doing, and I'd do it without Samuel." He gripped her hand. "Anyway, things are different this time. The operating and communication systems are cutting-edge!"

"Things always seem different." Her bloodshot eyes narrowed into a fierce squint. "What will happen when you run into the dragon, son?"

Flynn turned his head, considering the odd statement. "I'll kill him or bring him back in chains."

"You'll come back in a coffin, you damn fool!" She inhaled deeply, letting the breath out in a wavering sigh. "Oh son, if only I could make you see." She stared blankly at the ground. "What makes this mission any different than the last one? You think that if you're there, you'll just figure a way out of anything? You're so brave just like your father." Her tremor caused her head to wobble, but her eyes were steady. "Handsome, courageous, eager, and stubborn. He was a heroic man who lived to help those in harm's way." She smiled. "I was with him through it all—the Marines, your birth, and fifteen years at the fire department." Her face turned grave. "They had already lost one man in that blaze. They begged him not to go back in, but her screams were too much for his heart to bear." A tear ran down her face. "They found him, with her in his arms, ten feet from the exit." Her eyes pierced him. "Is this your inferno? Will you make it out?"

CHAPTER 12

July 13, 2012, Camp Leatherneck, Afghanistan

The C-130 cargo plane rolled to a stop, turbines moaning as they wound down. Flynn grabbed his gear and descended a rickety rollaway metal staircase, scanning the pitch-black surroundings as he stepped down onto the tarmac. It was mid-July, but the desert air was chilly.

As they congregated Stephen Rosenberg bent over, rubbing his back and stretching. "That was a long-ass flight. My back is pissed off."

Robin Barnes rubbed his stomach. "Back, hell! My stomach's done chewed through my backbone. If I don't get some chow quick, I may have to come over there and eat some of your pussy, Rosenberg." Barnes leaned back, cackling.

Rosenberg frowned. "Not you too. Come near me, you sick fuck. I swear to God—" He made a slicing motion across his throat.

Flynn glared at them. "You two assholes shut up and follow me. He turned and walked toward a large elongate pole-and-canvas structure barely visible in the dark desert night. As the distance closed, the shape of the tent became apparent; its three high points made it resemble a big top circus tent. A wonderful aroma of freshly fried food intensified as they approached. A makeshift plywood porch was haphazardly built up around the entrance. Standing on it was a dignified-looking officer in uniform. As Flynn approached the porch, the distinguished man descended the tiny staircase and extended his long arm, shaking Flynn's hand.

"Welcome to Afghanistan, men. I'm General Smith, the base commander here at Camp Leatherneck."

Flynn grinned, casting a sweeping nod over his shoulder. "Thank you, sir. I'm Robert Flynn, for better or worse, the commander of these louts. I owe you a debt of gratitude, General Smith. We appreciate you allowing us to land here so late. It means a lot to us that this is kept confidential."

General Smith waved the comment off. "It's my pleasure, young man. I can assure you only a handful of my men know what's going on." He offered a warm smile as if they were old friends. He looked to be in his late sixties. His shoulders were broad though his body appeared withered by the ravages of time. He had no hair and sparse eyebrows. The skin on his face and head was thickened and discolored from the scars of a rough life and years of the sun's radiation. General Smith cocked his head as he regarded Flynn and the others. "I've got several important things to brief you on after you eat. He motioned good-naturedly to a painfully thin man next to him. "My cook—er, my chef—Pete here is magnificent. He has the best chicken-fried steak, mashed potatoes, and gravy you've ever tasted. I'm ready for some myself," he said, rubbing his belly. "Enjoy it, men. We'll talk cowboys and Indians in a while." General Smith walked up the wooden stairs and held open the tent's main flap, ushering them in with an outstretched arm. "Come on, come on. Don't be shy."

The meal, as promised, was excellent. Flynn

washed down the thick steak with a huge glass of lukewarm water then stood and approached General Smith, who had also finished eating and was now standing near the entrance. General Smith scratched his chin, eyes tightening. "Colonel Kelley over at Camp Rose has signed up for another round, huh?"

"Yes, sir."

General Smith nodded. "You're in good hands with Colonel Kelley. I've known that man for thirty years. He took heat for the last go-round, but he'll come in swinging if he has to." General Smith leaned forward, his thin brows rising as he continued in a hushed tone. "You boys aren't welcome by high command. I don't know if you know what's going on around here, but I was told not to have anything to do with S&K Industries." He smirked, rubbing his hands together. "What they don't know won't hurt them." The moment of levity vanished, his expression turning serious. "I have to tell you, son, since we've drawn down our forces, it has been increasingly treacherous traveling outside of established cordons. We're operating with ten percent less manpower than we had two years ago in 2010." He glanced over his shoulder to the west. "The area you are traveling through is so saturated with terrorists, we don't even go west if we don't have to." He rubbed a hand over his bald head. "Samuel Khan picked a rotten time to send such a small team into that area again. The outlaws are floating in and out and attacking in numbers we've never seen. They give no quarter, just kill and loot. Word is that a powerful chieftain named Mullah Mehsud has moved in from a province to the northwest of here. We estimate he has over five hundred hardened and well-equipped foot soldiers at his disposal. Murders in the border areas of the Chagai Hills have tripled since your first platoon was killed there in early spring."

Flynn's face twitched. Tripled?

Bollick lurked nearby, turning around at the comment. He walked over, glaring at General Smith as if he were the enemy. "BRING … IT … ON! If Mullah Mehsud attacks this platoon, it'll be the last thing he ever does."

Flynn cringed as General Smith spun on his heels, face to face with Bollick. The general's voice rose. "I don't know who the hell you think you are talking to me like that, but you better throw those huge balls over your shoulder and keep 'em good and goddamn ready. You're gonna need 'em where you're headed!"

Bollick stepped back. "Huump!" He spat on the ground then turned and walked away.

General Smith frowned at Bollick, eyeing him for a moment before turning back to Flynn. "Mullah Mehsud's foot soldiers have been killing everyone in the valley. The decent people have fled. Only assassins now roam those hills." He pointed a crooked index finger at Flynn. "Remember that! You kill everyone you see if they haven't talked to you first." General Smith's eyes narrowed into a fierce squint. "I'm dead serious, commander. No hesitation. Wherever these sons o' bitches come from, they are the best goddamn ground troops I've ever faced."

Flynn's stomach roiled. "I'll keep that in mind, sir."

General Smith pointed to the west. "Out there, in the dark, are your transport vehicles with Salar Khan and his Pashtun tribesmen. When you're ready, gather your gear and two of my drivers will take you out to meet them." He crossed his arms. "I'll keep my ear to the ground. If you get into trouble, I'll help Colonel Kelley the best I can." He offered a tight-lipped smile. "I hope this isn't the last time I see you, but in any event, good luck, commander."

CHAPTER 13

In the predawn hours they clambered aboard the two trucks. The transports rolled quietly through the west gate then came to a halt. Flynn followed Izzy to the back of the truck and hopped out, landing in a crouch in the soft, deep sand. Flashlights danced as men approached. One of the beams illuminated an overweight Pashtun in tribal dress with a huge bushy beard and mustache. Izzy approached him, the men embracing. The man stood back, gripping Izzy's shoulders. "My nephew! Welcome to Afghanistan!" he said in perfect English. It was Salar Khan, Samuel's first cousin. The man spoke in a rowdy tone. "Life in the west has been good to you, Ishmael. you have your teeth!" Salar chuckled, flashing an edentulous grin.

Izzy glanced over his shoulder at Flynn. "This is Robert Flynn. He is my friend and the commander of our unit."

Salar stepped back, rubbing his thick black beard as he regarded Flynn. "Your brother from Helmand?"

Izzy nodded. "Yes, this is him."

The Pashtun walked over and grasped Flynn's hand, shaking it vigorously. "This is the lion I have heard of." He placed his hand over his chest. "I am Salar. I welcome you, Flynn."

Flynn's face warmed. "Thank you, Salar." Salar turned back to Izzy, and Flynn shifted his attention to the grim-faced Pashtuns who moved briskly, stowing the gear into multiple small white Toyota pickups. Two gaunt adolescent boys performed the lion's share of the task, moving efficiently from vehicle to vehicle, outpacing the adults. Flynn reached for gum for his dry mouth, breaking out the pack in full view of the two boys. The earliest morning light let him see he had captured the boys' interest, but they remained stoic, loading the trucks, pretending not to notice. Flynn waited for them to come back toward him then put out his hand. "Wait." The boys froze, their expressions hard, eyes wary but curious. Without emotion, he tapped out two pieces, handing one to each boy. They popped the gum into their mouths, their brown, almond-shaped eyes widening with delight as they chomped. To his dismay, the boys lost interest, returning to their frenetic pace and somber demeanor.

Izzy let out a sharp whistle then said something in Pashto to which the tiny birdlike men nodded in deference. "Flynn, I told them you're the commander and treat you like a brother. If they give you any grief, let Salar know. They're scared shitless of him."

Salar spoke with Izzy, switching from Pashto to flawless English, no doubt learned before the Soviet occupation and Afghanistan's disintegration into radical Islam. Salar spoke in anxious tones, looking to the west. "I have spent the last month securing a route toward the pass. My scouts have been living along the way to guide our passage into the Chagai Hills." He rubbed the back of his neck. "It has been very treacherous here. The smugglers that have moved in have excellent weapons. I have lost four men this week, and now my scouts aren't answering their radios." He pointed to the west. "My best man is Hamasa. He's out there somewhere, but I haven't heard from him in three days." His eyes tightened as he shook his head. "That is very unlike him. They are hunting him." Salar put his hand on Flynn's shoulder. "We must go."

Flynn put his fingers to his mouth and wolf-whistled. "Second Platoon, gather up! Men, we already have an issue. The Pashtuns guarding our path aren't answering their radios. Salar says they are being hunted down by a huge force of well-equipped smugglers. Prepare the grenade launchers, rockets, and all of the conventional arms we have in case our GPS is jammed."

The Pashtuns' white Toyota pickups were armed with .30-caliber machine guns welded to mounts in the back; light plate armor covered the most vulnerable areas of the vehicles. Salar motioned for Flynn and Izzy to get into the cab of his truck. Laster, Barnes and Sobieski hopped into the back as the trucks moved out along the bumpy, poorly demarcated road.

Ten minutes into the drive Rex Laster leaned over, tapping Flynn on the shoulder through a small back window in the cab. Laster pointed out the windshield, his arms covered in goose pimples. "You see all of these rock formations that are popping up? I feel like I'm in one of those movies right before the shit hits the fan—"

RIIP, TZING, RIP, RIIP. Tracers tore through the atmosphere, grazing the Toyota. Flynn flattened as the stream of glowing bullets passed above them, some bouncing off the plate armor covering the side windows. Laster was first to react. "Drive right at them!" he shouted. Laster disappeared for a moment then reappeared with an M203 grenade launcher in his hands. "Look out there on the horizon where the sun is rising. Do you see them up on that dune? Slow down and give me a shot!" Laster straightened his posture, squinting into the distance as the driver downshifted. Flynn spotted the red flashes of the enemy machine gun on top of a sand dune, four hundred yards away. Laster eyed the distance, estimated the angle of trajectory and fired. The round exploded wide right and fifty yards short. BOOM! Laster fired again. This one found its mark, exploding into the position, the gun and its mount flipping through the air. Flynn shook his finger toward the hood of the truck. "Drive! Drive!"

Barnes's laughter erupted from the back. "That's like a sore peter! Hard to beat, my friend, hard to beat."

Flynn nodded. "Good shot, Laster." The men scrambled into their battle gear as the Toyotas pulled deeper into the foothills. Rocks crunched and popped under the tires until the men were less than ten miles from the pass. Salar said something in Pastho to the driver, who stopped just short of a ridge hiding the topography behind it. He peered into Flynn's eyes with an icy stare. "Tell your men to be ready to fight." The driver eased over the natural ridge, revealing a sloping depression about the size of a city block. It was shaped like an hourglass, its sides formed by complementary rocky ridges. The valley narrowed to fifty meters at its waist.

Laster's head popped into the cab. "We're going to get ambushed."

Flynn studied the opposing outcroppings, hair rising on the nape of his neck. His speaker crackled in his ear and the screens on his HUD went blank. "What the—" Flynn keyed his microphone. "Anybody hear me out there?" Silence. Somebody just jammed our communications. His breathing quickened as he fumbled for the satellite phone. It blinked red: offline. He picked up the only piece of communications equipment left, the old UHF Marine radio. "Anybody out there?" A chorus of excited replies crackled back. "Everyone get ready. We're heading through." The lead truck was traveling too slow. It cleared the waist of the rocky formation, rolling out into more open terrain as gunfire erupted all around. Tak, tak, tak, tak. Dakka, dakka, dakka. It was the unmistakable sounds of the Russian-made PKM heavy machine gun. Like a starry night, hundreds of muzzle flashes twinkled in the early morning light. They lit up both ridges, accompanied by the contrails of the rocket-propelled grenades screaming in. Thoom! A strong concussion shook the truck, making Flynn's ears ring. Ping, ping, tzing! Bullets poured in, bouncing off the armor. "Drive! Drive!" Flynn screamed impotently as the first truck was destroyed, the explosion of an RPG burying its engine block into the sand. The human contents of the vehicle spilled out, the survivors loading into the remaining five Toyotas. The last three trucks veered left, behind the perceived protection of a spinelike rock berm, standing ten to twelve feet high. Only Flynn's Toyota and the one left behind him were in the fight on this side of the rocky spine. He scanned the area, his eyes locking onto a large crater near the center of the valley. It was about eight feet deep with soft dirt pushed up high around its edges. "Tell the driver to park in front of that crater." Salar's eyes followed Flynn's arm, his head nodding in recognition as he turned and jabbered to the driver in Pashto. Flynn held on as the man yanked the Toyota to the right, bouncing on the verge of crashing through boulders and a hail of bullets. The other followed, the two trucks sliding up to the hole, shielding the crater. As they scrambled to pull out the ammunition boxes, a murderous rain of AK-47 machine gun fire erupted from the cliffs above. Tracers accompanied the tearing sound of the supersonic rounds as they pierced the atmosphere, some pinging off the Toyotas, others thumping into the earth like meteors. Flynn keyed the UHF radio. "Mendez, how you holding up?"

Mendez's excited voice poured through. "We are pinned down! There's forty or fifty of 'em moving down the ridge. They're going to overrun our position."

"Pour as much fire back into them as you can until I can get there!" He assessed the variables of the situation, time slowing as his mind came online. His gaze ran across the crater to the ridge on his left. Barnes was already wedged between the lip of the crater and the bumper of one of the Toyotas, his M4 cracking thrice each time he pulled the trigger. Laster stood more exposed, firing the M203 at a machine gun nest. Bollick crouched next to him, prying open wooden boxes of hand grenades with his Ka-Bar.

Izzy sat on the ground next to Bollick, rubbing his ankle as he grimaced in pain. Flynn crawled over to him. "You hit?"

Izzy shook his head. "No, I twisted my ankle. I don't think it's broken, but I can't walk."

Flynn popped up for a second to get his bearings. The muzzle flashes crescendoed. Puffs of dirt were converging on him from every direction, forcing him to squat back into the crater.

Izzy's expression was harried. "I've never seen so much fire!"

"Mendez is about to be overrun. We're going to link up with him then head back this way," Flynn said, motioning frantically for Salar to come over. The Pashtun slid up. Flynn cupped his hands around Salar's ear. "I need men to come with me to charge around that berm and hook up with those three Toyotas. We'll knock out the machine gun and head back this way!"

Salar's radio erupted in excited chatter. He held out his arm, listening for almost half of a minute, his expression changing from surprise to horror. Salar pointed behind them, in the direction they had driven from. "My men say most of the enemy have disengaged from the ridge above Mr. Mendez. They are on the move, attempting to get behind us and close the noose."

Flynn leaned out, his eyes darting around the ridge as he keyed the old field radio. "Mendez, we're heading your way. Get your shit tight and ready to roll. Those bastards up on the ridge above you have broken away. They're going to get around behind us if we don't stop them." Flynn grabbed two of the small AT4 rockets and slipped them over his shoulder. Salar crouched nearby, surrounded by close to ten of his men.

Barnes slid on his butt down the dirt wall of the crater. "Where's everybody headed?"

"I'm leaving you four here as bait while I head off this ambush."

"You're going to do what!?" Barnes yelped.

"You have to hold the men on this side off long enough for Salar and I to stop the other group from getting behind us. We'll counter ambush and swing back and pick you guys up." Flynn pointed to the natural promontory they had first crested to enter the hourglass. "By the time we make it back over that ridge, I imagine they'll be on top of you. They'll be sitting ducks." He smashed his fist into his hand. "We'll cut them to pieces."

Laster emitted a booming laugh then pointed the M203 at him. "Just make sure you time it right. Get back before those knives cut us to pieces." Laster's eyes darted around the crater at the wooden boxes scattered around. "We've got good cover and plenty of ammo, but I don't know how long the four of us can hold off this many men with the high ground. There must be a hundred on this side alone. They're going to charge us as soon as you leave."

"Do your best. I'll be coming over that ridge like a banshee, I promise."

Mendez's voice surged through the radio. "They've got a heavy machine gun that's tearing us to ribbons." A burst of rifle fire erupted through the radio.

Flynn put the radio to his mouth. "Hold on, Mendez! We're coming! Barnes, cover fire!" he said as he scrambled out of the hole. He led the others up and out, ignoring the bullets impacting the dusty ground. He fought to build speed in the deep sand, pumping his arms and legs. He closed the distance, the seconds like hours, finally sliding around the tip of the spinelike berm. Salar and the Pashtuns skidded up behind him, taking up positions. The three Toyotas were parked nose to tail, Mendez and the others plastered against them, firing up into the ridge. A well-placed PKM machine gun controlled the rim, its barrel spitting hundreds of rounds into the Toyotas. Flynn slipped the AT4 rocket off his shoulder. He brought the tube up, flipped up the sight and armed the rocket. As the gunner turned to engage him, he positioned the PKM within the square window sight and fired. THOOM. The rocket wash created a deep roar, which changed to a tearing noise as it sped away. The position went silent, a thick cloud of dirt erupting into the air. Flynn ran to the Toyotas. "Can all of you move?" The wide-eyed men nodded. Flynn opened the door and sat in the driver's seat of the rear truck. Mendez and the others jumped in as Salar and the Pashtuns piled into the other two. He looked into the ridge, panic filling his being. No muzzle flashes, they're already behind us. Flynn backed up and spun around, stomping the gas. He sped into the entrance to the trap and stomped the brakes, sliding to a halt. All of them jumped down onto the sand. Movement to his left caught his eye. Close to ten enemy fighters were running away toward another small formation of rocks a hundred meters away. Flynn ran as fast as he could, struggling to arm the second rocket as his legs churned. The birdlike Pashtuns flew like Olympic runners, leaving him behind as if he were on crutches. Time stood still as he watched it unfold. The enemy was headed to a depression flanked by outcroppings of rock, not dissimilar to the larger formation they had just been ambushed in. The Pashtuns were taking the bait, running after the bandits directly toward the gulch. The damn fools! At the last moment, the Pashtuns did something unexpected. Salar's men didn't jump into the gulch at all. That's it! That's it. Yes, yes! The Pashtuns worked with watchlike precision, dividing their column like a zipper, one man leaping up into the rocks to the right, the next bounding up to the left. In seconds, the two groups of Pashtuns hopped, jumped, and ran deeper into the opposing ridgelines, firing down onto the unsuspecting foes. Multiple point-blank gunfights raged for several minutes. Before Flynn could even close the distance, the fight was over. Salar emerged with several Pashtuns, jogging over to him. "We've broken the separation attempt." He made a slicing motion across his throat. "We killed them all. Now what?"

Flynn held his hand to his ear. The gunfire sounded like it was in the crater. He pointed to the shallow ridge that led into the flats. "We'll arm up there then move back toward the crater. Get in the trucks!"

He held the wheel in a death grip as he accelerated to the rise, sliding to a halt just shy of the top. The Pashtuns surged out like locusts, pulling out every weapon they had. In seconds Sobieski and Mendez were setting up one of ORION's 81 mm mortars. Flynn scooted over to them. "What are you doing? GPS is offline. You can't guide those things in."

Sobieski looked up. "I know but I'm good enough with this weapon that I can still use it old school. We'll fire long and walk them back in."

Flynn brandished a finger at him. "Don't hit that fucking crater!" He raised his radio to his mouth. "Izzy, we've broken the end around. How you guys holding up down there?"

A frenzied voice he hardly recognized came through. "They hit us with a grenade, and Laster's bleeding out! We're down to a case of grenades and two clips for Barnes's M4." Bollick's voice boomed in the background. "Here they come!"

CHAPTER 14

Flynn stared down his line. A ragtag bunch of disorganized men, bristling with weapons stretched down its length. "Tear them to pieces!" He roared into the handset, running ahead of the rest toward the earthen berm. As he cleared it, the two Toyotas and the crater came into view. Flynn slowed at the sight. Men in dark, loose clothing were pouring down the rocks like ants, many on flat ground just meters from the crater. Long curved knives bounced at their waists as they sprinted toward Izzy and the others. I'm too late! He focused into the crater. They're still alive! Laster stood within a loom of tracer fire, shooting grenades into the enemy charge. Wuuummph! Sobieski's 81 mm belched behind him, snapping him back to reality. What's that? His eyes went to a black-shrouded man on one knee, aiming an RPG towards Izzy's side of the crater. In a smooth motion the tube of the AT4 was at his shoulder, the sight around the threat. He pushed the trigger. Thoom! The rocket exploded into the would-be assassin, killing him instantly. A cacophony of rifles, rockets, mortars and grenade launchers deafened him as his men unleashed their fury. The beheaders slowed for a second, caught off-guard by the counterattack. Their attack then became more furious, bloodlust and desperation trumping fear. As he fumbled for another rocket, a crackle in his ear caused him to halt. Bright light hurt his eyes as six of the quadcopters' POV cameras flickered back onto his HUD. Sobieski and Mendez had scored a lucky hit, knocking out a position high on the northern ridge that must have housed the jammer. Flynn growled with rage as he took control of his quadcopter. I'll take you all on! He gritted his teeth, pushing the UAV hard. In seconds he was two hundred meters above the crater. "Fire at will!" he screamed. Red dots populated the screen, painting the enemy scattered throughout the battlefield. Wuumph, wuumph, wuumph, wuumph. The thunderous orchestra of ORION's 81s ensconced him. He watched his visor. Red dots would disappear as the rounds were fired; new targets now eligible for acquisition. The mortar tubes erupting so close thundered like an artillery line. His feeling of panic eased as the shells rained into the blood-drunk killers, consuming them in huge fireballs and rockslides. The thermal images accentuated the power of the 81s. Warm bodies burst like water balloons, glowing bits of flesh and blood raining back and painting the earth. He focused the high-definition camera on the crater. Barnes had ceased firing, covering up against the side of the crater next to Izzy. Bodies were scattered from five yards from his position, all the way up into the left ridge. The killers on the ridge to the right had fared much worse. Laster and Bollick had delivered hundreds of grenades into the rocks, bodies littering their side. Laster was standing in the same spot, still firing his M203. Flynn keyed his microphone. "Izzy get that crazy motherfucker to stand down. There is no one left to kill."

Izzy responded in exasperation. "I've tried to. The senseless bastard's bleeding to death from his neck but he won't listen. He just keeps reloading the M203."

"Laster get your ass into the crater now! That's an

order!" Bollick pulled the weapon from Laster and threw it over the berm, putting Laster's arm over his shoulder and helping him sit down. Flynn ran to the crater to check on Laster. He's white as a fuckin' sheet. "Laster! Laster, are you okay?" Laster muttered something indiscernible.

Flynn knelt at Laster's side. "He's going into hemorrhagic shock! Someone bring me the medical kit." Mendez skidded up and pulled open the black bag. Flynn reached in, grabbing a bottle of saline and a pack of four-inch-by-four-inch cotton gauze pads and pressing them into the gash on the side of Laster's neck. "Laster—"

Laster put a handout. "Quit yellin'. I ain't dead yet, just weak as hell," he said, his head bobbing. "Jesus, I've never been in a brawl like that. Those men wouldn't go down unless I cut 'em in half."

Flynn took Laster's clammy hand. "Rex, you saved the whole unit with that stand, but you're in trouble. I need you to relax and stop talking so I can think."

"Um-huh."

Flynn put on a pair of the sterile gloves and washed out the grit with saline, working the gauze into the biological mortar of thrombosed blood. Fuck, it's where the jugular is. If there's shrapnel in there and I pull it out—. You have to do it. He dislodged the coagulate, dark blood and partly formed clots gushing from the wound. Good, there's no pulsing. Flynn probed the wound with his fingertip. "There it is." He dug out the surgical instrument known as Kellys, working the hemostats around the edge of the metal. Clip. I got it! Okay, take your time and wiggle it out. "This may hurt, Rex." He rocked it gently back and forth, working out a nickel-sized piece of jagged black metal. He stared at the laceration. It's still just oozing. He held pressure until the wound quit bleeding, then reached for the tube of Super Glue. He applied a thick bead to the wound, pushing the edges together then fanning it with his hand. "Mendez, stay here and hold pressure. If he starts bleeding again, call me."

***

Flynn scanned the battlefield. The fissures the bandits were hiding in had magnified the amplitude of the designer explosive, scattering pieces of men and their weapons in fan-shaped debris fields. The enemy movement was gone. The efficient soldiers had dragged off many of their wounded and vanished. He turned to the lanky man behind him. "Sobieski, I'm in no mood for surprises. Keep your UAV in the air." He keyed his mic. "Everyone, move in slow and gather up anything that looks worthwhile—documents, weapons, electronics, whatever." As the rest of the platoon walked toward the crater, the Pashtuns scurried up into the ridges, killing any of the beheaders still alive. Salar came up next to him, stopping next to one of the dead men. He knelt and rifled through the man's pockets. He looked up with a look of distaste. "Punjabi, not from around here."

"Pakistan?"

Salar shook his head. "I'm not sure."

Mendez's voice rang out. "I got me a Chinese sniper rifle with an electronic targeting system, some night vision goggles, and some expensive-looking radios over here."

Barnes bent down and picked up a box of pills. "Captagon! No wonder these motherfuckers wouldn't go down. They're eating speed." He threw the paper box to the ground and stomped it.

Jonny Chen held up an unusual-looking black electronic box. "Hey, I found something!"

Brian Bollick walked over. "Let me see that," he said as he jerked it out of his hands. He flipped the box over, grabbing the metal back and ripping it off. Pop! Metal screws flew through the air. Bollick peered in, studying the device. "Uh-huh, yep, it's a GPS jammer, all right." He grabbed a small edge of paper protruding from a slot deep within the device and pulled it out. He tore it off and studied the markings. "Flynn, come here and check this out." Bollick's finger trembled, making it hard to see what he was pointing at. "See this frequency spike?" He traced it out. "This is when they jammed our GPS system."

Flynn's hands grew clammy. Only professional, hardcore fighters used Captagon, men who fought for days without food or respite. *What the hell have we walked into?* And what about the electronics? "Salar, come here. Is this sophisticated hardware typical for Punjabi fighters?"

Salar's brow furrowed. "I'm not sure. These men are from far, far away."

A group of chattering Pashtuns drew Flynn's attention. They were standing around a large number of dead enemy fighters, murmuring and pointing as if terrified. Barnes walked amongst the Pashtuns and kicked what remained of a leg, the body part spinning through the air.

"Jesus, Barnes, that's fuckin' gross," Sobieski said, pulling an apple from his pocket and polishing it on his sleeve. Crunch.

"Aye, yi, yi!" Flynn's eyes darted to the sounds. The Pashtuns and Barnes were backing up like someone had a gun on them.

Barnes took off, screaming as he ran by. "It's a swarm of wasps, fuckin' huuuge motherfuckers! Hundreds of 'em." Barnes slapped his hands all over his head. "Get off me, you cocksuckers!"

The Pashtuns dropped to their knees and prayed.

Flynn went to Salar, who was now kneeling with the others, praying in a hushed tone. "Salar?" Salar continued to pray. Flynn whispered into his microphone. "Izzy tell me what the fuck is going on. These guys act like these wasps are harbingers of Satan himself."

Izzy approached, a puzzled look on his face. Flynn waited for him to get within earshot. "Jeez, what the hell is it?"

Izzy's voice quivered, his eyes huge. "Something supernatural. The wasps, I mean. I can't remember exactly, some ancient Arab belief. A pious man returns to see his death as a wasp?" Izzy bit his lip. "No, that's not it."

Salar got to his feet, his usually fierce eyes now wide and meek as a kitten's. He shook as he pointed at the wasps, as large as sparrows, hovering over the dead men's corpses. "They're so beautiful." He looked at Flynn, then at the sky. "In the days of the prophet, Muhammad had a trusted military commander who was surrounded on a hill by infidels. He was given the choice to surrender or be killed to the last man." Salar's features tightened into a fierce expression. "He did not surrender but instead they fought like lions, all of them killed. His name is known to many Muslims: Asim bin Thabit. When the infidel commanders heard the news, they demanded proof of Asim's death by presentation of his head." Salar shook his fist. "But Allah sent a swarm of wasps to protect Asim's corpse." His eyes twinkled. "They shielded him from the messengers who could not cut anything from his body."

Flynn scratched the back of his neck. "These dead men are no martyrs. They're common—"

Salar's voice thundered. "It is not for man to decide who is pious before Allah." He cast an encompassing hand toward the dead men. "These men have the blessing of an eternal afterlife with the Great One." Salar glared at him. "Perhaps you and your men are the true evil. You come to a strange land and kill its inhabitants as if it were your divine right." The Pashtuns moved behind Salar in solidarity.

Flynn recoiled from Salar, walking back to Izzy. "Izzy, the Pashtuns seem angry. I can't afford to alienate them now. Please tell them I didn't understand. Tell them they have my apologies." The hairs stood up on Flynn's neck as he looked over the Pashtuns and their murderous expressions. Izzy spoke in their native tongue, pointing to the wasps then clasping his hands together, offering a deferential bow. The Pashtuns relaxed; their attention redirected to a collective movement of the swarm.

"Here they come!" Barnes yelled.

The swarm hovered aggressively in a dense cloud ten feet above, their wings generating an intense drone. They didn't attack. As if placated by the American's submission, they left, disappearing one by one into the intense fireball of the morning sun. Flynn scanned around. His men had separated from the Pashtuns, their posture tense, hands on their weapons as if ready to fight it out with the guides. Flynn pushed his open hands toward the ground. "It's over. Get your hands off those weapons and load up the supplies on the dollies." He stole a glance over his shoulder at the Pashtuns. "Izzy, I don't know what just happened, but it scares the shit out of me. We gotta get out of here, and we have to do it now." A deep restlessness filled him. What if they had killed men of faith? Was he the real enemy here? "Gather up the gear. We're moving out as fast as we can."

CHAPTER 15

"Mendez, you and Sobieski fashion a gurney for Laster, strap it to one of those dollies, and do it quick," Flynn said. "Everyone else dock your quadcopters and change the batteries. I know everyone is tired, but we have to go the rest of the way on foot. From here on out, we don't move an inch without one of those sweethearts above us." The men loaded the purpose-built dollies with the three-hundred-pound avatars. Mendez and Sobieski hoisted Laster onto one of the dollies, which served as a makeshift ambulance. "How's that ankle, Izzy? Are you able to lead a team?"

Izzy worked the joint around in a circle. "It's just a strain," he said, his head down.

"Excellent. Listen up, men. For now, we'll break up into three teams. Izzy, myself, and Bollick are team leaders. We'll leapfrog each other, so to speak, each team covering the other."

Flynn led his team westward for thirty minutes then halted, scouring the screens for suspicious heat signatures as Izzy's and Bollick's teams moved past, taking the lead. The cool air was gone. The rising sun grew hotter by the minute, heat waves shimmering up, distorting the silvery desert floor. Flynn's lungs burned, struggling to provide the oxygen to match the feverish pace of the small Pashtun men. Their slight frames carried more weight than the Americans and at almost twice the speed. Flynn looked at the display of the GPS locator then spoke into the microphone. "We've already traveled three kilometers in thirty minutes. I know it hurts but we need to keep up with the Pashtuns. Keep pushing." A bolt of concern went through him as he realized that Izzy and Salar's group had stopped ahead. They stood side by side, Salar peering at something through binoculars. Flynn keyed his microphone. "What's going on up there?"

Izzy's voice piped through. "Salar is nervous as a cat. Hamasa is supposed to be around here waiting, but he's not at the rendezvous point."

The sound of children wailing poured through the audio of Izzy's helmet. "What's that?"

"It's the twin boys. Hamasa is their father."

Flynn recalled the toothpick-thin boys dressed in flowing cotton garments; their tiny feet wrapped in delicate linen sandals. He had mistaken their worry for serious work ethic. No wonder they worked like mules to get the vehicles loaded.

"Flynn, you need to get up here. Barnes just saw something."

***

Flynn slowed as he reached Salar, trying to catch his breath. Boom! A large-caliber rifle made him flinch. Boom! He scanned the high portion of his visor. The video feed from Barnes's quadcopter displayed the source. A lone figure stood at the opening of a tiny cave thirty meters up a rock spire less than a hundred meters away. Flynn crouched down, placing the baseplate of his mortar tube on the ground. Sobieski retrieved one of the 81mm rounds from a dolly, handing it to him. "Give me a bead, Barnes!" Flynn positioned the round at the top of the tube.

"Wait!" Salar's panicked voice boomed. He stood

with one arm outstretched to Flynn, the other holding the binoculars to his eyes. "Praise be to Allah! It is Hamasa!" Salar straightened and jumped up and down, his fists clenched as he started to run toward the formation. The boys rocketed past Salar and tore up the granite tower like mountain goats, soon reaching their father and embracing him. Flynn's focus went to a group of men in loose clothing who now emerged from the cave with Hamasa. In seconds they were clambering down the face, leaping and sliding from ledge to ledge. No wonder they weren't found. The way down looked difficult but reaching the cave must have been a herculean feat. As Hamasa and his men congregated at the bottom, Flynn got a good look at them through the quadcopter's high-definition camera. Hamasa had a serious patriarchal face motionless above his black beard. Even now at the point of his salvation, his face was grave, seemingly devoid of emotion. The Pashtun had a massive square jaw and stood almost two heads taller than the others. Even in his current condition, he walked with swagger. His chest bulged and his shoulders were wide. He looked strong enough to rip apart tires with his huge hands. The twins stood attentively next to him, barely reaching his waist. As Hamasa followed Salar back, the twins emulated their father's body language, their tiny faces feigning fierceness and the courage of lions as they strode beside him. Behind the moving group something stepped out, catching Flynn's attention. It was an emaciated large-breed dog staggering stiff-legged from a small alcove on the desert floor. Flynn's eyes creased at the sight of the creature. He studied the unusual-looking animal, clearly displayed on his screen. Its ears were cropped to the skull and it had no tail. Its brindle-striped coat was interspersed with pink burns and thickly matted hair. Even through the thick part of its coat, ribs were visible.

Izzy and Salar's group moved out first, Flynn's team covering them as they went. The tribesmen from the cave wobbled as if they hadn't been on their feet in days.

The malnourished canine stumbled under its own weight trying to follow them. Over the next five minutes the animal had fallen behind and was now right in front of Flynn. His mind went to Joseph Roddick's description of a powerful and cunning animal. Surely this pathetic sack of bones was not that dog. God, look at it. He refuses to give up, but how long can it last in this heat? The Pashtuns were indifferent, leaving him to languish. Poor thing. Why does it follow them at all? He nudged Sobieski. "That must be the tiger dog we heard about."

Sobieski's gaze narrowed. "Funny-looking, isn't he? It looks more like a starving hyena." He tossed a nod toward the animal. "Looks like the kindest thing we could do is put a bullet in its brain."

Sobieski was right. Perhaps a mercy killing was the kindest thing to do. Flynn put a handout. "If it needs to be done, I'll do it," he said. He gazed over the teams ahead of him at the changing topography. The wide expanses of sand were giving way to narrow corridors amid jutting formations of granite, thrusting hundreds of feet into the air. If the dog was having trouble now, it was only going to get worse as they closed in on the steeper foothills of the Chagai mountain range. Flynn keyed his microphone. "Izzy slow your pace. Your group is getting too far ahead."

"Ten- four."

Flynn approached Laster, still alive on the makeshift gurney. He knelt and felt his pulse. "Laster?" Laster didn't answer. His pulse was rapid, and his skin was clammy and cool. Izzy's voice came through the helmet. "Flynn, these guys are super rattled. Hamasa has been talking about mass executions of anyone this Mullah Mehsud band has captured. They won't even stop for a break. As tough as they are, these Pashtuns are terrified. Hamasa insists we keep moving to the safety of the pass."

"Negative. Laster needs to be stabilized. I have to give him medical attention. Find an acceptable area to set up the eLORAN grid. We'll move out in the morning."

"Okay. I'll try to calm them down."

Flynn's neck was already sunburned. The sweat and abrasive sand on the burning skin compounded the discomfort. He dreaded the daily patterns of the Afghan summer: chilly mornings, scorching days, and freezing nights. He ached for a drink of cool water and the shade of the cliffs. His mind drifted from his own discomfort back to Laster. I'll get an IV in him and give him some fluids. Maybe that will perk him up. He noticed the dog warily eyeing him. The animal seemed less stiff after walking for a while, keeping pace beside him as if already aware Flynn was the best chance it had. "Come on, tiger, just a little farther."

Flynn approached Izzy's and Bollick's groups, which had stopped under the shadow cast by a colossal piece of granite. It was almost perfectly square and leaned sideways, buried like a giant block that had been dropped into the sand. As Flynn followed Laster's gurney under the rock, the temperature changed precipitously. The microenvironment offered by the cool rock made it feel like it was still morning. He walked behind Sobieski and Mendez, who pulled Laster to an unoccupied spot and sat down the gurney.

The Pashtun men from the cave had flopped onto the soft sand, groaning and crying out while clutching their bellies. Flynn's nose wrinkled at the disgusting odor wafting from the tribesmen. The small space was cool, but it amplified their stench. He turned to Izzy. "What's wrong with them?"

Izzy's nose wrinkled. "Dehydration, I suppose. They were trapped up there with no food or water for three days." Izzy walked to one of the smaller supply bags, pulling out an armful of plastic bottles of water and distributing them to the thirsty Pashtuns. The men reached out, ripping the bottles away, gulping the liquid uncontrollably, some choking.

Flynn scanned his surroundings. "Sobieski, you and

Bollick take as many men as you need and get the eLORAN grid up while I care for Laster." He pointed to the top of the formation. "Park the UAVs with their cameras up on the rocks then grab as many snakes as you can carry." Flynn made a sweeping motion. "Spread them out in a circle and let them autolocate."

"Do you think he's going to make it?" Bollick asked, his eyes fraught with concern as he peered at Laster.

Flynn shrugged. "I'll do everything I can, but I need you two to get that grid up." He crouched beside Laster again, feeling for his pulse. It felt thready and weaker than before, his heart racing at one hundred and fifty beats per minute. "Laster!" He shook the red-haired man. Laster opened his eyes and mumbled something then tried to grasp some imaginary object. Flynn turned to Barnes. "He's in hypovolemic shock. Find that other medical kit with the IVs and tubing!" Barnes lugged the large bag over and set it beside him. Flynn unzipped it and dug for the blood pressure cuff. He pulled it free, wrapping it around Laster's arm. The manometer read 80/50. Flynn's stomach rolled. As a medic, he knew that hypovolemic shock from blood loss was the number one killer on the battlefield. It had been poorly understood for centuries until American and French researchers unraveled its pathophysiology during the Vietnam War. They called it ARDS (adult respiratory distress syndrome). Shock causes the lungs to leak, the alveolar membranes becoming thickened and stiff, unable to oxygenate the blood. Once the alveoli stiffened, even well-equipped hospitals struggled to keep the shock victims alive. Though shallow, Laster's breathing sounded clear; no wet raspy sounds could be heard. Laster's lungs didn't seem to be compromised—yet. Flynn reached for a large IV and an alcohol pad. He rubbed the pad on Laster's forearm, but the Viking's characteristic veins had disappeared. He decided to take the risk of puncturing the lung and go to the internal jugular. It was not a typical spot for an IV, but it led directly into the superior vena cava. Flynn took a deep breath and steadied himself. He looked for the long sternocleidomastoid muscle that runs down the front and side of the neck. The muscle splits into two portions as it inserts onto the clavicle. He cleaned the area then directed the stick toward the heart, pushing the needle between the two tendons. He felt the resistance of the tough outer layer of the vessel against the needle tip and popped it forward, piercing the right internal jugular vein. Relief washed over him as a flash of blood dribbled from the end of the IV. Flynn removed the sharp inner metal stylet, leaving the soft IV tubing in the vein. He screwed a tiny red cap over the IV and taped it down. Next, he rummaged through the supplies and pulled out a bag of saline mixed with glucose. He spiked the bag, attaching the tubing to the intravenous line and turned it wide open. The fluid drained in, but Laster's vitals continued to deteriorate. He needed blood and he needed it now. Flynn thought of Colonel Kelley and picked up his satellite phone. He paused, setting the phone back down as he did the math. If he called for a medevac, he would doom Laster to a delay in treatment but how much of a delay? An hour for the medevac team to get assembled, in the air, and to the site. Another hour to get Laster to the M.A.S.H. unit. If they didn't have O-negative blood, there would be cross-typing and matching the blood products. The realization struck him like a two-ton heavy thing. He turned to Barnes. "Barnes, what blood type are you?"

Barnes took a step back with a look on his face like he smelled something bad. "Huh? O-positive. Why?"

"I don't know Laster's blood type. If I give him the wrong type, it will cause an anaphylactic reaction that will kill him in minutes."

Barnes scratched his cheek. "What are we supposed to do then?"

"O-negative blood can go into anyone, no matter what their blood type," Flynn said. He pointed to the other platoon members. "Go! Find someone with O-negative." He rubbed his hands through his hair. Dear God, let these guys know their blood type.

Soon Barnes was standing next to him, Rosenberg in tow. "Rossi here's got O-negative, only man in the platoon." Barnes grinned as he shoved him toward Flynn.

Rosenberg glared at the Texan. "Barnes, you ruesome hayseed. What did you drag me into?"

Flynn beckoned him closer. "Your blood type is O-negative, which means your red blood cells are smooth, with no immunological markers. Any human body on the planet can take O-negative blood. Unfortunately for you, you can only take O-negative, so keep your head down," Flynn said. He pulled Rosenberg's arm but couldn't get the man to sit down. Rosenberg put his hands out. "What the hell do you think you're doing? I've never heard of something like this. Is this safe?" Rosenberg's face looked as pale as Laster's.

"Come on now. That's enough of this. Give me your arm!" Flynn grabbed Rosenberg's arm and pulled him over. "I'm not going to kill you. Sit down and quit acting childish."

Rosenberg's eyes turned in a circle. "Sorry, can you just give me a—OW!" he howled, squinting one eye tightly as he stomped his foot. Flynn, having found the vein, secured the access. "See? First stick. Nothing to it," he said as he taped the IV down. He looked to Mendez. "Mendez get over here and help Barnes stack up some of those ammunition boxes next to Laster. We have to lay Rosenberg higher up." They gathered a number of the sturdy wooden ammunition boxes, stacking them up next to Laster's makeshift bed. Flynn patted the stack of boxes. "Up here, Rosenberg." Flynn connected a line of clear IV tubing to Rosenberg's IV. Dark red blood moved quickly through the tube, pushing air in front of it. Flynn waited for the air to purge, blood now dribbling into the sand. He inserted the tubing to Laster's IV and twisted them together.

Rosenberg's eyes bugged. "That's a lot of blood going through that line. Do you know what you're doing?"

Flynn scratched his chin. "The tubing holds thirty milliliters. It took ten seconds for the blood to travel through the tubing." He did the arithmetic in his head. Rosenberg could theoretically give a maximum of two pints. He needed to let the makeshift transfusion run for no more than five minutes. He set the timer on his watch and waited, hoping that Laster's heart didn't act as a vacuum, pulling more blood from Rosenberg than anticipated. After the time had elapsed, he disconnected the tubing from Rosenberg's IV, holding it in the air as the last drops flowed into Laster.

Rex Laster opened his eyes, momentarily lucid. "Of all the people," he whispered, managing a weak smile. "Thanks, Rossi."

Rosenberg cut his eyes. "It's not like I was given a choice." His frown melted, eyes turning to concern as he took Laster's hand. "You just shake it off, okay?"

Flynn removed Rosenberg's IV, placing a small bandage on the puncture site. Laster closed his eyes and swallowed. "God, I hope I don't start pulling up and asking people if they have Grey Poupon."

"Don't worry about that. You'll always be a baboon," Rosenberg smirked as he patted Laster's hand. He steadied himself and hopped down. Unable to stand, he stumbled into Barnes, holding onto his shoulder. "Fuckin' vampires bled me good, didn't ya?" He frowned bitterly at Flynn.

"Come on, Rosenberg, admit it. You feel like a better person, don't you?"

CHAPTER 16

Leaning back against the cold stone, Flynn watched Laster rest. Though he was asleep, the effects of the transfusion were apparent. He was less pale and occasionally shifted his weight on the cot. Flynn scanned the area sheltered under the rock. The Afghans had consumed everything in sight, and most of them had fallen asleep twitching and snoring loudly. Not the dog. Flynn noticed there had been no concern for the mongrel. Not even the mindful twins paid him any regard. At this moment, he detested the Afghans. The pathetic creature had trembled, watching the Afghans swill the water and eat the food, and they had given him nothing. He had been too busy with Laster and the grid to do anything about it himself. The animal's body was ravaged by starvation, illness, and injury. It sat stoically but its jaundiced eyes were desperate. The pleading yellow eyes seized his, a rigor and a soft whine following. Flynn spotted the rations bags lying near Laster's cot. Careful not to disturb him, he reached into one of the black duffels, pulling out a small red container and a couple of the bottled waters. He tiptoed back to the animal and filled the bowl with water, setting it on the ground and sliding it over with his foot. He found himself returning to fill the dish multiple times as the animal drank his fill. The animal smacked his lips and laid his head down, eyelids growing heavy. The dog taken care of, Flynn's mind drifted back to the traitorous reporter's pirate transmissions. Joseph Roddick had described the animal in rich prose that had captured his imagination. The only trait he recognized now was the creature's spirit and its distinguished and proud demeanor. In the States, people would steal a regal animal like this, but here it was nothing, relying on morsels of kindness for its very survival. Flynn got up and brushed the sand off as he walked to his gear. A large canvas duffel held the provisions he had prepared to care for the dog. He knelt, dragging the bag out and pulling on the wide plastic zipper until the bag gaped open. Cans of dog food and veterinary medical supplies were neatly organized on one side, surgical instruments and debridement supplies on the other. He grabbed a can of food and opened it, letting a large glop of the paste ooze into a small container. He sprinkled deworming powder on top and mixed it with the potent broad-spectrum antibiotic the veterinarian had suggested. The desert dog opened its eyes and watched intently as he approached. Flynn set the bowl as close as he dared and returned to his bedroll against the rock wall. The wary animal's nostrils flared at the sudden aroma of the food. The desert dog craned its neck and consumed the can of food in several enormous bites.

Flynn picked up his helmet and keyed the microphone. "Sobieski, you and Chen climb up on top of this rock and take point on opposite sides for the first three hours then Jefferson and Rosenberg will relieve you two. Don't fall asleep!"

"Not a chance, boss."

Flynn sat and peered from under the ledge. The sun, now a half-circle of fire on the western horizon, shone around the formation. Trillions of particles of atmospheric dust reflected the light within the halo, transforming the sky into a kaleidoscope of colors. The heat of the sun was in full retreat, the bone-shaking chill of the desert night moving in under the cloak of darkness. He tightened his ballistic vest. The custom inside panels were covered in cloth, providing warmth and a reasonable degree of comfort. Izzy sat next to Salar and Hamasa, who were having an animated conversation in their native tongue. Flynn walked over and sat in an empty spot on the sand directly across from Izzy.

"Laster—is he going to make it?" Izzy asked.

Flynn looked back over his shoulder. "I think he's going to be okay, but we won't know for certain until morning. What have you guys been talking about for the last two hours?"

"About three weeks ago that drug lord that we've been hearing about moved in with hundreds of henchmen. Hamasa spotted the main horde coming in and soon him and his men were running from them, hunted like every other group in the area. He says Mehsud's men have sophisticated electronics able to localize the source of any type of electronic energy. They then track down the source and kill them. The Pashtuns threw away their cellphones and even their radios; however, they were still tracked down. They were right behind his group when they managed to escape."

Flynn cocked his head. "How did he give them the slip?"

"Hamasa came to that small cliff and recognized the impossibility of reaching the top cave. He used his superhuman climbing skills to get a rope up there. It was close, Flynn. He said his last man and the rope were pulled to safety as Mehsud's bandits arrived below them. The killers moved on, not realizing they were in the cave above. There have been so many of Mehsud's reinforcements pass through they had to wait for us to come through to rescue them."

"Hamasa may be happy to know we killed well over a hundred of them today." Flynn studied the giant Pashtun man. "How many men did he lose?" Flynn asked.

"He lost two teams of five. Fortunately, most of the Pashtuns were under Hamasa's wing. Salar says the Pashtuns look to him in these situations."

Flynn observed Hamasa, who was now settling down to rest. The tall man had broad shoulders and wiry, muscular limbs. "He's the biggest Pashtun I've ever seen."

Izzy looked at Hamasa as he spoke. "Can you believe the man used to be a doctor? I don't know what happened, but Hamasa is not keen on discussing it. Salar says he's the best at everything he does, but what makes him really special is his climbing skills. Salar calls him a wind walker, a man that has mastered a blend of balance and gravity to speed through the steep, rocky hills. It's an ancient discipline, passed down by the Steppe region's inhabitants long before the days of Genghis Khan. Salar says the only way to kill an enemy in the hills of Afghanistan is to turn his flank and get behind him. If your wind walkers are better than theirs, you can encircle the enemy force. Salar swears by it, and Hamasa is the best of the best—well, except maybe for his twin boys. Apparently, they also have the gift. He says Hamasa won't admit it, but he thinks the twins are faster than their father."

Flynn looked around for the two. "These twins, one of them is really expressive but he never speaks. What's his story?"

Izzy touched his throat. "That's Adam. His larynx was injured by a landmine when he was a child, rendering him mute."

"That explains the sign language."

"The other twin is Aamir. He's the translator for his brother. Adam won't let Aamir out of his sight." Izzy glanced at Hamasa. "Tell everyone to be careful around their father. He is protective of the boys and doesn't like them fraternizing with Americans, so be mindful. I'd hate to see the man angry."

"You and me both. He could tear a man apart with his eyes alone. What about the dog?"

Izzy's inner brows rose. "Would you believe it used to be a champion fighting dog? Hamed, his handler, was killed with the first platoon. It just hangs around now."

Flynn turned to look at the beast, lying on his paws, still watching him. "He's got a bullet injury in his left hip that needs to be addressed. I may have to tranquilize him to debride the wound."

Izzy stroked the whiskers on his chin, regarding the animal with interest. "He's pretty docile. You don't even know he's there. As a matter of fact, he kinda reminds me of Mac. You too, huh? That's why you're doting on him."

"I feel sorry for him. Big deal."

"Have you seen the teeth on that thing? He'll eat your ass if you try to dress that wound," Izzy said, stifling a yawn. "What is it with you and dogs?"

"Ah, come on. Don't start on me, Izzy. Besides, I'm quite sure you remember that nice lady from the Pentagon? You know, the one you made me look like an asshole in front of?" He cut his eyes at Izzy. "That woman liked me, and you totally cockblocked me with that 'Izzy of Arabia' routine."

Izzy's eyes widened. "Oh, is that what you call it?"

"I felt a spark with that woman." Flynn cut one brow low, the other rising. "Did you even get her number, junior?"

Izzy's face reddened. "She was a slippery one, I'm telling you. The only man she was interested in was Earl."

"Earl?"

Izzy smirked. "Earl LORAN."

Flynn snickered. "Whoever she was, she was connected, and she did suggest that we take care of the dog, right?"

"She didn't say you HAD to do it."

Flynn emitted a heavy sigh. "That's the problem with you brilliant people: You can't comprehend social cues." He put his hand on Izzy's shoulder. "Since you struggle in the woman department, let me give you some more tips."

Izzy stood up, running in place on his tiptoes while clapping his hands. "Oh, Big Daddy, please, tell me, tell me."

Flynn repressed a grin. "When a woman 'suggests' that you do something, she means that if you don't do it, she'll consider you an insensitive asshole. Assholes don't get favors, capiche?"

Izzy rubbed his chin, brows crunching in. "You know, she never offered to assist in getting the animal home. As a matter of fact, we have no idea who she really is. We are reliant on U.S. military transports to get home. That bitch just upped and vanished after she left S&K that day. We haven't heard a thing from her. Nothing."

Flynn's shoulders slumped. "So, I made all these preparations to help the creature. For what? So, I could get attached and leave it behind? Shoot it at the airport?" He stared at the ground. "Man, some things never change."

"Flynn, we need to talk about the dog." Izzy took a deep breath. "It's about a conversation I had with my father. He knows the dog's history, and all but him and I are worried about the liability. One bark could get us all killed. Maybe we should just go ahead and end its suffering. I don't want to, but I'll make sure it is clean and that he doesn't suffer," Izzy said.

Flynn studied the canine. "The Pashtuns don't appear worried about it. The mere fact that it is still here speaks volumes. Who knows? He may save our asses someday."

"I don't know, Flynn."

"Izzy, when have you known me to be wrong about these kinds of things?"

Izzy stared into his eyes for a second then looked back at the dog. "Fine, we'll roll with it for now and see how he does. God knows we have bigger things to worry about."

"Exactly. If he becomes an issue, I'll take care of it myself."

CHAPTER 17

Flynn's eyes adjusted to the first bits of light, the fog from his breath visible. Johnny Cash's "Folsom Prison Blues" drifted over from Barnes's headphones. He turned to Sher Dil's bed, but the tiger dog was not there. A slight chill went through him at the thought of Laster. He's not on his cot? He was fine two hours ago. He pulled his helmet from next to his bed mat, brushing the dirt from the fabric and shaking it out. He put it on, looking at the eight screens from the cameras Sobieski and Bollick had positioned around them. He reached back and grasped the edge of his UAV and flicked it into the air. He flew to altitude and gave the quadcopter full power, swinging around in an arc above the monolith. Laster, Sobieski, and Barnes were sitting on a small ledge, smoking cigarettes. He hovered ten feet above them. Laster turned stiffly, showing a victory sign as he grinned at the drone. Flynn felt happy and ultra-awake, rejuvenated with the group's good fortune. He pushed full power on the UAV, rocketing into the sky, Laster and the others becoming like grains of pepper on the colossal rock below. The bony tiger dog sat like a sphinx in front of the makeshift shelter. He brought the UAV back and slipped it into the holster, walking out toward the dog. Odd-sounding name, Sher Dil. Izzy said it meant "lion heart" in Pashto, earned from the dog's performance in the fighting pits. Flynn cocked his head with interest. The animal was regal in its own way. He sat next to Sher Dil, careful not to make eye contact. After a few minutes, he turned his head and stole a glance. Sher Dil made eye contact then sighed, placing his massive skull on his outstretched forelegs. The animal was emaciated but the length of his frame was longer than a man. He was graced with athletic lines and solid bones. With his triangular head, wide at the back and narrowing into the face, he looked like a hyena. The ears had been cropped to the skull, only what had been in the mutilator's grasp escaping the blade. The small slivers of cartilage had healed into fingerlike scars, adding a sense of menace. Maggots crawled from the bullet wound festering on the animal's left hip. The deep wound jogged Flynn's memory. The broad-spectrum antibiotic he had brought was called Augmentin, only effective if given every twelve hours. He looked at his watch; it was time for the next dose. He got up and walked back to his supply bag, returning with the bowl. He set it on the sand next to the animal then reached for Sher Dil's injured left hip. "Let's take a look, mister."

Clack! A blur of white teeth grazed his hand. Sher Dil emitted a resentful growl, his eyes burning into him. Flynn jerked his hand back, leaning away. "My apologies, sir. We can try this again later." He keyed his microphone. "Sobieski? Bollick?"

"Yes, sir?"

"Pick up the transmitters and collapse the grid. I want to move out and get to that pass ASAP."

Twenty minutes later Bollick came and sat next to him. "We're packed up and ready to move out." A troubled look came over him. "Something's bothering me. I couldn't stop thinking about those wasps last night. I hardly slept. We were just talking about it outside, and it has everyone upset."

"You too, huh? I didn't sleep either. I hate to admit it, but they scare me. I mean scared of being on the wrong side, you know?"

Bollick nodded agreement. "Do you believe in omens?"

"I don't know what to believe, Brian. I wouldn't have thought too much about it, but the reactions of the Pashtuns have me concerned that they may see us in a negative light. Like maybe we are the bad guys not the other way around."

Bollick's eyes tightened. "The sooner we get to the pass and get that grid up, the sooner I can relax."

Flynn's attention was drawn to movement on one of the screens. Hamasa held two rabbits he must have snared. Aamir and Adam bounded around their father as he walked up. In minutes he had deftly butchered and seasoned the meat, throwing it into a large wok like pan settled into the embers of the fire.

Flynn smiled at Bollick. "I guess we can wait just a little bit." The savory aromas drifting around made Flynn's stomach gnaw and complain. Hamasa smiled, handing him a large piece of warm flatbread, slathered with the stir-fry. Flynn's eyes widened with delight. He nodded in gratitude, taking the pizza like dish with both hands. "Thank you, Hamasa." Every once in a while, a soldier in the field might experience such delights. Here it was commonplace. I should have become a mercenary a long time ago. It was a mixed bag of feelings being back in Afghanistan. Before this mission Afghanistan had always been a simple place, one where a man knew what his role was. Now with the first team's death, the previous day's battle, and the wasps, it was anything but simple. He finished the food, pushing the thought of the wasps away as he looked at his watch. 0600. "Everyone, wrap it up, snuff that fire, and get ready to move. We march out in five." His eyes ran along the foothills of the giant Chagai mountain chain to the left and back to the endless flat desert to the right. A buffer of badlands a mile wide separated the two. It was strewn with ancient boulders and spires of rock that arose from the sand. Acacia bushes lined the runoff basins carved by the infrequent heavy rains. The deluges had created narrow channels in the sand, a maze they would have to walk through. "Izzy, same thing as yesterday, we swing around each other in teams until we get in the narrows. Hell, or high water, tonight we sleep in that pass."

***

The three teams spread out over two hundred meters, moving up in elevation without event. The landscape had changed precipitately from boulder-strewn desert to formations of granite, jutting higher and higher. The Chagai Hills rose from this point, the granite mountains beginning their ascent south into Pakistan. They entered a natural low spot where water pooled before finding its way into the channels that emptied into the natural granite crevices of the foothills. The unceasing wind intoned an eerie song. An unsettling feeling gripped Flynn. Enemy fighters could attack from multiple locations at any moment. His keen eye registered thousands of pockmarks from previous firefights all over the surrounding rocks. If they hit us again, it will be here. He keyed the mic. "Keep each other in sight, your UAVs in the air, and your shit tight." Flynn's heart thumped at the sight of Izzy. Izzy had stopped his group and was waving him over.

As Flynn approached, Izzy pointed to a crevice in the side of the mountain. "Salar says this is the entrance to the pass!"

"Barnes, you've got five minutes of juice left in your battery," Flynn said. "Fly your quad around and take a good look. A deep crevice split the mountain as it rose steeply. The nimble UAV sped around the canyon, first at higher altitudes, followed by lower probing runs into possible ambush sites. The incredible resolution of the lens made Flynn feel like he was on a magic carpet. The crisp grayish-brown edges of the chasm contrasted with the dark shadow of its charred center and the blue sky all around. Flynn closed his eyes, succumbing to a feeling of vertigo from the camera angle.

"I don't see a thang," Barnes said.

Flynn pushed up his visor. Salar was high above, standing on rubble, beckoning with his arm. Flynn turned to Bollick. "Follow me." They crouched low and crept over the immense pile of rubble. As he approached Salar at the top, the pass came into view. The opening was a hundred feet wide, growing narrower and steeper as it rose. The rocks here looked like charcoal, not granite. Flynn understood why an airstrike had been used against the first team. The pass would be easy to defend once the eLORAN grid was established. Any smugglers not well-connected enough to get through ISAF and Pakistani border checkpoints would likely attempt to come through this very corridor. His eyes returned to the soot-stained rocks. A shiver went down his spine, his senses heightening at the devastation the thermobaric warhead had wrought on the canyon. The awe turned to resentment as an image of Montacayo's face appeared in his mind.

Bollick scraped his fingernail on the sooty black stone. He pulled his lips back, baring his teeth like a beast as he stared up into the pass. At that instant Flynn hoped the man never got mad at him. Flynn reached Salar, who pointed up to the left. Hamasa and Aamir ran a hundred meters up the pass then climbed the steep face to the left with no harness, their stiff-soled linen sandals providing sure footing. They moved at unhuman speeds to a small horizontal slab a hundred feet above. Salar climbed slowly behind them until he stood with Hamasa and Aamir, waving down at the rest of them. Flynn nodded at Bollick and Sobieski. "You two stay here. I'm going to check it out." He followed the path behind Adam, who had waited for him. Something dark stuck in the rocks grabbed his attention. He reached down and grabbed the edge of a dark blue baseball cap, working it out and dusting it off. Interesting, a Yankees ball cap. I wonder where it came from. He read the initials B.R. written in black marker on the inside of the cap then stuffed it into his pocket. His brow furrowed, Adam made hand gestures as he showed which rock to grab and where Flynn must put his foot. Adam would jump up, grab an edge, and pull himself up, encouraging Flynn to do the same. Flynn was managing until he made the mistake of looking down. His vision tunneled as that old phobia returned. He pushed his face against the rock. You've got this. Calm down and take your time. He was eight stories off the rock bottom of the pass and the thought of jumping for the next ledge two feet above made him freeze. Adam waved encouragement. Flynn's limbs shook as he reversed, moving down several feet, placing his feet on a series of more natural steps.

Adam covered his face with his hands as if Flynn had failed a most basic test of manhood. "Huummph!" Adam made an animal-like grunt then turned and bounded up the steep face like a mountain goat.

"Little bastard," Flynn muttered. He spotted an easier angle and ascended the rocks, both hands on the face for balance. By the time he reached the rest of them, the Pashtuns had already taken positions in the upper faces with their Dragunov sniper rifles.

Salar ran his fingers over the slab. "This is a cave similar to the one your first team used." His dark eyes narrowed as he stepped back, frowning as he studied the rock façade. "It's shifted—almost a meter." He knelt, running his fingers along the bottom of it. "See this? This should align with this." He pointed to a hand-hewn ledge of stone eighteen inches below the slab. "It used to be the perfect hiding place," he said, his shoulders slumping.

Flynn bent down. The eighteen-inch-wide crack was just large enough for a man to slide underneath. It doesn't have to be perfect, just defendable. He reached over his head and grasped the thin edge of the UAV. He knelt and pushed the UAV under the slab, placing the aircraft up onto a dirty stone floor. He pulled his arm free, wiping the blackened dust on his pants. The quadcopter hovered in the roomy space, its thermal camera scanning the grotto. The heat signature of a rat scurried to the rear and disappeared into a dark tunnel-like void. Flynn landed the UAV on the cave floor and pulled off his helmet and bulky ballistic jacket. Barnes had made it up to the ledge, looking a bit out of place as he stood among the Pashtuns. "Barnes, get your gear off and help me out." He got on his stomach then wiggled up onto the cave floor. He pulled in his legs and lent Barnes a hand, pulling him into the small dark space. He grabbed a small flashlight from his belt and switched it on, the click of the switch echoing in the emptiness. The beam illuminated a dusty circular space approximately twenty meters across. The stench of human excrement hung in the air.

Barnes gagged. "Smells like the bathrooms in Teague Park in here!"

Flynn breathed through his mouth, walking to the back of the cave, shining the beam of light into different tunnels, which radiated out like spokes on a wheel from the main space. He examined the complex maze before returning to Barnes, illuminated by the sunlight shining under the slab.

Barnes stood, pinching his nose, still examining the main chamber. "I've never seen anything like this."

Flynn pointed down one of the tunnels. "There's a cave in the back loaded with someone's supplies." He slid back under the slab and leaned over the face. The rest of his men stood at the bottom with the gear. He cupped his hands around his mouth. "I want that gear busted down and set up ASAP." He turned to Salar. "Salar, I could use some help getting those supplies up here and spreading the transmitters. I need your Pashtuns."

Salar smiled a toothless grin before turning and yelling in Pashto to his skinny men. They responded instantly, scurrying from their sniper nests down the steep face to the loaded dollies. Flynn marveled at their impossible strength. Over and over, they ascended with weight he would be challenged to handle on flat ground.

Flynn spoke into the mic. "Bollick, I'm coming down with the Pashtuns. They're going to take us up into the canyon and help us set up the transmitters."

"Copy."

Salar, Hamasa, and Aamir were already halfway down, but Flynn noticed the mute boy was again waiting for him. Flynn smiled at Adam. "You're not going to make me look bad, are you?" He playfully pushed the lightweight teenager behind him. With the head start Flynn descended as fast as safely possible, occasionally jumping down to an available ledge for show. He wasn't winning any style points, but he was getting it done. His boots and clumsy technique created noisy rockslides accompanied by large puffs of talcum-fine dust. The white flash of Adam's loose cotton garments entered his peripheral vision. Adam ratcheted down the face, passing him in silence, not a single falling rock betraying his location. Trying to pick up speed, Flynn focused on his next step, a medium-sized rock with a nice flat top two feet below. He hopped down, his foot slipping on the fine dust. Adrenaline burned his skin as he lost his balance. His arms windmilled as he slid like a surfer toward the steep face. He was at least forty feet from the bottom and picking up speed. He gasped, closing his eyes as he lost his balance and fell.

CHAPTER 18

Flynn cried out as he hurtled through the air. Blinding pain shot through his neck as he hit something with his throat, the force knocking him onto his back. He dug his nails into the stone as something gripped him and stopped his descent. He opened his eyes wide. Hamasa, silhouetted by the blue sky, stood glaring down at him. The Pashtun looked like a giant, standing over him and admonishing his foolishness with a wagging finger. "I'm sorry," Flynn bleated, his face flushing with heat.

Hamasa's upper lip curled. He turned away and motioned for Flynn to follow. Flynn mimicked his moves until he arrived safely at the bottom. He approached Hamasa, who was now standing with Adam. "I'm sorry, Hamasa. Thank you for—"

"Stupid man are you," Hamasa said in a deep baritone voice, brows tightening as he crossed his arms. Adam mimicked his father, crossing his arms and glaring at him.

"God, how did that happen?" Flynn muttered with embarrassment. He saw the brim of the hat sticking out of his waistband. He pulled it free and tossed it to Adam. "Here, take this."

Adam caught the hat and examined it, his frown turning into a smile as he put it on.

Hamasa's eyes tightened. He yelled at Adam in Pashto, yanking the hat off the child's head and dragging him away.

Flynn sighed as Hamasa stormed off. He limped over to Bollick. "I feel like the biggest dumbass in the world."

Bollick offered an almost imperceptible shrug. "Hey, I'm just glad he was able to get to you in time. You should have seen that son of a bitch move. He must have been thirty feet below you when you slipped." Bollick handed him a helmet. "Here, take this one. You left yours up on the ledge."

Barnes's piercing voice shattered the morning calm. "There goes paradise! We've got bad guys movin' in!" Everyone scattered to hide as Flynn threw on the helmet, focusing on the image from Barnes's quadcopter. Three armed men approached from the desert. They wore traditional scarves wrapped around their faces and heads and were otherwise clad in camouflage military fatigues. All three held rocket-propelled grenades holding the Type 69 warhead, a devastating weapon in close quarters. The camouflaged men slunk along the mountain at the entrance to the path, entering the opening then creeping among the tons of rubble toward his position. Flynn targeted the three men off of Barnes's UAV feed. "I've seen enough. Who's got a round ready?"

"Ready to go," Laster piped back.

"Fire!"

***

The dead men were searched, but only handheld radios were found.

"Izzy, we planned on digitally mapping the pass and the surrounding terrain. Now seems like a good time to do it. How long will it take the quadcopters to pull it off?" Flynn asked.

Izzy looked up as he calculated the answer. "Four UAVs can map this four-mile cordon in thirty minutes."

Salar was standing nearby eavesdropping. "Digital mapping?"

Izzy pointed to the disc on Flynn's back. "We fly these over the terrain and take high-resolution digital images. Once we map the area, we will have the source image to match to scans done in the future. By using digital subtraction, we can highlight any changes in terrain down to a small stone out of place."

***

Over the next two weeks the complex of caves became a home of sorts. The equipment was neatly arranged and the varying caves each served a purpose. Two escape routes out the back had been discovered, a luxury the first team had not enjoyed. Flynn sat back in the safety of the space, admiring the sleeping animal. Sher Dil had put on twenty pounds and his coat was shiny, the hair growing back around the wound and burns. He had taken to the bed Flynn had thrown together, an extra bedroll bent in half and covered with one of the heavy blankets used to wrap the gear. More and more he reminded Flynn of Mac. Sher Dil was more personable though. He was a faithful companion that followed him everywhere. Each time he was fed, the animal would come over to say thank you by burrowing its big head under Flynn's arm then smacking his lips as he licked them, staring affectionately with his big brown eyes. He had proven Izzy wrong, never barking under any circumstance. Sher Dil had a severe look, but he was a good dog.

"What the fuck is this?" Izzy said. "Flynn, get over here."

Flynn hurried over, kneeling next to him.

Izzy's brows furrowed. "These are the scans from this evening. Now look at the original obtained the day we killed those three bandits." He dragged the more recent set of images over the top of the originals. They appeared different.

Flynn pointed to a collection of red marks on the digitally subtracted image that remained. "This pile of rocks by this cave, they weren't here before."

Izzy's voice cracked, pointing at the other side of the screen. "Here are some more over here! Flynn, that's less than three hundred meters from us."

A shiver went through Flynn. "That's an IED and it's in my pass! How could they have snuck in right under our noses?"

"And where the fuck are they?" Izzy asked.

The other men dropped what they were doing, gathering around, listening to the conjecture. The soft clinking of weapons and swearing filled the large cave, the men grabbing the mortar tubes and slipping new battery packs into the quadcopters.

Flynn secured his helmet and went through his checklist. ORION was fully operational, the eLORAN system operating flawlessly. He lifted off. "I'm taking a closer look." Like he was riding the quadcopter, he zipped up the pass. Within seconds the reliable little UAV hovered high above. The sun had set, the narrow pass drenched in darkness. He switched the camera to the heat-detecting FLIR mode, squinting as his eyes adjusted to the brightness. The UAV descended into the pass, stopping fifty feet off the ground.

"Holy shit! There are men in that cave!" Barnes said.

Flynn recoiled at the sight. Six men were crouching in the cave as if listening intently. He zoomed out, flying a little higher to survey the spot, then flying to the other area where rocks had been pushed out of a medium-sized cave. The heat signatures of several men holding rockets materialized. He spoke in an uncertain tone. "I watched those cameras myself. How did they get past me? I don't see any red bandanas, but they're sure as hell professional." He looked at Sher Dil. "I guess you get a pass since you're so far away, but you didn't help any either."

Sher Dil laid his head down and whined.

Izzy's eyes were freighted with worry. "Do you think these guys are the ones that killed the first platoon?"

Flynn's eyes narrowed. "Doubtful. I imagine these are Mullah Mehsud's death squads that General

Smith warned us about, perhaps the same group that Hamasa got away from, but I don't get the impression they have air support."

Barnes's voice cut through. "They know where we are. What the fuck are we waiting on? We need to kill these motherfuckers!"

"Simmer down, Barnes. ORION is fully operational. Let's sniff around for a bit," Flynn said.

Sher Dil walked to the entrance, sniffing under the slab. The animal stiffened, growling as it backpedaled to Flynn's side.

Barnes stated the obvious. "Oh shit! Even the dog can smell 'em, they're so close!"

Flynn's eyes were glued to his visor. A heatless human shape ran across the bottom of the pass to the alcove housing the improvised explosive device. "They are thermoneutral somehow! I just—"

"There's another one!" Barnes said. "What the—? It's the zombie apocalypse!"

Another humanoid shape, devoid of heat, ran across the screen. "They know we have FLIR imaging," Flynn said. "Everyone get their avatars out of the caves and into position!" Flynn landed his UAV close to his avatar. He concentrated on the avatar's screen, waiting for it to boot up. In seconds the robot was ready. He walked the robot out of the cave to a flat area surrounded by boulders on all sides. The robot squatted, knee joints locking at ninety degrees. A thick hydraulic stabilizing bar extended from the bottom of the robot, the flat plate hanging passively from its end flattening as the bar contacted the ground, settling solidly onto the rock. The robot reached back to the magazine on its back, securing two of the forty-pound 120 mm shells, one in each mechanical hand. The mortar tubes rose from the lower legs and stopped, the avatar now holding the rounds over the eighteen-inch Kevlar tubes, ready to fire.

"What now?" Barnes asked.

"Everyone move out of the cave to your hiding spots. One well-placed rocket-propelled grenade could ruin our day." He looked around at them. "Now! Take your 81s in case the avatars malfunction." The men's expressions hardened as they prepared for battle, moving out one by one from the cave. Cursors moved over the screens, dropping red dots all over the images from Barnes's and Laster's UAVs. "Fire!"

A thunderous roar shattered the night sky as the mortar rounds flew toward the enemy. The massive amount of CL-20 detonating in the narrow pass released enormous amounts of energy, the blast forces amplified by the narrow geometric confine. Flynn was flattened by a staccato blast of waves that tore through his position. Rock shrapnel shot around him with acoustic zips and zings, tearing past at thousands of feet per second. An endless rainstorm of gravel and rocks then showered him as he put his arms around his head. Excruciating pain erupted from his right ear, warm liquid oozing down his neck. He rubbed his finger through it, relieved to see that it was dark blood not clear spinal fluid. The blast had damaged his tympanic membrane. His ears rang and his head ached, but he was okay. "Everyone back to the cave!"

***

"Izzy, this fucking CL-20 is going to get us killed. Some standard comp-B or TNT rounds would be nice," Flynn said. He looked at the three blank screens on his visor's HUD. "Three of the goddamned quadcopters got vaporized."

Izzy sat on the floor rubbing his temples. "I think I have dust in my brain."

Flynn shook his head. His vision was still blurry, but his hearing was better. "Barnes and Laster, keep your UAVs in the air and watch my back. Bollick and Izzy, come with me. The rest of you hang tight." The three of them followed Hamasa, Adam, and Aamir down the face to the footpath below. Hamasa paced around the bodies with a look of distaste. "Punjabi! Bad men!" He pointed to one of the corpses. "Mullah Mehsud's bandits."

Flynn placed the edge of his boot under one of the corpses and rolled it over. The man was dressed in a thick insulated suit that had blocked his heat signature. "Where are they from?"

"Not here from." Hamasa said. He spat at one of the bodies as the twins scavenged through the corpses' pockets.

Flynn surveyed the carnage, stooping to pick up a bent rocket-propelled grenade, still loaded with a warhead. He illuminated the weapon with his small metal flashlight. Chinese symbols were stamped across the base of the grenade. "Chinese gear."

Bollick's face was covered in light-colored dust, making him look like a ghost in the darkness. He walked up, holding a small black box, similar to previous finds. He held it against his belly, examining it under the beam of his flashlight. "GPS jammer, just like the other one. These sons of bitches just won't learn their lesson."

"What do we do, Flynn?" Izzy asked.

"One of two things happens next. Either we did so much damage that they will find another route, or they'll be back in greater numbers. My fear is, if they come back, they'll have air support. Barnes, you have the most experience with the Stingers. From now on, you keep one close at all times, understood?"

"Yes, sir!"

"They must have had a good idea where we were hiding, the way those IEDs were placed. If we had chased them like they were trying to goad us into, we would have all been killed." The fatigue of combat crept in; his legs weakened by the experience.

CHAPTER 19

Flynn sat stiff and sore from the previous day's battle. His right ear felt like a seashell was pressed to it, but at least he could hear. Sleep had evaded him, haunting thoughts of the wasps and Mullah Mehsud's bandits tormenting him. The cacophony of snores and the smell of Sher Dil's gas didn't help. Flynn sighed, pulling his shirt over his nose to breathe. "Good god, dog." Sher Dil lifted his head, seemingly aware an insult had been cast his way.

Barnes propped himself up on one elbow, a look of distaste distorting his boyish good looks. "Your dog's ass is killing me, boss. Maybe you've been medicating him too much."

"He's not my dog."

Barnes rolled his eyes. "Give me a break. That thing latched onto you the minute we got here. Everyone here knows you two are smitten except you." He yawned and rolled over, going back to sleep.

Flynn cocked his head and stared at Sher Dil lying on the ground, his mind moving from the paint-stripping stench back to the latest enemy contact. The defensive positions of the caves offered a good degree of safety if ORION was operational. However, they would again become crypts in the event of an airstrike with a thermobaric bomb. He would move the men out today and establish defensive positions outside of the caves in the crags and crevices afforded by the terrain. He reached for the battery-operated coffee pot, pouring a cup of the hot black liquid. Flynn moved quietly to the entrance and placed the mug outside, pushing it out of his way before slipping under the slab. Sher Dil wiggled out behind him, stiffly ambling over and sitting next to him for what had become their morning ritual. His tail wiggled, eyes holding Flynn's without waver as he panted with happiness. I hate it when he looks at me like that. Barnes was right. He loves you and you're going to have to leave him behind or kill him. You know that. You're not his friend; you're a traitor. He scratched the animal behind his ears, pushing the guilt down again. "I'll do what I can to get you back with me." He told himself the same lie every day. Somehow I'll find a way. Somehow. He pushed the thought of shooting his new friend out of his mind, the idea too painful to bear. He put his arm around the beast, a single tear streaming down his cheek as he peered into the intelligent being's eyes. Sher Dil whined then pawed the ground, leaning into him, surely trying to offer comfort from the pain he was feeling.

"Morning, boss. No se puede dormir?" Flynn pulled his arm away from Sher Dil and wiped his face before looking over his shoulder. Laster had emerged from the cave.

"Mr. Rex Laster himself. How you feeling, wild man?"

Laster rubbed his forearms, mouth opening in a huge yawn. "My neck's stiff as steel, but I got my legs back and I'm ready to rumble." Laster tilted his head, eyes laden with concern. "You okay? You look like you've got a lot on your mind."

"That obvious, huh?" Flynn pointed to the rocks above them. "We need to relocate, at least for a while. These cliffs offer easily defendable positions on both ridges. We can spread out and secure the pass without actually being in it." He shifted his butt on the hard stone. "We'll get the robots positioned in the hills. If we get pinned down, they'll be our mortar batteries."

Laster pulled out his phone and held it up, focusing it for a moment. "Sounds good but first a picture of you two. Say cheese!" Laster snapped a couple of pictures and slid the phone back into his pocket.

***

Bollick walked along the top of the ridge, approaching Flynn. "We scouted the area as you ordered. I found a cave fifty meters from here that we could take cover in. It would make an excellent ambush position if one of those Cobras comes in."

"Show me," Flynn said. He followed Bollick along the ridge and crawled into the small cave. Two huge pieces of granite projected up into the air on either side of its opening.

Bollick pointed to an expansive corridor between the two mountains. "Look at the area we can cover from here. A helicopter pilot would have to come right at us to have a chance of destroying the position. The problem for him is he will fly right over us and expose his rear, not even knowing we are here." A glint of mischief shone in Bollick's eye. "We'll place some of the LED flashers in that cave in the distance. A chopper pilot would line up through this channel to attack the flashers. When we see the ass of the helicopter—" He made the motion of firing a shoulder-fired rocket. "Game over. If we can light him up right out of the box, we won't have to waste a Stinger on a helicopter."

"I see your point. A chopper may also use this channel to turn around for gun runs on the pass." Flynn scratched his chin. "What bothers me is that this channel is larger than it looks. It will be near impossible to hit a moving helicopter with a rocket if it gets too far down the line."

"You're right. We'd have to hit it right as it came over." He shrugged. "If the rockets miss, the tracers on the .50-caliber will walk it down and chew it up. It may not be an easy shot but it's a shot."

Flynn spotted Hamasa seventy meters up the pass, cleaning his weapon. He cupped his hands around his mouth. "Hamasa, come here." Hamasa nodded, moving like an apparition amid the rocks. In seconds he was by his side. Hamasa dropped his head slightly. "Fleen, I sorry for angry earlier."

"It's okay, Hamasa. I deserved it. Thank you again. I owe you my life."

Hamasa's lips pressed together, his massive jaw clenched as he gazed over the expanse. "What you plan?" he said.

"We thought we could kill any choppers if we could trick them into flying down this channel. What do you think?"

Hamasa grinned. "It good plan." He pointed up the pass. "Hamasa set PKMs up there. I kill any who make it that far."

"Hamasa, if we don't fire first, you and the boys hide. They'll be coming right past you," Flynn said.

"Yes, I hide." Hamasa slapped him on the back and disappeared into the rocks.

"There are at least four spots I found for the avatars," Bollick said.

"Let's hope Izzy and Salar are doing as well over on the eastern ridge." Flynn keyed his microphone. "Izzy, how's it looking over there?"

Izzy's enthusiastic voice piped in. "Looking real good. We've got more hiding spaces than we've got guns."

"Outstanding. Hamasa and his boys will be well up the pass to turn back any smugglers lucky enough to get up that far. I'm headed back into the desert to find spots to hide the Fat Boys." Flynn made his way back to the entrance of the path to examine his strategy from another vantage point. He neared the tons of rubble at the mouth of the pass, freezing at a sound behind him. His pulse hammered in his neck as he spun around. Sher Dil was pulling his haunches out of a hidden crevice not ten feet away. "Where did you come from?" Flynn walked over to investigate. The opening was obscured by the edge of a boulder pressed tight against the space. He got on his hands and knees and wiggled into the crevice, Sher Dil pressing back in behind him. The hidden grotto was twenty feet long and ten feet wide. *How did we ever miss this?* He scratched the animal's head. "Sher Dil, you are a genius." He eased out of the tight opening and continued the remaining fifty meters toward the desert, crawling over the rubble and out of the pass. He trudged through the sand for a couple of minutes then turned around. A huge alcove fifty meters from the entry was an intuitive staging area for any force planning to enter the pass. He would park one of the Fat Boys, disguised as a boulder, in the middle of it.

CHAPTER 20

Crash! The flimsy aluminum door to Colonel Pitts's tiny office burst open and slammed against the wall. Major Roberts charged in, his inner brows high. "Is it true? Tell me it's true!"

"What the hell are you busting in here blabbing about?"

"The U.S. airstrikes in Farrar! Rumors are pouring in that Ibrahim and all his foot soldiers are dead!"

Colonel Pitts put his hands behind his head and leaned back in his recliner. "It is true. I just read the report from High Command."

Bang! Major Roberts's clenched fist crashed against the metal ceiling. His face twisted in pain and embarrassment.

"Meathead. They carpet-bombed the whole complex yesterday morning. I spoke with Mullah Mehsud a moment ago. He said Ibrahim's thugs had been attacking ISAF patrols. Last month Ibrahim received an ultimatum to cease attacking ISAF forces or be destroyed. He attacked a convoy of ISAF vehicles outside of his village last week, which killed two CIA agents. That pissed off the chief spook over in Bamyan. He sent in B-52s."

"I gotta give it to Mullah Mehsud. I always thought he was dreaming, thinking he would ever control that area again. Now the U.S. Air Force has done all his dirty work." His eyes creased. "Where's all the dope? We're getting in on this, right?"

Colonel Pitts put a hand out. "Patience, my friend. Mullah and his foot soldiers got in soon after the B-52s left. They plundered the entire compound."

"How much?"

"Twenty tons of fully processed bricks, top-flight stuff, bundled and ready to go."

Major Roberts's jaw hung open. "Twenty fuckin' tons! That's more than we've moved in the last two years. What does that come to?"

Colonel Pitts poked his finger at him. "Don't start counting your money yet. We have to approach this delicately. We have to revisit that pass to get it through."

Major Roberts cringed. "That's Colonel Kelley's cordon. I hate traveling through that pass. I barely got out of there with my hide last spring. If we go back and get caught in the mountains with twenty tons of smack—"

"No, no, no. You're looking at it all wrong. The fact is that Colonel Kelley and General Smith have no manpower. Mullah Mehsud's horde has infiltrated this whole corner of the country and killed all of our competition. Say we do run into a shadow group in the pass. Colonel Kelley wouldn't know any more than us. Even if he tried to intervene, any patrol from Camp Rose would get killed before it even got near that shitty little pass." He reached for his glass of single-malt Scotch whisky and took a gulp, savoring the pungent liquid. His thoughts drifted back to the heroin. "What really bothers me is how pleasant Mullah Mehsud was the last time we talked. I know he needs help getting those twenty tons through the pass, but he was syrupy, handing out compliments, the whole bit. Something's going on but I can't put my finger on it."

Major Roberts's eyes narrowed. "Do you think he'll turn on us?"

"Hell yes, if he could. He hates me for controlling the border. I'm a foreigner in his land, and I have the upper hand. From his perspective, the twenty-five percent transport fee we charge is adding insult to injury. My mind keeps going back to that smuggler we interrogated last week. He said that over the last three weeks Mehsud had lost two large teams of men near that pass, but when I asked Mullah Mehsud about it, he flat-out denied it." He frowned. "Mullah is well-supplied with jammers and heavy weaponry. It's hard to believe that smuggler's story could be true." Colonel Pitts took another gulp as he peered at Major Roberts. "My gut says Mullah Mehsud is going to use a proxy force to try and kill us, lead us into an ambush or something. I've already spoken to General Syed about it. He says he'll make sure we're properly equipped. Hell, maybe he'll finally give me a bomb or two since I don't have anything left in inventory."

Major Roberts grinned. "Twenty fucking tons." The smirk vanished, his eyes widening. "How the hell am I going to get twenty tons up that steep-ass pass? It's covered in gravel. We'll have to carry it through with donkeys just like last time. We could be annihilated if we meet a force like that in the pass."

Colonel Pitts frowned. "Calm down. It won't be like last time. First, we'll send through a dummy shipment with as many of Mullah Mehsud's men attached to it as possible. If they survive, we'll go through with the real shipment. If they don't—" he put out his hands and shrugged. "I'll get two Cobra gunships from General Syed to cover your team as you lead the caravan through."

"Two gunships? That sounds more like it. When does he want to move the heroin?"

"Right away. I'll send the trucks to Farrar Province tomorrow. We'll move it to the jail here at Camp Rock for safekeeping then get started as soon as possible.

We'll have to make more than one run."

"What about Mullah Mehsud?"

 Colonel Pitts slammed the whiskey left in his glass. "As long as I'm in control, I'm inclined to play along. We'll let him think he has the upper hand."

CHAPTER 21

August 9, 2012, Nimroz province

Hamasa and his sons camped higher in the pass than the other men, their climbing speed and fighting skills making them the perfect goalies. Hamasa huddled with Aamir and Adam in the little windproof space, enjoying the heat radiating from the rock. Hamasa breathed easier as the eastern sky brightened with the early morning sun. Maybe the smugglers wouldn't come back. As he prepared the small string snare, he felt a stiff nudge in his ribs. Adam looked alarmed, pointing to the sky. Hamasa put away the snare and listened. He closed his eyes and cupped a hand behind his ear. Pfft, pfft, fup-fup-fup. The rhythmic, barely discernible sound grew with every second. Hamasa rose to his feet. "Adam, the radio!" Hamasa mashed the transmit button, speaking in Pashto. "Salar, a helicopter approaches from the west!" In seconds, the faint sound morphed into a resonant thump. Nothing good happened when helicopters approached from the west. Hamasa put his arm around Adam, peering into his large brown eyes. "Easy son, everything will be all right, but now we must hide."

***

Flynn picked up the satcom then put it down. The risk of the satellite phone exposing their position was too great, and besides, Colonel Kelley would have informed him if any friendlies were coming through the area. His mind went back to Camp Leatherneck, which seemed so long ago. General Smith's stern voice played in his head. "You kill any unidentified human being you see if they don't contact you first. I mean it, son." Goosebumps rippled across his skin as Barnes and the others whispered expletives through the audio. Flynn raced with Mendez and Sher Dil to the entrance of the pass, crawling into the Lilliputian cave the dog had crawled out of two days earlier. He pressed himself against the stone, eyes widening as Sher Dil crept to the concealed entrance. The beast's head rose in the air, huge nostrils quivering. His body stiffened, a soft baritone growl filling the space as he crept backward, never taking his eyes off the entrance. They must be close! Flynn's diaphragm quivered as he inspected the images from the quadcopters that had survived the debacle in the canyon. The early rays of morning sun illuminated a glittering caravan of men and donkeys approaching from the west. The colossal line meandered like a serpent slithering through the desert.

Mendez fingered the St. Michael medal hanging from his neck. "There's so many of them," he said, flattening against the stone wall. "This is the part I hate the most."

Flynn's eyes remained fixed on the HUD. As if a door from another dimension had opened, the roar of two helicopters mixed with the braying of donkeys, shattering the morning calm. The caravan of men in Afghan clothing was led by six agile commandos already moving over the rubble mere meters away. Red bandanas waved boldly around their upper arms. The noise of the nearest helicopter exploded as it resonated directly above. Flynn's senses heightened as his heart thumped at the epiphany. "It's them."

Izzy's voice came through the helmet. "Salar says this is exactly how it happened with the first platoon in the spring. The Cobra gunship covered the commandos as they came through, clearing the pass for the caravan." Salar's voice could be heard in the background. "Praise be to Allah I'm not down there. They stretch as far as I can see."

"Be alert!" a stranger's voice warned from outside.

Flynn froze, swallowing hard as the images on his visor flickered and disappeared as the GPS feed for the communication link was jammed. Before he could stop himself, he leaned out, a black flash visible as the boots of the point man moved feet from his face. He stiffened at the thought of Sher Dil growling. Sher Dil's eyes locked onto his and the creature blinked slowly, remaining silent and perfectly still. Flynn exhaled as Izzy fired up the eLORAN grid, the camera images flickering back on.

Barnes whispered through the helmet audio. "I say we let them get strung out in the canyon and kill every one of them."

Flynn keyed his mic. "Shut up, Barnes. Everyone stay perfectly still and keep those quadcopters out of the air. These guys are twitchy. Let's draw them in and get to know 'em." The lead group of commandos moved higher into the pass toward Hamasa and his sons. The donkeys in the middle of the caravan began neighing and curveting as they passed the small cave, no doubt sensing the tiger dog. The smell of livestock filled Flynn's nose as the oblivious handlers drove the suspicious animals past, whipping them and cursing them in Farsi. The commandos searched the nooks and crannies of the pass, throwing grenades into caves as they led the convoy, slipping and sliding up the pass. Over the next thirty minutes the lengthy caravan filled the pass, the thunderous resonance of the two gunships ever present above.

Eventually the last team of man and beast passed Hamasa and the twins. They disappeared south into the increasing elevation of the narrow gorge, the gunships following them into Pakistan. The noises of the convoy gave way to a sepulchral silence. Flynn keyed his mic. "I heard the lead man speaking English with a drawl as bad as Barnes's."

Izzy's voice dripped with disappointment. "We should have done something. Those motherfuckers killed our friends and we just sat here like cowards. We let them waltz right through."

"We could have wiped them out," Sobieski complained.

Flynn growled into the microphone. "Quit your bitching. That's the first real shipment we've observed, and now we know our enemy. We're going to get one shot at this. If we have only an instant, we're going to do something huge, something earth-shattering."

"I agree," Bollick said. "Those men were expecting a fight. They'll be back soon enough. Now that we know their capabilities, we can lay a proper ambush."

"Fair enough," Izzy said. "We could report this to Colonel Kelley, but he'll pull the plug. If Central Command couldn't catch them before, how will they catch them this time? I say we keep this to ourselves, stay here, and wait for them to return."

"I agree," Barnes said. "I've got a Stinger antiaircraft missile in my hands. We'll call Colonel Kelley if we have to."

Montacayo's smiling face flashed into Flynn's mind as if to bless the notion. "Good. Let's prepare a welcome party for these bastards. I have a hunch we'll see them soon."

CHAPTER 22

August 10, 2012

Flynn slipped under the slab, sipping his coffee with Sher Dil in the cold morning air. Clouds passing under the bright moon cast ghostly shadows, flickering as they drifted across the ridges. Looking at the face of his filthy watch, Flynn took a long slurp of the scalding, bitter brew. 0523. He closed his eyes, feeling a sense of urgency as if something momentous would occur over the next few hours. I have to be sharp today. No mistakes, no mercy. He stood up and headed back towards the dimly lit lights in the cave to address the others, all of whom were awake. "Okay, men, gather round." He took a knee, peering up at them as he spoke. "Let's go over this one more time. If this goes off, it's gonna be a long day."

Barnes crossed his arms, standing with his chin stuck out. "If they show up, it'll be a damn sight longer for those motherfuckers."

Flynn regarded the group around him. Their eyes burned like a pack of hungry jackals sensing weakness in their prey. At first, the collective emotion had been fear and doubt. Through the night, that emotion had become an indignant fury that grew thorny and bitter, hardening into a cold primal instinct for retribution. This wasn't an ambush; it was a reckoning. Flynn picked up the long sturdy staff Salar used for climbing, smoothing the dirt out again with his boot. He used the tip of the stick, marking the map: north, south, east, and west. Next, he traced a meandering line along the north-south axis. "This is the pass. Hamasa, Aamir, and Adam will be here, high in the southern portion closer to Pakistan. By the time the lead commandos get to Hamasa's position, the rest of their caravan will be strung out throughout the pass." He ran the stick along the line in illustration. "Salar, when the time is right, you are going to spring the ambush." He crossed an "x" on the eastern ridge a half-kilometer into the corridor. "Salar, this is your position, fifty meters from Bollick and Laster, here. When I give the order, you lean over the edge of the ridge and make a commotion. Tell them whatever it is you guys say to really piss each other off. After you do, empty a clip out of that AK-47 into the middle of the caravan. Pick up your RPG then run like hell to join Bollick and Laster in the cave. You'll be safe from the Cobras if you can make it."

Bollick and Laster stood opposite him. Flynn poked the stick at them. "Hopefully, Salar will make it over to help, but if he doesn't, the entire success of the ambush will depend on you two. God willing, they will only have one gunship this time. You have to take out that helicopter! Preferably in the rear fuel tanks."

Bollick nodded. "We're ready. The LED flashers are in the bait cave. We'll draw the copter into the canyon and smoke that son of a bitch with our AT4 rockets."

Salar leaned back and crossed his arms, breaking into a toothless grin. "I'll make it. I will show how them how the descendants of Genghis Khan fight."

Flynn smiled at the Pashtun leader then looked back to the dirt map. He pointed the gnarled stick to the bottom of the map. "Here, out in the desert, just fifty meters to the west of the entrance, is an alcove that enemy forces will instinctively stage in before they crawl over that rubble and enter the pass. Sobieski has one of the covered Fat Boys parked right in the middle of it. Flynn cupped his hand. "The wall of the alcove pointing toward the desert is like a parabolic disc. When that Fat Boy goes off—" He mimicked an explosion motion with his hands, a ripple of evil laughs filling the cave. "The other two Fat Boys are closer to the middle of the pass, here and here, one between Laster's and Bollick's position on the eastern ridge, the other closer to Hamasa's location way up here high in the southern pass. After the rockets kill the gunship, the Fat Boys will go off." He scanned the group. "The rest of you stay hidden, operating your avatars from the ridges. Use the thermal cameras; the dust is going to be thick. I'll take Mendez to the entrance where we hid yesterday and cut off any stragglers trying to escape back into the desert." He looked at his watch. 0537. "The sun will be up in seven minutes. Everyone get to your posts."

They broke apart, quickly disappearing among the rocks. Flynn checked his quadcopter's batteries and grabbed his M4 and several grenades, moving toward the front cave, Mendez and Sher Dil in tow. He thought of Montacayo, leaping off the platform surrounded by blue sky. His chest heaved as he fixated on his enemy. He wished for nothing more than to tear these men to pieces. They arrived at the tiny cave as the first illuminating rays of sun peeked over the horizon. Flynn followed Mendez and crawled into the tiny space, taking a seat against the cold granite. Sher Dil flopped next to him, laying his massive head on his thigh.

***

The old UHF U.S. Marine radio used by the Afghans crackled. Flynn picked up the bulky black radio, turning down the sound as Hamasa's excited voice jabbered in Pashto. Salar's voice followed. "A gunship comes from the west!" Flynn's senses heightened, the fury rippling just below the surface. In seconds he could hear a single helicopter, coming fast. Only one helicopter! His mind exulted. The UAVs high above the entrance showed a meandering line of men and beasts coming from the desert led by the same six commandos, their body language more confident and relaxed than before. The resonant boom of the Cobra became cacophonic, the vibrations tickling Flynn's cheeks as it hovered above the entrance, bristling with its 30 mm Gatling gun and rockets, eager to deal death. He thought of the armor-killing thermite grenades that S&K had designed for the quadcopters and keyed his microphone. "Hey, Izzy, maybe I should try one of those thermite grenades. I know I could fly right up on this loser and stick one to his engine bay. He'd never know."

"Sweet Jesus, Flynn, I'm trying to concentrate." Flynn could hear Salar's muffled voice

through Izzy's microphone. "Allahu akbar! They're everywhere!"

Flynn scanned the HUD, finding the camera above Hamasa's position. Hamasa and the boys were lying flat behind a wall of rocks, the commandos still far below, closer to the entrance. He studied the screen showing Salar's position as he gripped the UHF radio, waiting for a moment longer when the commandos would be out in the open. When the last one stepped out, he keyed the radio. "Salar, fire." The tubby Pashtun moved, crouching as he went, small rapid steps propelling him to the edge. He leaned over and screamed something, holding the Kalashnikov high over his head, pointing it down over the ledge. Orange bursts of fire filled the screen as the twenty-five-round clip cycled through the rifle. Salar easily escaped, running to Bollick and Laster's position. Bollick and Laster both crouched low on one knee, rocket tubes at their shoulders, Laster's red beard whipping from under his helmet like a perturbed cat's tail.

The entire valley exploded into gunfire and ricochet as the caravan members shot blindly up into the rocks. The AH-1 Cobra's turbine roared as it accelerated into the pass, searching for targets. "Laster, ready with those flashers!" Flynn yelled. The Celt's timing was impeccable. The pilot, seeing what he thought were muzzle flashes, pulled the yoke hard, swinging the helicopter up and away from the perceived threat. The Cobra thundered with anger, arching around in a long loop, its turbines screaming ever louder as it came back for a gun run. A resonant boom hit as the powerful machine flew over, lining up then dropping into the narrow corridor. The Cobra released two rockets, smoke trailing them as they approached the flashers at incredible speed. While the rockets annihilated the flashers, two new contrails tore toward the aircraft. Flynn's heart skipped a beat as both rockets missed high, streaking over the canopy. The savvy pilot reacted instantly, accelerating up into an evasive turn. Flynn quit breathing as three more rockets shot up toward the escaping helicopter, two of them impacting the rear fuel tank. The petrol of the doomed machine ignited, a huge fireball illuminating the pass. For a second, the climbing helicopter hung in the air as if suspended like a puppet then dropped and impacted at the mouth of the cave. The shrieking of the twisting metal filled the canyon as it clanged down the face, crashing onto the rocks below.

"Hamasa, fire!" Flynn shouted into the radio. He peered through the high southern camera. Hamasa and his sons strafed the exposed lead commandos with PKMs. Two of the men fell like trees after bullets tore through their necks and chests. Flynn surveyed the other screens on his visor. The entire caravan was in the pass, minus a reserve group in the alcove west of the entrance. "Sobieski, detonate the Fat Boys!" Thunderous blasts accompanied the massive CL-20 bombs as they detonated in daisy-chain fashion. Even though Flynn had his helmet on, the warheads hurt his damaged eardrum. He ignored the sharp pain. "Avatars! March out!" The robots marched out and squatted, stabilizing bars extending to the ground. The robots reached back, grabbing a round in each hand. Small red dots filled the screens as targets were selected. Within seconds the massive rounds were tearing into the atmosphere, crashing through the gorge and inflicting devastation throughout its recesses.

***

Mullah Mehsud's hands trembled at the increasing ferocity of the attack. He stood with fifty of his personal guard, assembling to protect the rear of the caravan. He turned to Fahran, his lieutenant. "The ghosts in the pass!" The helicopter was silent, and the explosions were growing in force, coming closer to the entrance. Mullah Mehsud felt an urgent danger. He turned to the open desert and ran, urging his men to follow. Suddenly he was in a different dimension, surrounded by light, enveloped by the sensation of immersion in ice water, electricity surging through every nerve in his body.

***

Major Roberts lay at the head of the convoy, trapped by the barrage of bullets from the machine guns above. He barked to Bennett, the one man still alive next to him. "We have to charge that gun nest!" He raised the new airburst rifle, careful to stay out of the line of fire. "Bennett, give me covering fire!" Major Roberts rolled out from the protection of the rock as Bennett emptied his carbine. He pushed the laser range finder and squeezed the trigger, the 20 mm airburst round exploding perfectly over the target. "Let's go!" Major Roberts screamed, pulling the man up by his collar, pushing him in front. They vaulted the rocks in an adrenaline- fueled surge, soon on top of three men in Afghan dress, one an enormous middle-aged Pashtun, the other two scrawny, boyish-looking teenagers, one of whom was bleeding from his shoulder.

The flash of Bennett's rifle barrel raising entered his peripheral vision. Major Roberts drove his elbow back into Bennett's face. "You dumb bastard! They're our ticket out of here! Get them up and move!" They struggled with the dazed Afghans higher into the steep pass. Out of breath, Major Roberts turned into a small stone alcove. He spat the metallic taste from his mouth then yelled into his radio. "Mayday! Mayday!"

The radio crackled back. "What the hell is going on over there? I can hear explosions here at the base!"

He said through panting breaths, "Déjà vu, Colonel. The whole convoy has been annihilated. I'm trapped up in the southern portion of the pass. You gotta send a chopper for us or we'll never make it out!"

Colonel Pitts was silent for a moment. "Major, I'll have Serpon turn around and head back with the helicopter."

"Goddammit, there is no Serpon! They killed him first!"

Alarm filled Colonel Pitts's voice. "Who killed him? What are you talking about?"

"I'm not sure who they are, but I captured three of the son of a bitches, and if we're ever gonna find out, you'd better get that Huey over here quick!"

"I'm grabbing the pilot and coming myself. Turn your beacon on and find a suitable pickup point. I'll be there in five minutes."

CHAPTER 23

Flynn struggled to breathe, the cloud of stone dust and the poisonous smell of the CL-20 filling the air like toxic sludge. The echoes of wild gunfire had ceased, replaced by ghostly intonations of the howling wind driving cyclones of dust and smoke up and out of the mountain crevice. Flynn followed Sher Dil out of the space, crawling on his hands and knees, taking small gasps until he found fresh air. He propped himself against the rock. "Is everyone okay?"

"We're all still here," Izzy said.

Bollick's voice chimed in. "We're okay."

"Everyone stay hidden if you can. They could send in another attack helicopter or they may have drones as well." Flynn threw his quadcopter into the wind and methodically surveyed the pass. The donkeys had escaped but clusters of motionless human forms lay twisted and mangled a half-mile up the path. He flew around the wreckage of the Cobra, looking for markings, but it was burned beyond recognition. He parked the UAV, setting it down on a nearby perch of rock. "Sobieski, hand me that ninety-thousand-dollar satellite phone you're using for a chair. This mission is over. I'm calling Colonel Kelley."

Sobieski carried the case over, setting it on the ground in front of him. Flynn dialed and listened.

Click. "Corporal Lewis speaking," a boyish voice declared.

"This is Commander Robert Flynn. Put Colonel Kelley on the line." A rustling came through as the receiver was put down.

"What the fuck is going on over there, Commander? I'm getting reports of heavy fighting in my southern cordon."

"It was us, sir. Yesterday we observed a huge caravan of what looked like heroin go through the Chagai Pass. Whoever it was had two unmarked Cobra gunships and sophisticated equipment that jammed our GPS system. I elected to observe them, but this morning they came back. We just wiped them out."

The tone of Colonel Kelley's voice changed. "Are you and your team okay?"

"By the grace of God, we took zero casualties, but I'm concerned about the similarities to what happened to our first platoon in the spring."

Colonel Kelley scoffed. "No shit, Commander. I see why you're the leader. Jesus Christ!" Flynn could hear the sounds of glass breaking through the phone. "I knew I shouldn't have agreed to this shit again! Commander Flynn, I've had it! I'm ending your mission. We have to get you to Camp Leatherneck as soon as possible."

"No argument here, sir, but we have a dilemma. I can't escape into the desert because I have no vehicles or cover. Our only option is to stay holed up like the first team or head high up into the pass under the eLORAN grid. What's the chance you can send me a helicopter?"

More profanity poured through the line. "I only have two Apache helicopters on the base and they have no extra seats. Our two Black Hawks are at Camp Leatherneck for repairs."

"That's okay, sir. We're not picky. An Apache

could watch our asses until we can get transport out."

"I'm sorry, Commander Flynn, but they are providing support for a company of Marines pinned down ten miles from here. I can't spare them." An uncomfortable silence grew over the line. "Commander, you were sent in with two Stinger antiaircraft missiles, correct?"

"That's the rumor, sir."

"Excellent. If any questionable planes appear on my radar, I'll contact you and you blow them out of the sky. You said you wiped them out? Are you free to move?"

"Yes, I just didn't want to end up on the wrong end of a thermobaric weapon, so I figured I'd call."

Colonel Kelley took a deep breath. "If they had access to light bombers, we'd have known it by now. My advice is to hunker down in those caves until I can notify General Smith and get some men to escort you out."

Flynn cleared his throat. "I don't know, Colonel. I think we better get out of these caves. They know exactly where we are. I think our best option is to stay in the grid and move up the pass toward Pakistan and hide there."

"Commander, I have already dispatched a truck in your direction. If I can't secure a chopper, you'll have to risk another trek all the way back to meet my MPs in the desert. How many of you are there?"

"Twelve men, forty of our Pashtun guides, and a dog, sir."

"What dog?"

"He was with the Afghans, but we've been utilizing him as an early warning system."

"I can get your twelve men out. The Pashtuns and the dog are on their own."

"I'm taking my team up the pass. We'll walk back down if it comes to that."

"It's your call, Commander."

"Sir, a scout team of six commandos led the smugglers in. They were American. They passed two meters from my position. One of them spoke English with a southern accent."

Colonel Kelley was silent for a moment. "I see. Commander, you let me worry about that. For now, I'll stay glued to this phone. Godspeed, young man."

Flynn put the phone in its cradle, turning around to face the men, now gawking at him. "Colonel Kelley can't provide immediate air support or withdrawal and recommends we hide in the caves until transport out of here arrives."

"Maybe that's best," Izzy said.

Flynn shook his head. "I don't think so. There are too many variables beyond our control. We'll move under the grid toward Pakistan and find a more secure location where we can take shelter. In the event a bomber shows up, we'll be gone. Worst-case scenario, we march back down when Colonel Kelley's MPs arrive in the truck. Besides, Barnes will be in a better position to defend us if we can get up this mountain. If there is a bombing attack, they'll do the same thing they did last time and zero in on the last location of that satellite phone. They'll hit the ground we are standing on."

"You're right. Those Stingers would target better if we got out of these crags," Izzy said.

Salar's Pashtuns scurried around, collecting the intact bundles of heroin, throwing them into a huge crevice for later retrieval. The elder Pashtun's eyes darted around as Flynn and the others moved toward him. "There is a cave we can take refuge in only two miles away. Please, just a few minutes more," Salar said.

Izzy marched over, jabbing a finger in his uncle's face. "These drugs will get all of us killed! You idiots can stay behind and get slaughtered, but I'm leaving with my team."

Flynn cupped his hands around his mouth. "Sher Dil, let's go!" The animal emerged from a small space, panting as he trotted over. Flynn felt the blood drain from his face as the realization hit him like a truck. "Hamasa and the twins! Has anyone accounted for them?" He had lost track of them during the melee. He picked up the UHF radio. "Hamasa…" Flynn flipped his visor down, the haunting feeling now a physical pain as his gut twisted. He flew his UAV over their position. It was empty. He burst up the pass, running and crawling on all fours through the slippery gravel. He closed on the location to a pile of large stones, hopping and jumping toward Hamasa's position. As he closed on the final steep rise to the wall hiding the PKMs, he froze. Two dead commandos lay in the middle of the path. Flynn ground his teeth and began praying as he scrambled up and over the stone wall. He scanned the small space, his eyes locking on to a puddle of congealed blood and a tiny linen sandal.

CHAPTER 24

Major Roberts cupped a hand around his ear. "The Huey is on its way."

Bennett wiped blood from his broken nose, glaring at him for a moment before he spoke. "I think the boys are this big son of a bitch's sons. They look like identical twins."

Major Roberts regarded the boys, then the man. He took his Glock .357 Sig from its holster and took a step toward the injured boy. The elder man and the other boy straightened, their eyes growing as he pressed the gun's barrel to the injured child's head. The boy was barely conscious, too confused and weak to react.

"No! No!" The wiry youngster cried from under his father's arm.

The towering Afghan removed his arm from around the boy and stepped forward. He dropped to his knees, clasping his hands together. "He is my son. Anything I do, anything I tell you. Please, please don't my son you hurt!"

Major Roberts spat out a mouthful of metallic-tasting blood and holstered the pistol. "Bennett, help me get him up. We're getting out of here." Major Roberts fought the terrible soreness in his rib cage, grimacing with pain as he picked up the injured boy.

The Huey thundered in. He closed his eyes as the helicopter flared the rotors, a low-pitched whoosh accompanying the stinging blasts of sand-laced air. The Huey hovered inches from the rocks. Bennett crawled in first, helping the uninjured twin and the father into the aircraft before turning and grabbing the injured boy. Major Roberts growled in pain as he grabbed the edge of the door bay and pulled himself in. "Up, up, up!" He yelled, jackhammering an outstretched thumb. He settled back in his seat, pointing his finger at the pilot. "Don't you even think about taking a look-see at that pass. You fly us straight to Camp Rock."

"Yes, sir, straight back."

"Where the fuck is Colonel Pitts?"

"Camp Rock. He said he wasn't coming."

Major Roberts reached for the radio's handset. "Alpha Zulu, this is zero-nine, come in."

Colonel Pitts's voice piped through. "You got the prisoners?"

"Yes, I do. Pashtuns, a father and his identical twin sons." He cast his eyes on the Afghan. "It won't take long to get what we need."

The first building that come into focus was the aircraft hangar, the largest at Camp Rock. Smaller tubelike structures were built in series along the south end of a short airstrip. The pilot set the helicopter down softly next to one of the curved metal half-pipe buildings. Colonel Pitts opened his office door and hobbled down the steps into the swirling vortices. He motioned toward the building. "In there!" he mouthed.

Major Roberts crawled out, reaching in for the injured boy. With one hand he grabbed a handful of thick black hair; with the other, he gripped the back of the boy's clothes at the waist. He yanked him up, a knifelike pain tearing through his chest. I must've cracked my goddamn ribs again. He took small stilted breaths as he lumbered up the stairs and over the threshold, tossing the boy headlong onto the floor. Thuud! The boy landed on the wooden planks in a crumpled heap, a cloud of dust rising into the air. Bennett led the other two in at gunpoint, separating them from the wounded one. Colonel Pitts limped in behind and locked the door. He looked at the big Afghan, then at the injured boy on the floor. He covered his mouth and nose with his hand. "Good God, they smell unhuman!"

"No shit. You oughta ride in the chopper with 'em." Major Roberts pointed to the boy now clutching himself on the ground. "He's hurt pretty bad. Won't speak. Hasn't said anything since we pulled them out of that gun blind. The little bastard just glares at me." A perplexed expression came over Major Roberts as he walked to the injured boy, standing over him. "What's this?" He said, pausing to examine something. He bent down and pulled a blue hat from the boy's waistband. He unrumpled it and turned it around, examining it. "You gotta be fucking kidding me!" He held the hat in the air. It's my fuckin' Yankees hat." He clenched his teeth, glaring at the father. "That bastard must be affiliated with that same group we killed last spring."

Colonel Pitts's eyes narrowed as he scrutinized the trio. "I doubt it. They probably came through later and found it in the rubble. No one could have survived that thermobaric blast, not stuck in that little canyon."

Major Roberts shoved the hat in the pocket of his fatigues.

Colonel Pitts regarded the injured boy. The gangly teen's clavicle jutted up out of the skin, striated red muscle fibers contracting with each raspy breath. "I think he has a punctured lung." He nudged the boy with his wingtip. "What's your name?" he asked, circling him like a shark. The boy remained silent, his eyes locked in a defiant stare. "Major Roberts, give me your rifle." He took the M4 carbine, gripping the rifle with both hands wrapped around the end of the barrel. He extended up high before driving the rifle butt deep into the boy's shoulder. Crack! Colonel Pitts grinned as the boy howled in pain.

"Shit, you're going to kill him," Major Roberts said.

The father dropped to his knees and wept, bowing in a praying motion.

Colonel Pitts sighed. "You people almost have me feeling sorry for you. Almost." He walked to the Pashtun man, alternating glances between him and his crying son. "I see your son means a great deal to you."

"Yes!" The man bawled, tears streaming down his face onto the floor. The man looked capable of great fierceness but was now putty in his hand.

"What are your names, and where are you from?" Colonel Pitts stamped his foot on the floor. "Answer me!"

The Pashtun looked up, making eye contact before directing his tear-stained face back to the floor. "I am Hamasa of Nimroz, father of Aamir and Adam." Hamasa rubbed his hand over his own throat then pointed to his son on the floor. "No he speak."

Colonel Pitts scoffed. "That's some royal title. You must fancy yourself an important man. What are you? King of the sand fleas?" He passed the rifle to Major Roberts then went to one knee, eyes burning into the trembling Afghan. "Look at me Hamasa of Nimroz! Get it straight. You are nothing. Your sons are nothing. The only reason the three of you are still breathing is those thieves in the pass. You're going to lead me to them, and I am going to exterminate them." He spat in the Pashtun's face then stood back up. "Adam and Aamir. Nice-looking boys. A credit to their mother, no doubt." Colonel Pitts turned his back to the prisoners and took a step toward the door, rubbing his chin as he stared out of the dirty window pane. He wheeled around and drew his .45 pistol. "Hamasa of Nimroz, father of Aamir and Adam, time is of the essence!" He shook the gun. "Tell me now. Who you are working with? Who are these men that have attacked me without provocation? How are they overcoming our jammers? Where are they hiding?"

The conflicted Pashtun's eyes darted back and forth.

Bang! An ear-shattering explosion rang out as Colonel Pitts shot Adam between the eyes, splattering the boy's gray matter over the floor and the faces of his father and brother. "Who are you working with?" Colonel Pitts thundered.

"Uuuuuuuuuueeeeooooooowwww!" The slumping father and the living twin shrieked ghastly wails at the site of Adam's slight corpse settling onto the floor. The boy looked even more tiny as he took a final agonal breath and was quiet.

"This one is for Aamir!" Colonel Pitts stepped toward the other boy, placing the pistol to his head.

"I help Americans, a new weapon system, they are testing—the pass," the father stammered, pointing to the east.

"Were they here last spring?"

"No, that was different team. They all killed."

"That is because I killed them," said Colonel Pitts. "How many of them are there now?"

"Twelve Americans and forty Pashtuns."

"Why are they here, Hamasa? I want the truth!"

"Yes, truth. They testing GPS mortars." Hamasa made flying motions with his hands. "Fly up and enemy look at and kill."

"That's a lie! The GPS jammers had no effect on them."

Hamasa kept his face down. "The group killed in spring use GPS but now they use different." Hamasa shook, searching for the words. "I don't know what it called," he cried.

Major Roberts stroked the thick scar on his chin as he stared at Hamasa. "That would explain a lot."

"Hamasa, these Americans have taken something valuable to me, and you are going to help me get it back. If you don't—" Colonel Pitts pointed the pistol at Aamir. "Tell me how to beat them. If you do, I will let you and Aamir live."

"Okay, yes, anything," Hamasa said, a flicker of hope in his voice. "They can use weapons only in range of transmitters." Hamasa pointed. "Path far up, by Pakistan runs into the pass." He made a "T" shape with his hands. "Out range of American transmitters."

"You're saying that I could ambush them if I could get them to head toward Pakistan then get in front of them?"

Hamasa hung his head. "Yes," he said.

"You are doing well, Hamasa." Colonel Pitts waved the firearm nonchalantly toward Adam's corpse, his brain matter hanging between the planks of the wood floor like strawberry jam. "Had you said that first, Adam over here would still have a head." Colonel Pitts walked to what was left of Adam then glanced at the pistol in his hand. "Amazing what a .45 does at close range. Hamasa, what other types of weapons do they possess besides guided mortars?"

Hamasa counted on his fingers. "RPG, grenade, and machine gun."

"Is that all? Are you certain?"

"I swear on the name of Muhammad!" Hamasa lost control, weeping and struggling to breathe as his abdomen became rigid, the muscles visibly seizing with involuntary contractions.

Colonel Pitts handed Major Roberts the pistol. He walked over, placing his hand on the grieving man's shoulder. "Calm down, Hamasa. Calm down. I am not a monster. I will do Aamir and you no harm if you help me take back what is mine."

Hamasa's tears puddled onto the dirty wood floor. "Yes, I what you say do."

"Who is the commander? What is his name?"

"Mr. Fleen."

"Major, how many men do we have left?"

Major Roberts rolled his eyes. "Oh, my God. Bennett, you and myself. That's it. Three of us."

"You forgot about Hamasa here. Hamasa? Will you kill these Americans? Will you be my man?"

"I kill them all."

"Major, if we don't kill these son of a bitches, we're finished! Our fingerprints are everywhere. This Fleen character will be moving south toward the border to get away from the airstrike he anticipates. It's what I would do if I were in his shoes. If we can get in front of them and set up an ambush, we can turn this around. I'll report that we suffered losses when we stumbled across their smuggling operation and chased them into the hills." His eyes widened as if he had finally found a way out. "You and Bennett get these sacks of shit up, collect the weapons, and meet me on the chopper!"

CHAPTER 25

Colonel Pitts leaned toward the pilot, screaming over the noise. "Take us to the northern rendezvous point in Pakistan." The experienced pilot stayed low, hugging the mountains south into Pakistan. He then circled back, dropping into a small, well-protected shelf insinuated into the mountain. Bam! The aircraft hit the landing pad and the pilot killed the engine. "Out of the chopper. Let's go!" Colonel Pitts yelled over the unwinding of the turbine.

Major Roberts kicked Hamasa in the back, knocking him out of the aircraft. He jumped out behind him, holding Aamir in a headlock, his pistol buried into the boy's scalp.

"We may be headed back this way in a helluva hurry." Colonel Pitts jabbed his .45 at the pilot. "Keep your ears sharp and your head on a swivel. You fire this bird up the instant you see us."

"Yes, sir," the pilot said, his hands up.

Colonel Pitts crawled out and followed the swiftly moving pack, his right hip throbbing. He tried to keep up, but his burning lungs forced him to walk. He cleared a rocky ledge into an open space, spotting the others. Bennett was kneeling over the .308-caliber M60 machine gun, mounting it to the tripod. Colonel Pitts limped over to him. A long straight channel that descended away from him came into view. Hamasa was fifty yards down, leading Major Roberts, who was still holding the child. Colonel Pitts got on his hands and knees to better examine the lie of the erosion channel, carved into the granite by millennia of sand-laced windstorms and infrequent deluges. It was fifteen meters wide and over a hundred meters long, situated perpendicular to the larger main pass, which led into Pakistan. He peered up at the mountains behind him. Through the centuries the mountain had shed an enormous mound of thick, flat slabs piled up haphazardly on the flat ground. He leaned down and peered into the giant pile. There were multiple spots large enough for a man, ample space to set up a firing position. Across from the pile to his left was a huge boulder. He would place Hamasa and the boy behind it so he could shoot them if they tried to run. He crawled into the juxtaposed slabs, estimating the angle he would need to shoot the enemy as they walked into his line of sight. Major Roberts and Hamasa were walking back. As Major Roberts came within earshot, Colonel Pitts waved him over. "In here we can set up lying on our bellies. Drag our carbines and one of those airburst rifles under there while I go check out the other end." He crawled out, wiping the sweat from his brow. He meandered to the end of the channel where the main pass intersected. He stepped carefully over a pile of large rocks and small boulders, looking down to his left into the winding pass where the thieves would emerge. He cocked his head and listened: no men, just the moans of the wind.

The pass they would be coming up was narrow and steep. Unfortunately, it had an overhanging ledge they could hide under. He scratched his chin, imagining what he would be thinking if he were this Fleen character. He walked into the kill zone, looking over his right shoulder back at Major Roberts, who was sliding the weapons in. It was a good angle, though the kill box was smaller than he had hoped for and the rocks he had chosen to fight under were too far away. He needed more firepower and he needed it much closer. There had to be a spot for Bennett and the belt-fed M60 machine gun. He walked up the main pass, through the kill box, all the way past his channel's opening. He then turned around, examining the area from this perspective. He had not seen it before but from this position, he could see a small alcove just large enough for Bennett and the M60. He closed his eyes, visualizing the ambush. Bennett must wait as long as possible, letting the men walk past. When the box was full, Bennett would shoot them in the backs. He and Major Roberts would then engage from the side with their rifles. They should be able to cut them to pieces in the first salvo of the L-shaped ambush. If anyone was left, he would use the airburst rifles to get around the shelter of the overhanging ledge. He studied the ledge the bandits would cower under. Would the airburst rounds truly get to them? It hung out twelve to fifteen feet over where the rounds would detonate. We've got to kill them all in the first salvo. Colonel Pitts waved Bennett over.

As Bennett dragged the M60 into the alcove, Colonel Pitts hobbled back toward Major Roberts. To counterattack, the interlopers would have to walk through direct fire from Bennett's machine gun as well as his and Major Roberts' position. There will be no counterattack if I strike first. This was it, all or nothing.

***

The images of the cameras flickered and went out. A woozy feeling washed over Flynn as the GPS feed was jammed. He turned to Izzy. "Get the eLORAN network online and do it quickly."

Izzy shook his head from side to side. "I would've already had it up if I could, but we're just past the edge of the eLORAN grid."

Flynn flipped his M4 to FIRE, motioning his men to spread out. He walked just behind Sher Dil, trailing Izzy, who was on point. As they walked, the beast would sniff the air, moving in short cautious bursts if the route was safe, digging in his heels and blocking Flynn if more investigation was in order. As they moved, a comforting rhythm developed as Sher Dil led him up the pass. We're getting close to the top. He waved Barnes over, shouting over the wind. "Barnes, take the radio and one of the Stingers and crawl up on top of that rock formation. Keep your eyes glued to that radar array and watch our asses!" He slapped Barnes on the shoulder as the man turned and scampered away. Flynn continued up the slippery gravel slope behind Izzy and Sher Dil to an unusual formation with a huge rock shelf covering most of the pass. The formation split the wind like a reed whistle, filling the channel with ethereal moans and groans. As he tiptoed past the ledge, the opening of a small path veered off perpendicularly to the right. Flynn ran into Sher Dil, who had stopped. He dug his front claws deeply into the ground, pushing back against Flynn. Sher Dil's hackles rose from neck to tail. Though he couldn't hear them, Flynn felt the growls resonating through Sher Dil's body.

Flynn ripped his helmet off, cursing it. He reached for Izzy, but Sher Dil wouldn't budge. "Izzy!"

Izzy turned around. "What?"

Flynn pointed at Sher Dil then put his palm out. "Stop!"

Izzy shrugged then pointed ahead, turning and walking a few more steps.

Sher Dil was now low to the ground, staring into the path and snarling. Flynn's senses honed as his heart and breathing increased, adrenaline pouring into his veins. He flinched as Sher Dil leapt like a jaguar, bounding over the pile of rocks and disappearing into the gap.

CHAPTER 26

Colonel Pitts's breath came in stilted gasps, his diaphragm quivering with anticipation. The last of the evening sun shone on Hamasa and the stick-figure boy, hiding behind the adjacent rock. "Goddammit! Hurry, you fools!" he muttered, gazing through a shoebox-sized opening in the rocks at Major Roberts and Bennett. Their heads bobbed as they took their time setting up the machine gun. Major Roberts stopped moving then bolted upright as if he had heard something. He stepped over the pile of rocks and craned his neck, peering down the pass. Get back over here, Major! Instead, Major Roberts crept further into the pass, standing on his tiptoes, looking down into it. "You damn fool, get back over here!" Pitts shouted.

Major Roberts scrambled back over the mound of rocks and ran toward him, diving into the slabs. "Give me my rifle!" He took the carbine, aiming the barrel as he spoke out of the side of his mouth. "There is a column of men coming, and they have a fucking dog. Fuck, fuck,

fuck!" he said, eyes darting around. "Hamasa over there was telling the truth."

"He didn't say anything about a goddamned dog. How many of them are there?"

Major Roberts's eyes were huge. "Thirty or forty, maybe more. I sure hope Bennett gets this right. Maybe I should be down there."

Colonel Pitts heard a sound like tires spinning in the dirt. He jerked his head to the left to see Hamasa and Aamir disappearing back toward the helicopter.

"They're getting away!" Major Roberts yelled.

"To hell with them. They've served their purpose." Colonel Pitts placed his eye back to the rifle scope. Bennett fell into a crouch, disappearing into the alcove as if he were hiding from someone. Colonel Pitts's skin burned from adrenaline as a single crouching silhouette moved into sight. A large dog came next, followed by a second man. "Come on, come on," he whispered. The dog and the second figure stopped, only the point man still moving forward. The animal craned its neck, sniffing the ground and then the air. The animal's hackles rose as it peered directly at Bennett's position.

Major Roberts elbowed him in the side. "Should we fire?" Just as he said it, the huge dog lunged forward and jumped the rocks, disappearing into Bennett's position.

Flashes of light illuminated the area as Bennett's M60 erupted in a deafening fury. Tracer rounds enveloped the two lead men, slamming into the rocks around them, ricochets bouncing everywhere. Several drumlike thumps echoed out as the point man was shot in the chest. The man stiffened then fell like a tree. The second figure moved on his hands and knees, grabbing the back of the point man's vest. Colonel Pitts moved his eye back to the end of his M4. He placed the boxlike sight around the second figure, steadying his aim. Sudden movement next to his target distracted him. It was the point man, who had suddenly sat up, firing a handgun into Bennett's position before falling back limp. Bennett's M60 fell silent; only the dog going berserk could still be heard.

"The M60's out!" Major Roberts yelped.

Colonel Pitts refocused. The second man had somehow pulled the point man to cover and already picked up Bennett's M60! He stood in the open like Rambo, the heavy M60 at his hip. Before Colonel Pitts could fire, the M60's rounds tore into the slabs. A chaos of impacting bullets and stinging bits of rock made it impossible to return fire. He inhaled a lungful of heavy stone dust, coughing violently as he covered up.

Major Roberts peeked through a crack in the rocks. "He knows where we're at. He's coming!" Several long seconds later, the roar of Bennett's M60 and the ricochets stopped. "Fucker's out of ammo!" Major Roberts bellowed.

Colonel Pitts raised his head, peering through the tendrils of dust as they blew away. The berserker had tossed aside the M60 and was now thirty yards away, striding toward them, discharging a handgun as he advanced. Colonel Pitts squinted down the barrel of his M4 as the bullets struck all around him. He lined up the iron sight with the man's chest and pulled the trigger. The man spun around but continued advancing. The bolt of the advancing man's pistol locked back. "Out of shells! He's out of shells!" The berserker threw down the pistol and drew a large combat knife from his belt and sprinted toward them.

"RPG!" Major Roberts screamed.

Colonel Pitts looked away from the unusual display of courage. "RPG?" His focus went to a man with a long red beard, whipping in the wind. He sat crouched with a rocket where the point man had fallen. Seemingly in slow motion, a rocket emerged from the shoulder-fired tube, the contrail approaching. Colonel Pitts could only close his eyes. Thooom! A resonant concussion blew out his eardrums as the slabs of rocks fell in, stone dust filling the air. He held his breath as the winds mercifully pulled the unbreathable air away. Somehow he had not been crushed. When he looked back up, Redbeard was gone. A huge man had appeared now, dragging the knife-wielding berserker back behind the ledge. "Give me that airburst rifle!" Colonel Pitts fumbled with the bulky weapon and placed the red laser dot on the edge of the protective ledge, "127 yds," the display read. He picked a spot next to the overhang and pulled the trigger, the round exploding next to the edge of the shelf. Boom! A violent resonance shook the pile of slabs, darkness enveloping him. Boom! The ground shook again and again. He rolled into the fetal position, clutching himself as the barrage of shockwaves tore through him. He was helpless, as if pinned under water and unable to breathe. A powerful hand clamped around his shoulder, pulling him free of the slabs and onto his feet. It was Major Roberts. Colonel Pitts threw his arm around the man's sturdy neck as he assisted him back toward the helicopter. He struggled to focus on his partner's face. "What happened?"

"Grenades," Major Roberts said, not looking up as he chose his steps. As they rounded the bend, the turbine whined, the crescendo of the blades soon developing into a roar. In seconds, Major Roberts was pulling him into the helicopter.

"Where's Bennett?" the pilot shouted.

Colonel Pitts motioned for the pilot to take off. "Dead, just like us if we don't get the hell out of here!" The pilot's knuckles whitened. He turned and slammed the throttle to full power, the helicopter wobbling as it rose into the air.

Colonel Pitts felt more alert as they pulled away from the shelf in the mountain. "Fly low so they can't get a missile off on us."

"What now?" Major Roberts said. "The heroin is still in the pass!"

"Fuck! I can't believe I'm about to do this. Give me the phone!"

The line rang twice. "Camp Leatherneck, Corporal O'Malley speaking."

Colonel Pitts took a deep breath. "This is Colonel James Pitts. I have an emergency here at Camp Rock. Put General Smith on the line now!"

CHAPTER 27

"Yes, that Colonel James Pitts!" General Smith said. "I never thought I'd hear that son of a bitch ask ME for help, but he did just now, and I'm afraid your contractors are right in the middle of it."

"I just talked to them," Colonel Kelley said. "What did that slimy son of a bitch have to say?"

"He claimed he was attacked by a large ring of smugglers he observed acting suspiciously outside of Camp Rock. He attempted to detain them but ended up chasing them into the Chagai Hills. He claims they ambushed his forces, luring his commander into a trap that killed almost all of his men. He is demanding an airstrike on that little pass."

"Airstrike!? When hell freezes over. That no good son of a bitch!"

"I told him I'd get back to him right away," General Smith said.

"That man is lying! General Smith, my PMCs work hidden from sight. They have not left that canyon since they arrived almost a month ago. There's no way they were out of their nest snooping around Camp Rock. And another thing, if Colonel Pitts thought the group was so suspicious, how come he doesn't report it to me? That's my fucking cordon and he damn well knows how I feel about it. There's not going to be airstrikes on that pass as long as my PMCs are in it."

"You said you talked to them?"

"Yes, Commander Flynn called me less than two hours ago. This morning, they engaged a huge band of smugglers being led through by a Cobra attack helicopter, just like last spring. They intercepted tons of heroin and wiped out the whole operation. My guess is Colonel Pitts got his smuggling operation busted by my mercenaries, now he's trying to turn everything around."

"Interesting to hear you say that because Colonel Pitts says that he knows the name of the commander, called him by name—Flynn, but he said it with a funny accent. How he knows that disturbs me. That's his name, Fleen or Flynn, right? Your boy from Pennsylvania, the private military contractor with the high-tech gear? I met him a little less than a month ago, heading to those granite foothills, hush-hush, night flight."

"Commander Flynn. Yes, that's him," Colonel Kelley said.

"I liked him. I remember him well, hard young man, polite with sad eyes. Whatever really happened, we don't have much time. Those boys need to be taken into custody before they're all dead."

"The first team, now this. It's all starting to make sense."

General Smith went silent for a moment. "Colonel, this isn't the first time I've tussled with James Pitts. Last spring I got tangled up with him. Nosecones loaded with heroin, that's how he was doing it. The audacity of that man, flying those loaded planes in and out of Camp Leatherneck, right under my goddamn nose. Long story short, it was investigated by the local CIA asset, who died under suspicious circumstances at Camp Rock. Nothing ever happened to Colonel Pitts, but I know in my heart he orchestrated that whole grim affair."

"General Smith, when I spoke with Commander Flynn, I told him to sit tight but he insisted on hiking up the pass. He's convinced an airstrike is in the cards. Unfortunately, I can't come up with a bird to fly them off the mountaintop. The best I could do was send a transport truck with two of my best MPs. Now those poor saps will have to trudge all the way back down."

"Colonel Kelley, I don't think that's a good idea. Without backup, those MPs could wander into danger. It may be prudent for you to order them back to Camp Rose. Let my commandos do the dirty work."

"How long will it take your team to get there?"

"At least an hour, maybe two."

"That's an awful long time, General. My MPs are probably there by now. If it's all the same to you, I'd rather have them wait out in the desert, just in case."

"I can live with that. I'm having my own logistical challenges over here at Leatherneck. I'll get a chopper prepped and contact the CIA."

"Just get in there as fast as you can. I'll do what I can from this end."

CHAPTER 28

Colonel Pitts shook off the cobwebs as the Huey careened upward, his senses sharpening as it pulled into the sky. He was beaten. Of his core group, only the pilot, he, and Major Roberts remained alive. Were there any moves left? His explanation was shaky, and his men's bodies and the heroin would be discovered before he had time to remove them from the pass. He was quiet, like a man coming to terms with his fate, yet the stubbornness in him would not allow him to give up. "Major Roberts, if those are truly Colonel Kelley's affiliates that attacked us, they probably realize by now an airstrike isn't in the cards. All day, Colonel Kelley has been begging Camp Leatherneck for air support. If he has no bird, he would have to send a truck, right?"

He turned to the pilot. "Turn around and head back toward that pass!"

"Say what!?" Major Roberts pointed at the pilot. "Don't listen to him."

Colonel Pitts cast a stare of deadly intent, pointing his .45 at Major Roberts's face. "You shut your mouth!" He stole a glance at the pilot. "Back to that goddamn pass." He kept his eyes locked on Major Roberts as he lowered the pistol. "If Colonel Kelley did send a truck, it has to be close by now." Major Roberts's eyes creased. The man's lack of intellect frustrated him. "Think about it. He's out of options. The truck is the backup plan."

"Wait a minute. You just called Camp Leatherneck. General Smith is probably sending a unit of commandos as we speak." Major Roberts bit his lip. "You shouldn't have done that. Now we're fucking hosed!"

Colonel Pitts waved him away. "It's going to take time. He's not locked and loaded with the assets to just hop up and charge out here." His eyes tightened. "General Smith is two hours from that canyon. We have time to intercept that truck if we can find it. If we can switch places with Colonel Kelley's MPs, we may be able to capture those 'heroin smugglers' without a shot." He nudged the pilot in the back of the shoulder and pointed down at the desert. "Take her down low along the side of the mountain and head out over the desert." Colonel Pitts's stomach went into his chest as the pilot increased the power and pulled the stick to the left, pushing the Huey into a pitched sideways dive. The cab smelled of kerosene as the turbine thundered, gravity helping the helicopter accelerate along the rocky face of the mountain. The pilot leveled out, flying one hundred feet above the desert floor. Colonel Pitts pointed to the darkening desert, the sun beginning to set. "Take us out ten to eleven miles then turn back toward the pass in a lazy circle."

***

They were almost back to the pass, and they had seen nothing. The anxiety burned like a hot coal in his stomach. What if—the thought was interrupted by the sight of Major Roberts straightening as if he'd seen something.

"What is it?" Colonel Pitts asked.

"A dust trail!" Major Roberts pointed to the front glass. "Ya see it? About ten to eleven o'clock, two clicks out."

"I got it," the pilot said. They sped toward the rooster tail, skimming over occasional outcroppings of rock that rose up as if they would swat the presumptuous machine. Soon the familiar taillights of an M939 transport truck came into view.

"It's a transport. I knew it!" Colonel Pitts drove his fist into his hand. He turned to the pilot, rubbing his palms together. "Set us down in front of that truck. It's time for the ol' 'switcheroo.'" He turned to Major Roberts. "How's your acting?"

Major Roberts blinked rapidly. "Why are you fucking around like this? Why don't we just kill them? Especially after what they did to us today."

Colonel Pitts sighed. "That would be most desirable; however, they are still armed and won't be taken by force, and there are too many other loose ends. I want to take them to Camp Rock and throw them in the jail with the remaining heroin. We'll burn them alive along with all the heroin we caught them with. If they're not around to talk, there is probable doubt." He nudged Major Roberts. "It worked for us with the nosecones and it'll work for us again, but we have to get those men to Camp Rock."

Major Roberts frowned. "I can't wrap my head around this."

"It will work because they'll never expect it."

The helicopter slowed, passing over the truck. The pilot pulled hard, flaring the rotors. As the ground sped toward him, Colonel Pitts clenched his seat and closed his eyes, a hard jolt racking his spine. "Smile and wave," he said. "Move real slow. Let them know you're friendly." Colonel Pitts waved like a tourist at the wide-eyed men, now leaning over the truck's dash, the whites of their eyes visible. He crawled out of the helicopter, ignoring the pain in his hip as he initiated a disarming display of stretching and knuckle-cracking as Major Roberts climbed out behind him. Colonel Pitts walked slowly to the M939. As he approached, he could see the facial features of the men in the cab. There were only two of them, both young and sturdy, probably in their late twenties. He stopped twenty meters from the truck, hands raised. The dark-haired MP in the passenger seat had an M4 trained on his forehead.

The blond MP in the driver's seat frowned. "Colonel Pitts? Is that you?" The young man's face lit up as he pushed the other MP's rifle barrel down. "Colonel Pitts, you really gave us a fright, dropping in on us like that."

The dark-haired MP leaned in front of the driver to look out of the driver's-side window. "I'm sorry for pointing that rifle at you. What's going on? Did Colonel Kelley contact you?"

Colonel Pitts shrugged as he pointed to the Chagai Hills. "That's why we're here. I heard over the radio that something was amiss." He turned and acknowledged Major Roberts. "I brought my best man, Major Roberts here, to see if we could offer some assistance." He decided to take another gamble. "We made radio contact with the group in the pass. They are on their way back down." Colonel Pitts scrutinized the MPs' faces for deceit, moving closer to the truck to hide his hands. He ran his fingers over his Glock .45 pistol, feeling the rough texture of the handle as he measured their expressions.

A curious look came over the driver's face. "You talked to them? Did they tell you anything?"

Colonel Pitts smiled. "I—"

Somewhere in the truck, a satellite phone chortled loudly. Colonel Pitts watched the driver turn to pick it up. His heart accelerated as he gripped the pistol, moving slowly toward the door of the truck. Colonel Kelley's voice blared through. "You two stay out in the desert for now. I may have you turn around and head back to base. I just talked to Camp Leatherneck. It appears the base commander of Camp Rock is implicated in all of this. For now, you two park in the desert and wait for General Smith's commandos. Over."

Colonel Pitts was up on the side of the truck, holding the cold barrel to the young man's head as Major Roberts did the same to the other. "Easy," he warned in a low, relaxed tone. "Acknowledge and tell him you will wait for further instructions."

The MP's hand shook as he brought the phone to his face. He hesitated then spoke. "Acknowledged. We'll wait out here."

CHAPTER 29

"Uumph!" Sher Dil impacted the foe. Sounds of scraping nails and grunts of tremendous exertion came from the dark alcove as Sher Dil's roars blended with the shrieking of a human being. Bang! Bang! Bang! Deafening automatic weapon fire accompanied the luminescent flashes streaking from the darkness of the alcove. For an instant a shadow of Sher Dil shaking a man by the throat shone on the rocks. Ripping noises, like paper being torn, accompanied the stream of burning slugs, hurtling out of the void like dragon's breath. Flynn tracked the stream of tracers hitting the canyon wall above, his eyes widening as the bullets marched down toward him and Izzy. Time slowed as he flexed his knees and sprang into the air, his arms and legs stretched out as far as he could stretch them. Tracers passed above and below him like a shower of sparks. "Huummmph!" the air burst from his lungs as he slammed into the rock. Flynn put his hands on the granite, raising his head as two rounds tore through Izzy's chest, a sickening drumlike sound echoing through the passage. Flynn gasped, the blood draining from his face as Izzy's vest smoldered, unable to defeat the rounds at such close distance. Izzy reached out for Flynn, standing like a statue then falling like a tree. Izzy sat up and pulled his 1911 from its holster. He raised the pistol, clumsily firing the weapon, the last round leaving the barrel as he collapsed.

"Nooooo! Please, God! No!" Ignoring the tracers, he crawled over to Izzy, his fingers wrapping around the thick Kevlar collar of the vest. Flynn turned around and dug his boots in, pulling Izzy behind the cover of the ledge. Izzy made an agonal, guttural noise and was silent. Flynn clasped Izzy's hand between both of his. The thick blood pouring from Izzy's mouth had all but stopped, his beautiful green eyes already growing cloudy. "What have I done?" Flynn screamed impotently. His chest heaved as the realization of Izzy's death sank in. The faces of Laster, Bollick, and the others flashed through his mind as a volcano of hate exploded from some dark cauldron deep within his soul. "I'll kill you all!" He jumped to his feet, a sweet feeling of release unbinding him of mortal concern. His concentration was razor-sharp, fear was nonexistent and his body was rejuvenated with supernatural strength. He stepped into the channel and leveled his M4 at the muzzle flashes erupting from a pile of rocks at the back of the passage. "There they are!" hissed the demon that had awoken within him. He emptied the M4 in seconds and threw the rifle down, reaching for Izzy's carbine, discharging it as he walked toward the alcove Sher Dil had charged into. He fired the last round from Izzy's M4 as he cleared the boulder. Bright red blood dripped from Sher Dil's snout as he shook the dead man by the throat. The most beautiful thing that he had ever seen stood nearby, a mounted M60 with a full belt of bullets. He rushed to the sleek black weapon and disarticulated it from the tripod. The eighty-pound weapon was light as a child's toy. He held the rifle on his right side, bullets draped over his left arm as he stepped out into the hail of tracers, zeroing in on the origin. "Kill them!" the demon screamed. Flynn strode forward as he mashed the trigger, spewing a stream of molten tracers into openings in the slabs. He continued to advance as the M60 cycled through its belt and quit, out of ammo. Flynn threw the machine gun to the earth, drawing his 9 mm Beretta, emptying the clip as he ran. The demon smelled the cowards' fear, hiding like children in the granite slabs mere meters away. The slide of the Beretta kicked back as the last round left the barrel. Something like a hot baseball bat hit him in the right shoulder, spinning him around. He threw the Beretta at the pile, reaching for the handle of his Ka-Bar, the demon roaring with laughter. He could sense the kill as he drew the combat knife, crouching low as he sprinted toward the heap of slabs.

Thoom! A disorienting concussion knocked Flynn to the ground, stinging bits of rocks embedding into his face. Darkness and ringing in his ears enveloped him. He was back at his father's funeral, hundreds of uniformed men, standing solemnly with their hands over their hearts. He came to and tried to stand but something powerful jerked him back down. He fought the force, pulling against it, but it was like a hoist was attached to back of his vest, mercilessly dragging him away from his prey, robbing him of his kill. Flynn's senses returned, his own screaming shattering the air as he was pulled around the ledge to where he had initiated the charge. "Damn you," he screamed. He looked up, focusing on Brian Bollick's red face, huffing and puffing, trying to catch his breath. Spittle flew from Bollick's mouth as he roared like a lion. "Are you trying to get yourself killed?" Bollick slapped his face. "Don't you ever do that again!"

Bollick had robbed him of the chance to avenge Izzy. For a moment Flynn wanted to kill Bollick. The rage faded as his eyes fell on Izzy's corpse, lying against the ledge. Flynn rolled over and scrambled on his hands and knees to Izzy's side. He unstrapped Izzy's helmet and pulled it off, brushing the thick, black hair from his eyes. Blood had poured from Izzy's mouth, caking his face and matting his hair. He wouldn't like that. Flynn pulled a handkerchief and a bottle of water from his pack, cleansing Izzy's skin and hair of the plaster of thrombosed blood and sand. Salar and several Pashtuns stood solemnly, observing the washing. The rest were packed tightly against the east wall, strung fifty meters down the pass. Boom! Flynn fell on his back from the concussion of the airburst shell exploding above him. A few particles reached the hiding space through an elongate hole in the roof. The cowards had survived his onslaught. Flynn studied the skylight-sized opening in the ceiling. "Brian, get over here!" As Bollick slid over, Flynn pointed to the opening. "That hole in the rock up there. Could you throw a grenade through it?"

Bollick's brow furrowed as he examined the hole. He bit his lip and glanced around at the others. "I don't think I can do it. They must be four hundred feet up that channel!"

Flynn grabbed Bollick by the throat. "Bollick, we have to get back down into the eLORAN grid, but we can't let these guys get behind us on high ground on the way down. We have to counterattack now, or we'll never make it back into the gr—"

Boom, boom, boom. Flynn released him, covering up as airburst shells detonated all around the edges of the safe haven.

"If I miss, the grenade will bounce right back into us." Bollick pointed at Sobieski. "Or down the hill towards them." Sobieski's eyes widened. He turned and ran like a stork, leading a shuffle of men back down the pass.

"They just killed Izzy. Hit those motherfuckers!"

Bollick's lips pulled back into a snarl as he glared at the opening. He pulled a grenade from his belt, feeling the weight of the iron bomb hiding somewhere in his huge hand. He warmed up his arm, moving it in wide arcs and gentle throwing motions, gradually building in speed and amplitude. He stopped, took his place and peered for several moments at the crevice then closed his eyes, nailing down the enemy position in his mind's eye.

Flynn held his breath, hoping an airburst shell didn't explode over the opening.

The Afghans now lost their composure, following Sobieski's cranelike figure, lurching down the pass.

Ping. Bollick released the pin. With a quickness belying his size, he hopped forward, knuckles dragging the ground as he exploded into the throw, spinning around like a discus thrower. Flynn winced as the grenade skimmed the edge of the elongate opening. Ping. Bollick pulled the other pin and did the same with the second grenade. Ping, ping. Flynn popped the pins off two more grenades, handing them both to Bollick. The grenades became specks, climbing after each other and disappearing into the darkening sky.

Flynn peeked around the ledge. Boom, boom, boom, boom! The grenades impacted the pile of slabs like laser-guided missiles, the airburst assault ending. Only the moans and groans of the wind remained. He turned to movement in his peripheral vision. Sher Dil limped over the pile of rocks to him. He smiled, body tingling at the sight until he saw Salar swaddling Izzy's bloody corpse in blankets for the trek down.

Flynn felt the loss of blood from the gunshot wound in his shoulder, his vision tunneling. The bullet had passed cleanly through the muscle, but the swelling was worsening, his arm throbbing in pain with every beat of his heart.

"Alhamdulillah! Alhamdulillah!"

Flynn jerked his head around. Salar stood arms stretched to the sky, tears streaming into his black beard. He pointed to a large wasp flying over Izzy's corpse. "Alhamdulillah! Alhamdulillah! All praises are due to Allah. Lord of the Heaven and the Earth!"

***

The mania of combat mode gave way to its progeny, sheer mental and physical exhaustion. Flynn stumbled along with the others in a clumsy rush down the pass. Soon the screens on his HUD flickered to life, muted cheers arising from the men. Flynn ducked into a small alcove and pulled open the satellite phone. He punched in the code for Camp Rose.

"Get Colonel Kelley. Tell him it's Robert Flynn."

"This is Colonel Kelley. Tell me you boys are all okay!"

The question was like a dagger to Flynn's heart. "No, we're not okay. We were just ambushed at the southern rendezvous point. Izzy Khan is dead, and some of us are wounded." Flynn looked over his shoulder at the empty pass behind him. "We've made it back into the grid, and we're moving toward your MPs at the entrance."

Colonel Kelley's voice softened. "I'm sorry, Commander. I know I advised you not to go, but don't beat yourself up. I didn't know what the right move was myself. We never know about these things until it's over. That's the great irony of life, son. What do you know of the group that just ambushed your team?"

"I know they are Americans, at least the leaders. Whoever is in charge knows what I'm going to do before I do. I don't know how he keeps coming back. We wiped his forces out this morning. He even anticipated my move back up the pass and managed to get ahead of me."

"Commander, were any of your scouts taken hostage earlier today?"

"That's it! We did lose three Pashtuns, a father and his twin boys."

"Colonel Pitts must have questioned them and made the link with S&K. It must have been him that dropped the bomb that killed the first team. That's how he knew you'd head back up the pass."

"Who the hell is Colonel Pitts?"

"Colonel James Pitts commands a tiny forward operating base known as Camp Rock twenty miles east of your current location. Less than an hour ago, he called General Smith at Camp Leatherneck and reported that he followed a bunch of smugglers into a pass in the Chagai Hills. He said they annihilated his forces. He even named you as the leader to Central Command, but he called you Fleen."

The information must have come from Hamasa and the twins. Flynn was overcome with fatigue and grief, collapsing in a heap on the ground. He sat up and rested his forehead on his knees. He thought of Hamasa and the sons that the man loved so dearly. What had they done to deserve this? What torture had they endured? "He's a liar, sir. I haven't left these hills, and you know it!"

"Easy, son. I know, I know. You don't have to convince me or General Smith. We know the score. You just get back to the mouth of that pass so we can get you out of there."

CHAPTER 30

Flynn's vision tunneled as he stumbled, not able to keep up with the others. The tenderness in his right shoulder was growing worse. The swelling now extended well into his forearm, the pain pounding into his fingers with every pulse.

Bollick walked over, his eyebrows drawing together. "Flynn, put your arm over my neck."

Flynn draped his left arm over Bollick's neck, leaning against his rugged frame as they moved. Bollick carried most of his weight as he faded in and out of consciousness. He was imprisoned in a living nightmare, disturbing memories of Izzy playing over and over again. "I think we should stay here … we should stay here … ." Izzy's trusting smile flipped to his death mask. The more distant memories were more merciful. Izzy smiling, driving his car, yelling to him during combat in Helmand. His good-natured jealousy.

Bollick lowered Flynn to a seated position. "You rest. I'm going to look in on ORION." Bollick opened Izzy's bag and pulled out the laptop.

Sher Dil came and flopped down. The animal licked a long wound on his front left leg sustained in the struggle with the gunner. Flynn scratched him behind his mutilated ears. "You saved us, Sher Dil. Well done."

Bollick studied the screen. "The GPS is still being jammed, but the eLORAN grid never went down. Let's look around before we go any farther." Bollick reached over his shoulder and grabbed his UAV. The whir of the quadcopter returning to the sky was comforting. When Bollick was satisfied, he holstered the UAV, walked over, and extended his arm. Flynn gripped his hand and stood. They walked farther down the rocky pass, the desert floor growing as they descended. Soon they moved past the small grotto where Flynn had taken refuge during the attack on Colonel Pitts's forces. They slowed, stepping deliberately over the boulders that clogged the mouth of the pass. As Flynn reached the top of the pile, the full scope of the desert came into view. Tendrils of foul-smelling black smoke drifted from the alcove where one of the Fat Boys had detonated earlier in the day. Flynn's legs buckled at what he saw next. A hundred meters out sat a single M939 transport truck. Two MPs, a short one and a taller one, stood in front of the truck, arms crossed. "We're going home," he said. Sher Dil came and sat beside him, peering at the MPs and growling.

Flynn removed his arm from Bollick's neck. "I need to sit down and rest."

"Are you going to make it?"

"Yeah, I'll be fine." Flynn held his sore arm, watching the MPs as they pulled out bottles of water and other supplies. It was finally over. His eyelids fluttered with overwhelming exhaustion as the two MPs rushed over. The short one wore a ball cap, had wire-rimmed glasses, and walked with a limp. The other was taller and dark-haired. The man was burdened with a thick scar extending diagonally from his forehead to the floor of his mouth.

The short MP spoke with excitement as he adjusted his glasses. "Here, take these," he said, tossing about bottles of water. His eyes widened. "We heard about what happened. Colonel Kelley wants all of you brought to Camp Rose ASAP." He touched his chest. "My name is Chuck Cobb." Cobb acknowledged the taller MP with a nod. "This is my partner, Tom Zenke."

The scar-faced MP shook Bollick's hand then extended his hand to Flynn. "It's an honor," he said.

Clack! Sher Dil moved in front of Flynn, his jaws slamming shut inches from the MP's fingers.

"Whoa," the scar-faced man said, yanking back his hand as he glared at Sher Dil.

"Sher Dil! It's okay," Flynn said.

The scar-faced man's glare turned to a sheepish smile as he raised his hands. "My bad. I shouldn't have approached you guys like that."

The short MP stepped forward. "I apologize for asking you this, Commander, but Colonel Kelley ordered us to confiscate your weapons and cuff you for the trip over to Camp Leatherneck."

Barnes's voice rang out. "Ain't nobody cuffing me! Nobody!"

The scar-faced man nodded agreement, looking at the short MP as if vindicated. "That's what I think. How is it good to have a truck full of men with only the two of us armed? What if we get ambushed on the way back? Forget the stupid cuffs. Let them keep their weapons. We'll all be safer."

The small MP shrugged. "I know. It doesn't make sense to me either. I'm just following Colonel Kelley's orders. He said cuffed and disarmed." He took a step toward Flynn, but Sher Dil lunged again. The short MP's demeanor was less restrained than that of his partner, his fingers gripping his sidearm.

Bollick raised his rifle at the short MP's head. "Motherfucker, get your hand off that piece."

The short MP stepped back, startled by the speed of Bollick's reaction, his eyes widening as his fingers released the pistol grip. He pulled his hand up away from the gun, a muted smile appearing. "My sincere apologies. I was attacked by dogs when I was a boy. I'm jumpy around big ones like this fellow." He blinked repeatedly, eyeing Sher Dil.

Flynn reached down for Sher Dil, patting him on the head. "It's okay, boy." Sher Dil continued to growl, never taking his eyes from the short MP. "Salar, come here please," Flynn said. "Hold Sher Dil until we get on the truck. I don't want anyone to get hurt." Flynn's lower lip protruded, tears welling as he stared into Sher Dil's brown eyes. "You're on your own now, buddy. I'm sorry." Flynn pulled the Beretta from its holster then pushed it back in. I can't do it, not after everything that's happened. He looked at Salar. "My friend, watch over him. Promise me you'll feed and care for him."

Salar looked at the dog then sighed, his form slumping. "I promise." He hugged Flynn then stepped back. "I pray for your safe return. Salaam, my brother." He grasped Sher Dil by the loose collar, leading him over to the Pashtun tribesman standing guard over Izzy's body.

CHAPTER 31

Flynn floated feet above his body, disassociated from reality. The men around him seemed like actors he watched from afar. The hard wooden bench seat made his back ache, and diesel fumes wafting through the floor turned his stomach. The rough-riding truck accelerated then hit a pothole hard. Bollick flew up, striking his head against one of the metal hoops supporting the canvas top.

Bollick winced and rubbed his head. "These MPs drive like shit!" He stomped the floor of the truck, bellowing toward the front. "Slow this motherfucker down!"

A string of expletives erupted to Flynn's right. Barnes was hanging by one arm from one of the ceiling hoops, pointing to the front of the truck. "That's the setting sun coming through the cracks in the cab!" The tendons in Barnes's neck stood out, his pulse visible. "Camp Rose is to the north. The sun should be on our left."

The realization hit Flynn like a freight train, knocking him from the mental fog. His posture crumpled. Sher Dil tried to warn me, but I was too out of it to understand.

Laster stomped the floor of the transport. "We gave up our fucking weapons! Fuck! Fuck! Fuck! How could I have been so stupid?"

Barnes's eyes darted around. "We'll jump them and overpower them when they stop the truck."

"With what, Barnes? We have no weapons and our hands are tied," Rosenberg said.

"We do what it fuckin' takes!" Barnes said, his upper lip shaking. "I'm not dying like a chump. If I die, I die my way!" He raised his zip-tied wrists in front of him. "I'm going to guillotine Scarface with these." He made a motion of putting his bound wrists around a neck. "This zip tie can be turned into a garrote. I'll alligator roll once I get my wrists around that big bastard's neck. The rest of you hold him down while T-Rex chews his goddamn throat out before I get gutted by that Ka-Bar hanging off Scarface's waist." Barnes scanned around, eyes crazy. "Another team will do the same to the smaller one. We can do it if we work together."

Flynn motioned for him to take it down. "Barnes, if it comes to that, I say that is a good strategy and I'll fight right next to you but for now, it's too risky. He could have killed us already, but he didn't. We'll have to wait for the right opportunity."

Bollick's steely gaze locked onto him. "Flynn, Barnes is right. These are the men that killed our first team, and they're going to kill us too."

Flynn's body lurched as the driver took his foot off the gas. The texture of the road changed from soft dirt to gravel crunching under the tires. The brakes squealed then ground as the M939 slowed to a halt. Flynn strained his ears, faintly hearing a man's voice. "Welcome back, Colonel Pitts. What is left of Mullah Mehsud's men are guarding the shipment at the jail."

"Good. Any calls?" Colonel Pitts asked.

"Yes, Hoyt Green, the CIA chief in Bamyan. He left this number."

The lorry lurched as Colonel Pitts put the truck into gear and released the clutch. He pulled in a wide arc then rolled to a stop. The diesel engine bucked and rattled then fell still. Pffffffff. The air brake was set, and one of the cab doors swung open with a creak. Someone agile jumped from the truck. Footsteps crunched hurriedly toward the back.

Rip! Fresh air hit Flynn's sweaty face. The scar-faced policeman was now a snarling, impatient man at his breaking point. He lowered the barrel of his M4. Scarface wore a blue Yankees cap. "Out, you motherfuckers!"

Colonel Pitts limped up beside him. "Major Roberts, get these scumbags into the jail cell." Major Roberts jabbed the barrel at them. "Single file all the way to the building, assholes!" He kicked open a set of twin metal doors, pointing his carbine to a cell in the back. "Everyone that wants to live for another five minutes, get your ass into that cell." His fingernail blanched against the M4's trigger. "Or you can die right here. Your choice."

Flynn shuffled into the small cinder-block jail cell. Stacks of the same bundles the couriers had carried into the pass filled the back half of the cell. Three huge rows of them were neatly stacked, wall to wall and floor to ceiling. With all the bundles of heroin, the space was cramped as they squeezed in. The heavy metal door slammed shut like a gunshot.

The base commander's dark eyes burned into them. "So, you are the son of a bitches that have made my life hell?" He limped back and forth in front of the bars, stopping occasionally to stare with those murderous eyes. "Who's in command?"

Flynn raised up his bound hands. "I command this platoon, and I assume you're that traitor, Colonel James Pitts."

The weight of his dark stare settled on Flynn. "You're calling me a traitor? You're that thief I heard about. Flynn, perhaps?"

Flynn glared in silence.

A huge vein emerged across Colonel Pitts's forehead. "I don't have time to play games. Why are you here?"

Flynn stared back but said nothing.

Colonel Pitts pulled up his shirt, revealing the pistol's black holster. He put his palms together in front of his chest, interlocking his fingers and cracking his knuckles. In one smooth motion, he pulled the pistol from its holster and pointed it at Bollick's face. "Speak or the big man dies!"

"We're private military contractors here to test some hardware, but we never intended to get twisted up with you. We didn't even know you were out here."

Colonel Pitts moved the gun away from Bollick, frowning as he holstered it. "Who's your sponsoring commander? Is it General Smith at Camp Leatherneck?"

"No, Colonel James Kelley out of Camp Rose."

"Oh, that prick." He wandered a short distance away then turned around. "Why wasn't I notified of this? This could have all been avoided."

"First of all, we were in Colonel Kelley's cordon, whom we did notify. Secondly, after our first team was killed, we kept it secret from all but a few. None of us wanted to end up at the business end of another vacuum bomb."

"I see your point, but I command this border, not General Smith and not Colonel Kelley! How dare you operate in those hills without my consent?" He stammered as he searched for words, his face turning beet red. "Do you have any idea, any idea at all how hard it is to control this area? For two years I have succeeded at it while I have been denied the resources to accomplish it. And you come in without warning and steal my cheese." A satisfied smile came upon his face. "You see the measures I go to when someone steals from me. No matter where they go or what they do, I'll find them. I may seem like a monster to you but I'm not. I am a patriot. My methods may be hard for you to reconcile, but the men who occupy this godforsaken place are as cruel as the land." A peppered brow rose. "You may have learned that already. They respect nothing but the iron fist of brutality, and brutality is how I control them." He laid his hand on his chest. "I thought your team were nothing more than bandits after they killed my men and stole the shipment. What was I supposed to think? You call me a traitor. Tell me, why should I place my men in constant danger at the behest of the warmongers that manipulate us? Why should the common soldier not profit from his risk? And if he does, why is he a traitor?" Colonel Pitts shook his head. "It is a line of bullshit fed to all of us in uniform, from top to the bottom. I recognize those inequities for what they are: lies." He burst out in sarcastic laughter. "They have the gall to talk about honor. We die face down in the dirt while our families starve on our meager pensions. In the meantime, the people who run this shitshow sign hundred-year leases to strip-mine Afghanistan's mineral wealth. All the profits from this conflict go right into their philandering pockets!" Colonel Pitts held his arms wide. "Look at us. Every man in this room is a chump. We are cannon fodder, mere human fertilizer. We return from our service, wounded in body and soul, just to be denied benefits. Every one of you knows it's true."

Flynn stepped forward. "No doubt there is truth in what you say, but the way you have gone about rectifying the situation has become unhinged. Your indignation is contrived, and you have no empathy for those common men you presume to speak for. You just lost many of your own men and killed my best friend, and still you're only worried about what you've lost. You're a common criminal, and you know as well as I do that you're going to pay for it. Sooner or later, karma catches up to all of us."

Colonel Pitts stepped back, bemused as he regarded Flynn. "Karma? Did you just say karma?" The tempestuous man emitted a deep laugh. He turned to his scar-faced accomplice. "Major Roberts, two five-gallon cans of jet fuel on the double."

Scarface grinned then trudged out of the jail.

"Killing us will solve nothing," said Flynn. "I spoke with Colonel Kelley before we boarded that transport. He and General Smith both know you're behind all this. A whole company of Marines is headed from Camp Leatherneck to secure that pass. They're probably already there."

"Wishful thinking. I've got another half-hour at least."

Wuup, wuup, wuup.

Colonel Pitts turned his head, eyes growing wide as he cupped his hand to his ear. The blood disappeared from his face at the deep resonant thump of a large helicopter approaching. He raised the .45 and fired it into Flynn's chest. Bang! The gunshot in the small space was deafening. Sparks of burning gunpowder accompanied the pain in his chest as Flynn crumpled to the floor.

"Burn them!" Colonel Pitts screamed.

CHAPTER 32

Colonel Kelley peered over a file cabinet at the freckled redhead. "Corporal O'Malley, tell me you've reached Cobb and Jenke."

"I'm sorry, Colonel Kelley. I'll keep trying."

"What about Commander Flynn? Or Colonel Pitts, for God's sake?"

Corporal O'Malley fidgeted. "No answer from Commander Flynn. I've left a message at Camp Rock, but I've heard nothing from Colonel Pitts either."

Colonel Kelley's stomach sank. His PMCs must be in terrible trouble. What had happened to them? General Smith's team was, bare minimum, two hours away. It's up to me. I have to get them help. But how? The piece of paper from Senator Ryan! It has the cellphone number of Samuel Khan's brother.

Where was it? He racked his brain. The oak desk in my office. It's in the desk drawer, crammed to the back. Yellow with red ink! Colonel Kelley rushed in to the dank office, tripping the light switch as he hurried to the desk and plopped into the chair. He yanked the drawer open and dug through it. "Ha!" A curled scrap of yellow paper. He pulled it out. 0118675309. His finger trembled as he tried to dial the number.

"Salaam," said a sad baritone voice.

"Salar Khan?"

"Perhaps?"

"My name is Colonel Kelley. I'm the base commander at Camp Rose."

"You are the man who had them arrested and taken away. I know who you are, and I don't like you. Why do you bother me?"

"Mr. Khan, please, I need to know where they are."

"You took them, you fool."

"No, I didn't. My military policemen are not answering their phone, and I cannot reach Commander Flynn!"

The Afghan's tone softened. "They left traveling north thirty minutes ago."

Colonel Kelley's shoulders dropped. "Do you remember what the two MPs looked like?"

"An old one, short and ugly with a limp. The other was a beast of a man, a huge scar running across his face."

Colonel Kelley's heart pounded against his rib cage. "Salar, you just described the two men running a small base to the west of your position called Camp Rock."

The line went silent for a moment. "That is the man that captured my friend Hamasa and his sons. The son of a bitch killed one of his boys. Hamasa and the living son escaped and rejoined my force minutes ago. He knows where they are. Hamasa could lead us in if you could get us transportation. I have heavy weapons and forty men. My Pashtuns could capture that base in minutes!"

"Mr. Khan, I'll call you back."

"I'll be here Colonel. Salaam."

"Salaam," Colonel Kelley said. He thought of the lanky young CIA operative new to the area. What's his name? He picked up the receiver again and dialed the agent.

"Axl Herron speaking."

"Axl, this is Colonel Kelley from Camp Rose. We met last spring when you came through investigating the thermo-baric bomb."

"I remember. You sound upset. What's wrong, Colonel?"

"Axl, I have a dire situation here in Nimroz, and I must have your help."

"If I can help, I will."

"I'm sponsoring a twelve-man team of private military contractors here in Nimroz. I have reason to believe they have been kidnapped and are being held prisoner by Colonel James Pitts, the commander of Camp Rock. The team was accompanied by forty hardened Pashtun guides. The Pashtuns are still in the Chagai Pass, less than seventeen miles from Camp Rock. If you can provide a chopper, you could fly them to Camp Rock well before General Smith's commandos arrive from Camp Leatherneck."

"You want me to attack a U.S. outpost with native Afghans?"

"You're goddamned right I do! They'll be under your command. What's the problem? It's the only way to surprise Colonel Pitts and rescue my PMCs—if they're still alive."

"I can't do that without authorization."

"Well, call Hoyt Green and get authorization."

***

Colonel Kelley snatched the phone on the first ring. "Colonel Kelley!"

"Colonel Kelley, this is Hoyt Green. I just got off the phone with my new agent there in Nimroz. I hear your PMCs are in trouble."

"They're in a lot more than trouble."

"No contact whatsoever?"

"None, and to make matters worse, I sent my two best MPs in a transport to pick them up. They're not answering either."

"Those PMCs you speak of, are they Samuel Khan's team from S&K Industries?"

"Yes, sir. They're testing a new weapon system with the help of a band of Afghan guides. Salar Khan, the leader of the guides is Samuel Khan's brother. He never came stateside and still lives here in Afghanistan."

"Samuel Khan, the progenitor of ORION, yes, I've heard all about him. I understand time is of utmost importance but give me a rundown of what's going on."

"It depends on who you talk to. This morning, my PMCs watched a band of heroin-laden smugglers come through a pass they were dug into. There was an enormous battle, and the smugglers were routed. Things got hairy when the base commander at Camp Rock called General Smith at Camp Leatherneck. Colonel Pitts claimed he observed my PMCs acting suspiciously near Camp Rock. Thinking they were smugglers, he said he followed them to the pass where they wiped his forces out."

"I see," Hoyt said.

"I just spoke to Samuel's brother, Salar, less than ten minutes ago. He watched my PMCs being taken into custody. His description of the MPs matches Colonel Pitts and Major Roberts from Camp Rock."

"Agent Herron is headed to that pass in a Black Hawk helicopter. Tell your guides to be ready with their weapons and assembled at the mouth of the pass. In the meantime, I'll assemble a group of operators straightaway and get them on a jet to Camp Rock."

***

Hoyt Green hung up the phone and leaned back in the plush leather recliner. Colonel Pitts was a good soldier who worked closely with General Syed, a Pakistani air force general who was one of Hoyt's best double agents. General Syed reigned on the southern side of the border, Colonel Pitts on the northern side. The tandem had proved fruitful, dominating the Nimroz border for the last two years. Colonel Pitts was a valuable an asset, but eLORAN was far more important. He would sacrifice Colonel Pitts. Hoyt picked up the phone, speaking to his secretary. "Have Agents Gibbs and Schillings report to my office immediately."

In minutes a hard knock came on his door. "Come in," he said.

The hulking Randall Gibbs walked in, followed by a plain-looking Agent Schillings. Hoyt motioned for them to sit in the Queen Anne's chairs opposite his desk. Hoyt looked the giant over. It was amazing how ugly Randall Gibbs was. He looked like a giant Fred Flintstone, unkempt and standing almost seven feet tall.

"I'm sending you two on a mission to save a group of PMCs being held at Camp Rock."

Randall frowned, his eyes bitter. "That's Samuel Khan's team!"

"So?"

"Why would you help them?"

Hoyt's face reddened. "Randall, your failure to acquire the eLORAN data in the first place is part of the reason we're in this mess here in Bamyan. Now you have an opportunity to rectify your failure." Gibbs sat unconvinced, like a brooding child.

Hoyt thrust his finger at Randall Gibbs. "We must have that operating system, and we must have trained men to run it. Look, Randall, 'Switchblade' has been a great addition to our force and I commend you for it, but it has run its course. I know, for you personally, ORION is the enemy, but we must acquire that operating system. Your orders are simple. Swallow your pride, rescue Samuel Khan's team, then I'll convince them to help us."

Randall Gibbs nodded his understanding.

"You two will spearhead the operation. Colonel Pitts has kidnapped Colonel Kelley's team. We don't know if they are alive or dead, but it's likely Pitts is holding them at Camp Rock. You two get in there and kill anybody that gets in your way. Go in like you give a damn, like knights in shining armor. Make an impression. It will come in handy when I have to travel with my hat in hand to Pennsylvania to ask Samuel Khan for help." Hoyt eyeballed Randall. The man had a history of uncontrollable rages—intermittent explosive disorder, they called it. He had put up with the behavior for the genius of Randall Gibbs. Without him, the concerto of communication between the elements of his forces would not be possible.

Randall started to speak. "But—"

Hoyt cut him off. "Any chance for us here in Bamyan hinges on finding these men and securing their safety. You know that. The question is, are you capable of putting your country's interests above your own fucking ego? Randall, as unpalatable as you can be, you are the most capable man I have. Nevertheless, you must control that rage of yours. Some of those men may not respond well to your penchant for bullying." Hoyt's eyes narrowed into a squint. "Behave yourself, or I swear to God I'll kill you myself. You are not in charge. You are my representative, and don't you fucking forget it."

Randall's head dropped. "Yes, sir."

"Good." Hoyt glanced at his watch. "Secure Camp Rock and get those men on the plane and back to the States. DO NOT let me down."

214

CHAPTER 33

Wuuumph, wuuumph, wuuumph, wuumph. Hamasa came and stood next to Salar as the blinking lights of the Black Hawk drew closer. Hamasa's eyes burned with an intensity that made Salar uncomfortable. He squeezed Hamasa's shoulder. "My friend, please don't do anything foolish. Aamir needs you, and I need you."

Hamasa brushed his hand away and stepped into him. "Are we true friends or am I your servant?"

Salar's bushy eyebrows scrunched together. "What do you mean? Of course you are my friend. Why would you—?"

"When we capture Colonel Pitts, he is mine. If you ever had a morsel of respect for me, you will give him to me! You promise me now." Hamasa shook with rage. "PROMISE ME!"

Salar's instinct warned that Hamasa would kill even him if he got between the two. Salar swallowed hard as he nodded, glimpsing Hamasa's eyes. "I promise, my friend. Allah willing, the fiend will be in your grasp by morning."

An animalistic growl came from Hamasa's throat. "I show him Pashtun hospitality." Hamasa cast a fierce stare into the darkness. "The camp is small. It won't take long to find the beast."

The helicopter's blinking red lights grew more intense, the roar of the turbine changing to a whistle as the aircraft plunged toward them. With an impressive flare of the rotors, the Black Hawk scrubbed speed, sandblasting them as it settled into the earth with a wiggle of its tail. Salar squinted against the stinging rotor wash. A young dark-haired American approached. "Are you Salar Khan?" he shouted.

"Yes."

Axl pointed to the helicopter. "I have orders to gather you and your men and fly to Camp Rock."

Salar turned and pointed to Hamasa. "This is Hamasa. He knows the layout of Camp Rock. We will follow him in."

They slid weapons in until the bays were full of RPGs and a mixture of medium and heavy machine guns. Axl and the pilot secured the load and stepped into the helicopter. "Come on! Come on!" Axl encouraged, beckoning the Afghans into the belly of the Black Hawk. "You here, you there," he said, ushering the scraggly-bearded Pashtuns to their seats.

Salar followed Hamasa into the cab and sat down next to him. His eyes widened as Sher Dil jumped on, lying on the floor.

The pilot stomped his foot, wringing his hands like a drama queen. "We don't have time for this shit. Someone kick that fleabag in the ass and get it off of my bird!"

Salar looked at the pilot and made a biting motion with his hand, then extended his palms in mock helplessness. Axl nudged the dog with his foot. "Out! Out!"

Snap! Sher Dil bit at Axl's leg.

The whites of Axl's eyes showed as he jerked his foot back. He turned to the pilot. "Fuck it! Let's go!"

The pilot shook his head as he turned around and applied power, the turbines pulling the fully loaded UH-60 Black Hawk higher and higher, rising to an altitude of five hundred feet before dipping the nose toward Camp Rock.

"I hate helicopters," Salar muttered. He shut his eyes and gripped the edges of the small seat, sweat dripping down his cheek.

Wiiiiiiiii! A dreadful electronic warning filled the craft. Salar's stomach flipped again, eyes widening at the yellow light flashing on the display. "What is it?" he shouted.

The pilot waved him away. "You don't want to know. Just ignore it."

Axl's eyes widened. "That's the fuel gauge!"

The pilot shrugged. "I was told I had no time to get gas. I guess she didn't have as much as I thought."

Images of crashing into the earth filled Salar's imagination. The anxiety lessened at the sight of lights in the distance. The pilot dropped even lower, flying in a counterclockwise turn as they approached the base.

Axl yelled to the pilot. "Put us down close to the hangar—"

Pling! Ping! Slap! Bullets tore into the Black Hawk's side as the pilot approached the ground. Multiple muzzle flashes surrounded a small cinder-block building. A row of eight to ten Afghan-looking men knelt in tight clusters of three to four, directing small-arms fire into the Black Hawk. The rounds stopped hitting the Black Hawk as the chopper set down behind the cover of the large steel hangar between the airstrip and the stone building.

As the Black Hawk touched the ground, Hamasa leapt out of the helicopter, opening the weapons bay and struggling to extricate his PKM. The Pashtuns followed him like piranhas, grabbing weapons and yanking them free, stripping the bays empty in seconds. Salar tried in vain to keep up, grabbing an RPG and hurrying behind Hamasa and the band of fleet-footed Pashtuns, following them to a small earthen berm in front of the cinder-block building. Salar huffed over and flopped down next to the others, lined up on their stomachs in a shallow ditch behind the berm. Hundreds of bullets tore over his head, some popping up dust as they struck the top of the tiny berm.

Hamasa pointed toward the structure. "That's the jail. That's where we will find him! There's a front office and two cells in the back. It has a heavy metal door at the front and another in the back." He reached out and patted the RPG in Salar's hands. "You have to hit that metal door." Hamasa rolled over and pulled back the bolt of the PKM, inserting the belt of ammunition and closing the bolt. He rolled back and set the rifle barrel over the berm, raising his head to aim.

Salar gasped. "Hamasa, stay down!"

Pfft, pop! Rounds hit the dirt berm, tracers skimming centimeters from Hamasa's forehead. Hamasa was oblivious, holding the heavy gun steady then pulling the trigger. Salar looked on in disbelief as Hamasa stood upright, directing fire into the combatants. Salar grabbed Hamasa by the pants and yanked with all his might. His fingernails ripped off in the cloth as Hamasa tore from his grasp, walking toward the jail as the PKM annihilated anyone with the courage to stand against him.

The momentum was changing. In a fluid motion, Salar sprang up and centered the RPG's square peep sight on the metal door and squeezed the trigger. A plume of smoke followed the warhead as it streaked over Hamasa's shoulder and slammed into the heavy metal door, blowing it off its hinges in a ball of fire. Hamasa's audacious attack was too much. The Afghans guarding the jail dropped their weapons and fled into the night. Hamasa manhandled the bulky PKM, cutting every one of them down as they left. Salar's pulse hammered, his courage buoyed by Hamasa's wildness. Hamasa strode toward the jail, emptying the PKM through the opening as he advanced.

He reached the entry and ducked through the cloud of dust, disappearing into the structure. Salar followed, running bent over to the jail. He stepped inside, his sandals growing wet, overwhelming fumes of jet fuel burning his eyes and nose.

CHAPTER 34

A flash of fire accompanied the excruciating pain as the .45-caliber slug dissipated all its kinetic energy into Flynn's chest. He dropped dead-weight to the ground, ears ringing, unable to draw a breath for his paralyzed diaphragm. The pain built in an intensifying crescendo, radiating throughout his rib cage. Brian Bollick knelt beside him. The man's hand pushed under the vest, finding the soreness near his sternum.

Bollick looked down at him, a look of concern turning into a grin. "Fuck yeah! The vest stopped it!" He shook his head. "I thought you were dead for sure."

Flynn slid his hand under the vest, his fingers finding the source of the pain. A small lump to the left of his sternum. He sat up and looked around. Colonel Pitts and Major Roberts had moved away. Their voices drifted in from the front office.

"It's a goddamned Black Hawk! They're pouring out of it! What are we supposed to do?" Major Roberts cried out in desperation.

"Put fire onto them! We'll slow them down until we can break out the back and make a run for it." Sounds of the two men slapping the clips into their rifles gave way to chaos as they opened fire.

Flynn covered his ears, still confused. "What's going on?" he shouted.

Bollick pointed to the front then cupped his hand around Flynn's ear. "A helicopter just landed out front and, judging by their reaction, not one they expected. He and that scar-faced son of a bitch are firing on it."

A moment later return fire erupted. Ta-ta-ta-ta-ta-ta. It was the unmistakable sound of a PKM heavy machine gun. Its deeper, thunderous explosions dominated the chattering of the other automatic weapons. The rounds slapped into the cinder-block jail, blowing fist-sized holes through the cinder blocks, bits of stone and grit stinging Flynn's skin. He held his breath, waiting for the inevitable hit as bullet holes turned the walls to Swiss cheese, plumes of choking stone dust filling the space. Mercy came as fresh air poured through the voids, whisking dust out of the cell. The air was like water to a thirsty man. Flynn scooted on his butt to the cinder-block wall. He put his mouth to one of the holes and took a lungful of the clean air. He closed his eyes, a voice booming from the back of his conscious mind. They are here because of you. Do something! He gritted his teeth, positioning the plastic zip tie against the sharp edge of one of the jagged holes, sawing furiously. Pop! The plastic tie broke and he yanked his wrists apart. He scurried around on his hands and knees, breaking the plastic ties of the rest of them. Flynn crawled on his stomach, pushing the bundles of heroin in front of him. "Stay down and help me build a wall of these things!" He slid the bundles across the floor to the other men. They worked quickly, stacking them three deep, chest high in a protective horseshoe shape. In minutes they were done, huddling together like a nest of chicks in the makeshift shelter. The outer gunfire shifted, impacting different parts of the building and the bundle wall as the combatants outside engaged different parts of the structure. Flynn held his arms around his head as hundreds of bullets ricocheted around him. Puffs of white heroin dust accompanied the zings and pops of the bullets striking the stacks of drugs from every direction but the rear.

Suddenly, the deafening bangs of Colonel Pitts and Scarface's guns ceased. "We gotta get out!" Major Roberts bellowed. The man ran down the hall and threw open the heavy back door, a gust of wind stirring up more of the choking dust. Colonel Pitts limped behind him and disappeared into the darkness. Major Roberts stepped in, stopping in front of the cell with a five-gallon can of jet fuel. He stared down at them, his scar twisting in delight as he took off the cap.

Flynn swallowed hard. "Don't do this, Major!"

The man broke out in an evil laugh. It grew deeper and more sinister as he unscrewed the bung and dropped the can on its side, the liquid spreading into the cell with a glug, glug, glug sound. The growing ring soaked the bundles of heroin, the cold liquid running around Flynn's boots, the fumes overwhelming. Scarface then followed Colonel Pitts out the door. Flynn could hear Major Roberts's baritone voice clearly through the holes in the cinder-block wall. He squatted low and moved on to the wall, finding a bullet hole to peep through. The two figures stood mere feet from him.

"Lighter, lighter! I need one!" Major Roberts yelled. Colonel Pitts looked pained, patting his pants and pulling out a lighter, which he handed over. Colonel Pitts pointed to the south of the base. "That jeep over there, we've got to get to it. We can slip off the base! Come on, light that shit. We gotta go." The crippled man left Major Roberts with the task, turning and hobbling with impressive speed into the darkness. Flynn looked in horror at the red lighter in Major Roberts's hands. The man came back through the rear door and knelt down, out of view. Click, click, click. Click, click, click. "Give me a fuckin' break!" Click, click, click.

Flynn's mother's voice rang in his head. He thought of his dad and the little girl, burned to death ten feet from the exit. He closed his eyes and prayed.

Click, click, click. Click, click, click. "Fuck it! The gunfire will set it off," Major Roberts yelled as he stomped out.

Flynn pressed his eye back to the bullet hole. The man was sprinting off behind Colonel Pitts, disappearing into the blackness. He exhaled at the sight just as another burst of PKM fire slammed through the front of the jail and into the makeshift heroin wall. He covered up and scampered back to the nest as more lung-clogging white heroin powder burst into the air, overwhelming the ventilation offered from the bullet holes. They sat in a cluster, fighting for air, coughing uncontrollably. Flynn pulled out the handkerchief stained with Izzy's blood and covered his mouth and nose with it. The metallic smell was like a portal to a different dimension, bringing his friend back, like he was standing there before him. As if Izzy had anointed him, Flynn felt a sense of warmth and well-being, like everything was going to be okay. Like magic, his aching arm and throbbing fingers felt fine. Suddenly the firefight died. Flynn fought the somnolence of the narcotic as he wiggled on his belly through the cold, wet fuel to the cinder-block wall. He pressed his ear close and listened. In the distance a single jeep started up and headed south, initially at a relaxed pace before accelerating, the wail of the engine fading. "They're already outside the base," Flynn said. His concern dissolved as a violent blast hit the cell. The terrific concussion was worse than the .45, making his ears ring with pain. He covered his mouth as more choking dust blew into the tiny refuge. The blast was followed by another string of gunfire, then silence. He held his breath, waiting for the jet fuel to ignite. Whistling gusts of wind rushed through the newly ventilated structure, their eerie tone suggesting imminent demise.

"He, he, he...ha, ha, ha!" Bollick sat on the floor, holding his gut as a seizure of laughter gripped him. The giggling was infectious and felt good.

Pop. Crack. Noises, like men walking on glass, came from the front. They stopped laughing, frozen in a state of wide-eyed alarm. More footsteps crunched closer to the cell. A voice whispered something in Pashto behind the impromptu wall. Movement next to him drew Flynn's attention. It was Bollick, stooped over as he made his way to the front of the horseshoe. Bollick popped up over the bundles and then back down. He covered his mouth and giggled.

"Bollick!" Flynn motioned for him to stop. A cautious voice he recognized spoke softly from behind the wall.

"Commander Flynn?"

"Salar! We're in here!" Flynn yelled. A chorus of voices exalted and laughter turned to hysterical celebration as they clutched each other and hopped up and down like teeny boppers at a concert. Flynn recalled something Samuel Khan had said long ago. "When things go bad, there's no one you'd rather have by your side than a Pashtun." Flynn stood, grinning at Salar and Hamasa, standing outside the cell. "Samuel was right, and it's damn good to see you two!"

Salar shook his head as he looked at the fuel on the floor. "Truly Allah's loving hand is around you!" He walked up and pulled on the metal door. "Humph." He scratched his chin and said something to Hamasa. Hamasa walked into the front office, soon returning with a chrome ring, holding multiple large brass keys. Salar tried all of them but none fit the lock on the jail door.

Flynn tried to snap his fingers, settling on pointing instead. "Salar, um, you're going to have to go outside and get in that truck." He pointed to the adjacent wall. "Um, ram this western wall." He swayed, eyes widening as he wagged his finger at Salar. "Don't crush us!"

Salar's posture tensed as he walked outside. In seconds the M939 fired to life.

Flynn and the others moved back as it crept around the building. At first the impact was too light. Flynn listened to Salar back up the truck and hit the gas much harder this time. He turned and covered.

Boom! The wall crashed inward, cinder blocks flying, some tumbling over his boots.

Flynn lay back and enjoyed the fresh air. Moments later Salar stood above him, offering a hand. "Let me sleep," Flynn complained as Salar pulled him to his feet. He leaned against the thick Pashtun, coaxing his legs to work as Salar helped extricate him from the cramped, rubble-strewn space.

As Flynn stumbled into the open, a mass of fur hurtled toward him, impacting him and pinning him to the ground. Sher Dil pawed at his chest and licked the powder from his face, whining with excitement. "Sher Dil, you're the last thing I thought I'd see." For a moment the joy he felt made him forget about his troubles. He grabbed the dog's heavy neck and pulled himself up to the seated position, looking over Sher Dil's shoulder into the jail. Hamasa stood with Salar, who was running his hands over the bundles as if caressing a beautiful woman. Salar pumped his fists high in the air. "There're tons of it!" He put his fingers to his mouth and whistled. A line of Pashtuns stood up from behind the berm and entered the jail. Salar's head swiveled as he spoke quickly, pointing to the truck, then to the bundles. In seconds the wiry men arranged themselves in a fire line, handing each other the yellow bundles, some spilling powder as they bounced along the line of men up into the M939.

Flynn pulled on Sher Dil, using him to stand. The spectacle of the Pashtuns stealing the heroin pleased him.

Laster squatted in a bowlegged posture, eyes wide, body swaying as he pointed to the birdlike men. "They're stealing Colonel Pitts's heroin!" He slapped his knee, degenerating into an infectious snorting laugh.

"He's not going to be happy." Bollick said in a singsong tone that the others found hilarious. Soon even the sober Afghans were laughing along with them, enjoying the moment. All except Hamasa.

Hamasa stood stone-faced, his eyes fearsome as he directed the loading process. Flynn sobered at the thought of the Yankees cap. He cautiously approached the man and looked into Hamasa's emerald green eyes. "Adam?"

Hamasa cast a furious glare upon him, like he was mad enough to kill Flynn, his eyes then relenting and filling with tears, which spilled down his cheeks. Seeing the proud man cry was unbearable. The pain contracted his core. The ache in his abdomen told him the truth. The grinning boy—that playful, innocent child—was dead, and in a way, it was his fault. It was unbearable to look Hamasa in the eye. The truth was that Hamasa was a better man than he, a man who had paid the ultimate price for his loyalty. Hamasa was right to be suspicious of him and any influence he had on the twins. Flynn summoned his courage, looking into Hamasa's eyes once more. "I am sorry, Hamasa."

Hamasa stepped away, resuming the loading as if he wanted nothing to do with Flynn.   Even under the influence of the narcotic, Flynn was filled with shame, the guilt hitting him like a flood of water. Flynn meandered over to Salar, grasping the man's shoulder to steady himself. He pointed to the southern entrance. "Colonel Pitts and his accomplice escaped through the south gate less than five minutes ago."

Salar smiled. "That man has no friends in this area. I've already put out the word. He'll be in our grasp soon enough." Salar looked at Hamasa for a moment before turning back to Flynn. Salar's lips tightened. "Adam is dead. Colonel Pitts shot him in front of Hamasa and Aamir. I've promised Hamasa that if we find Colonel Pitts, he can have him." His brows rose. "I hope that is okay."

"I'll take it to my grave. Just find him."

CHAPTER 35

Flynn bumped around what was left of Camp Rock's jail then staggered outside again like a drunk who had just awakened. He stood among the Pashtuns, surveying the situation. A tall, slender man in U.S. uniform was getting out of a small jeep like Colonel Pitts's escape vehicle. Flynn limped over to Salar, pointing to the serviceman. "Who the hell is that just got out of that jeep?"

"That's Axl, the CIA man that brought us in his helicopter." Salar ran his fingers through his long beard, studying the man. "He must have tried to catch Colonel Pitts." Salar's eyes bolted open, his body stiffening as if threatened by some acrid epiphany. "I must leave before he discovers what is loaded in the truck!"

Honk, honk. Hamasa sat in the passenger seat, pressing the horn. He leaned out, waving frantically for Salar to hurry.

Salar hugged Flynn then stepped back, cracking his toothless grin. "I go now. I promise I see you later." He turned and moved like he did when he was in a rush, taking short steps to the transport, pulling himself into the cab. Salar stuck his head out of the driver's-side window. "Makha de gulunah, my friend!" He waved and hit the gas. The truck sat low on its springs, clawing for forward momentum as the engine toiled. The transport lurched and shook with each shift, gears grinding as the transmission struggled. The M939 bounced through the northern entrance and cleared the lights of the base, the taillights growing dim as it drove into the cool desert evening.

Flynn staggered to the group in front of the jail. The uniformed man approached him, an RPG launcher at his side. His eyes darted from Flynn to the distant tail lights. Axl flicked the switch arming the RPG. "That could be Colonel Pitts driving away in that truck!"

"No, no, those are friendlies. They're trying to get out before the authorities arrive. Don't worry about them."

Axl stared at the vanishing taillights for an uncomfortably long time. He shrugged then lowered the RPG as he turned to Flynn. "Robert Flynn?"

Flynn rubbed his hand on his sleeve then shook hands. "You must be Axl!" Flynn whistled. "If you'd been a minute later, that maniac would have burned us to death in that jail cell."

Axl seemed not to hear. He leaned over, eyes narrowing. "No offense, but are you guys covered in heroin?" Axl wiped some of the light-colored powder off Flynn's shoulder, putting his finger to the tip of his tongue. Axl's eyes widened. "Damn, that's some amazing shit."

Flynn tried to explain, but his tongue was as heavy as his mind was sluggish. "Colonel Pitts was holding us prisoner in that jail." He swayed, pointing to the vicinity of the small jail. "It was filled with bundles of heroin. Bullets came in and hit the packages." Flynn fell on his butt. He held out his hand. "Help me up." Flynn grasped Axl's hand and pulled up.

Axl smirked. "I get the point," the agent pointed to the north of the base. "What do you know about that truck that just hightailed it off the base?"

"They're friendly, just trying to get away from this mess."

The agent rolled his eyes. "No chance anything extra was in the back? It looked overloaded."

Flynn straightened, offering a salute. "Absolutely not, sir."

Axl pressed his lips together and crossed his arms. "I guess I'll ignore that twenty-foot trail of powder leading from the jail to where it was parked."

Flynn rubbed the back of his neck. He was stoned but aware of the delicate situation. "I'm sure it's just a … just a coincidence."

Axl stared at him for an uncomfortable moment then shrugged. "No matter. I've got more pressing issues."

"Yes, you do!" Flynn said, crossing his arms and rocking in place. "Like catching Colonel Pitts." Flynn pointed to the southern gate. "During the firefight, I saw them slip out in a jeep. I bet they're going to double back and head to Pakistan."

"Not if I have anything to do with it!" Axl trotted over to the pilot, who was dumping the remaining jerry cans of fuel into the helicopter's fuel tank. He cupped his hands around his mouth. "We're going after the son of a bitch—"

A ground-shaking roar enveloped them as a Boeing 737 thundered over, gliding down onto the runway. Six commandos burst from the plane, followed by two men dressed in suits. One man was enormous, standing close to seven feet tall.

Flynn studied the giant. Something about the man was familiar. What was it? He turned to Axl's Black Hawk helicopter as it rose steadily then dipped forward, its blinking lights gradually disappearing into the abyss.

Flynn and Sher Dil now stood alone, the others already amassing at the plane the commandos had exited. He meandered along behind them. "How the hell did you get on the chopper?" he said, scratching Sher Dil on the head. He put the thought of any mercy killing out of his head forever. He would simply do whatever it took to get Sher Dil on that plane and get back to his mother. He continued, moving stiff-legged toward the jet, Sher Dil at his heel. As he got closer to the plane, he realized something was wrong. Even in his inebriated state, it was obvious the gigantic man was having a meltdown, shaking his fist and standing in a threatening posture to Sobieski, who looked like a stick figure next to him. As he drew close, the giant's attention turned to him. Flynn's jaw dropped. Jay Black stood mere feet in front of him. "Jay Black? What the hell are you doing here?"

The hulking man took a step toward him, speaking with a tone of frustration. "I was sent here to take you guys home. Instead, I've spent the last five minutes playing babysitter and taking shit from a ravenous heroin addict." He flipped a nod to Sobieski. "I'm going to knock that son of a bitch's teeth out."

"Huh? Why are you so angry?"

"I told this drugged-up prick fifty goddamn times—I. Don't. Sell. Tacos."

Flynn looked at Sobieski, completely out of it, chewing on the back of his glove.

Jay Black backhanded Flynn's shoulder, a white cloud floating away. "You too? That must have been some party."

Flynn slapped at Black's hand. "Keep your grimy hands off me!" Flynn cut his eyes at Black. "I always knew there was something putrid about you. You didn't cover your tracks well. We knew you were a spy, just not for whom, until now."

The ogre danced on his tiptoes, punching the air with his index fingers. "You're a spy, you're a spy," said Black who stepped into him, knocking him backward. "I was much more than a spy. I was the best goddamn operator in that bunch, and I had it taken away from me by you and that baboon!" Black pointed at Bollick, seated cross-legged, playing rock, paper and scissors with Barnes. Black looked as if he were going to cry. "Five million dollars I missed out on. Five million dollars! It ruined my life. You think I'm going to make it on the agency pension?" His upper lip vibrated. "My superior had me cleared all the way in to test ORION." He poked his finger at Flynn. "I know you called the police. You tried to get me on attempted murder."

Flynn stepped back, his brow creasing. "Black, I never called the cops. I was in jail when that happened. I never tried to sabotage you. Don't you remember?"

"Don't try to act like you were on my side," Black sneered. "You never liked me!"

"So? Nobody liked you, but you brought it on yourself, intimidating every other man in the platoon." Flynn nodded at Bollick. "You tried to bully him, and he broke your damn arm, but that had nothing to do with me not liking you." Flynn jabbed his finger at Black. "You fucking psychopath, you almost blew Bollick's balls off with that flash-bang in the commode. What was S&K supposed to do? Make you commander? Double your fucking pay?!"

Black's wide-set eyes burned with a devilish glint. "Flynn, do you realize if I had been with the first platoon as planned, that thermobaric strike would have never happened? Are you smart enough to connect the dots?" Black sneered "My superior would have been watching over us and would not have allowed it. Those men would have never died, and Izzy Khan would be still be alive." He shook his head, looking down at Flynn, his smile growing more satisfied. "I'm sorry, but you killed them." His voice softened, becoming apologetic. "You killed them, Flynn."

"Yeah, well, that's what I'm good at." Flynn put his middle finger in the man's face. "Fuck you, Jay Black."

The hulk lowered his chin. "My name is Randall Gibbs. Quit calling me Jay Black." The huge man stood with his fists clenched. "I was going to be nice about this, but you just had to push my fucking buttons, didn't you?" He pushed Flynn in the chest then made an encompassing gesture around the team. "I hate you motherfuckers." He smirked. "You guys are in a heap of shit, I tell ya. The bigwigs may not yet know what the truth is but at this point, you boys have been accused by a respected base commander of smuggling, murder of U.S. personnel, and treason. Now we can add drug charges."

Flynn opened his arms wide. "Come on, man. We couldn't do anything about it. We're lucky we didn't all die of a heroin overdose!"

Randall Gibbs made a sweeping arm motion. "I heard the story from the other 'cool guys' on your team— and I don't believe any of it."

Flynn stepped toward him. "You wouldn't because you're a complete asshole."

Gibbs spat at Flynn's feet. "You best learn to respect, boy!"

"Your mouth smells like the outhouse on a shrimp boat. You best learn hygiene, boy!" Flynn turned and gagged.

Randall's face reddened, his lower lip jutting out as he shoved Flynn toward the plane, the cold, hard barrel of a pistol poking into Flynn's ribs. "Up the stairs!"

Grrrrr. Sher Dil's hackles were up, gleaming rows of teeth visible.

"What the hell is that?"

"He doesn't concern you," Flynn said.

"Shut the fuck up and move," Randall replied, jabbing the barrel deeper as they walked up the rickety rollaway staircase and into the plane. Randall looked over his shoulder, keeping tabs on the dog. "What's with the dog? He can't get on the plane, you know. It's government policy."

Flynn stopped, the gun barrel almost cracking his ribs.

"Oh no, you don't! All the way to the back, loser."

As they passed Bollick, he stepped into the aisle, placing himself between Gibbs and Sher Dil, now up the staircase on the threshold of the plane. "That dog saved our lives today. We'd appreciate some forbearance here."

Randall gave a surprised look as if considering the request. "Oh, I see. You guys think you're gonna gang up on me? Try to get me to change my mind by intimidating me?"

Bollick's shoulders slumped. "What? No one is trying to intimidate you. Please, Randall, we know you're in charge here—"

"You mean to tell me what's up? How it's going to be, huh?" Gibbs scratched his temple with the barrel of the 9 mm. "Well, let me inform you guys of a few things. Number one, this plane belongs to the federal government. Number two, Mr. Green is allergic to dogs, not to mention the quarantine issue." He displayed a wide grin, at once smug and triumphant. "The dog stays." Randall Gibbs jabbed the pistol into Flynn's back, pushing him down the aisle. "Take that seat."

An indignant fury ignited within Flynn like a gasoline fire. He calculated the distance between himself and Gibbs's head. He was still incapacitated by the narcotics, clumsy and weak, but his arm no longer hurt. He had to make a move. It was Sher Dil's only chance. He took a deep breath and lunged forward.

Randall Gibbs spotted the clumsy attack, twisting at the waist to avoid the strike. Flynn tried to compensate, his fist missing its mark, glancing off the top of the giant's skull. Randall spun around unhurt, smashing the tip of the gun into Flynn's face. A searing pain flashed as the metal split his eyebrow, warm blood streaming down his face. Flynn staggered, using the back of the chair to stay standing. He fought to stay conscious, his vision unfocused.

Sher Dil uttered the same guttural growl as he had when he killed the gunner. The tiger dog leapt into the air, latching his massive jaws onto the back of Randall's lower neck. The giant fell to one knee as Sher Dil hung fast, shaking his hundred-and-sixty-pound body violently.

Randall shrieked. "Get him off! Get him off! UUUUHHHHHNNNN!" He bellowed like a bull elk caught in the jaws of a hungry grizzly. Suddenly, Randall Gibbs flipped. His intonations of surprise and horror transformed to sounds of determined rage as he reached for the 9mm he had dropped on the floor. He grasped it, bringing the barrel around, trying to stick it into Sher Dil's fur.

Flynn's heart dropped. He was powerless to do anything but watch the inevitable.

At the last possible moment, Sher Dil unclamped his teeth, retreating out of the fuselage and down the staircase, his claws clicking on the metal as he descended. Randall Gibbs followed and leaned out of the plane, aiming the pistol.

Bollick moved into the aisle, grasping a big black camera. "The hell you do!" The camera accelerated in a blur, disintegrating with a loud thwack against Randall's ironclad skull, hundreds of pieces flying all over the cabin.

The ambush ended the attack against Sher Dil, but the giant was unfazed. Flynn's adrenaline spiked as Randall pointed the gun at Bollick. His eyes were crazy as he pulled back the hammer and squeezed on the trigger.

"Randall Gibbs!" Flynn roared like a commanding officer. Your mission is to help get those men out of there!"

Randall blinked then took a step back, his arm wavering. He put the hammer back down and put away the pistol. "Everyone in their seats! It's over!" He wiped the back of his neck, his hand coated in blood. He shook his head then turned and approached the rear door, slamming it shut and locking it down. Randall spun back around, eyeing them but keeping a safe distance as he reached for a small blue phone on the wall. "Rear hatch is secure. We're ready for takeoff."

There had been hope before, but it was gone. Flynn collapsed into the seat, his heart screaming with despair. The 737's engines whistled as it lurched forward, rolling to the end of the asphalt runway. The pilot held the brakes for a few moments, the plane shuddering as the engines-built power. The pilot applied full throttle and released the brakes. Flynn scooted to the small glass window, looking desperately for Sher Dil. He spotted him near the edge of the runway, sitting with his muzzle straight in the air. Sher Dil was howling.

CHAPTER 36

Colonel Pitts's head swam as the sweat dripped from his chin. He was pressed close to Major Roberts, the two stuffing the back seat of the black Russian Lada. The jalopy creaked and hit the frame, its shocks and springs flaccid as it bounced east down the dirt road toward Islamabad, Pakistan. He craned his neck to see the topography out of the dirty glass pane, but it was futile. The night was dark as pitch. Even the side of the road was difficult to see. Colonel Pitts closed his eyes. He felt naked with only his .45 pistol on his lap. His pulse quickened as he studied the driver. The man sat rigid behind the wheel and made little eye contact. When he did, his pupils were wide and black.

Major Roberts leaned into him. "I don't like this," he whispered. "We don't even know these guys. How do we know they're working for General Syed?"

Colonel Pitts wasn't in the mood to entertain Major Roberts's paranoia. "We should be across the border soon." He shrugged. "It's out of our hands. Just relax."

"I can't. We're marked men. I bet there are bulletins all along the border to watch for us. God knows how much the reward is."

"No matter. We'll get across. We just need one more stroke of good luck."

Major Roberts sighed, dropping his head. "What good is money if I have to live like this? I wish I'd never heard of Camp Rock."

Colonel Pitts nudged him. "You're acting like it's over, like you're beat. I know we're in a vulnerable spot. I don't like it either, but we'll get through it. I've got cash we can exchange for gold, and right now nobody knows where we are. Once we get to the safe house in Islamabad, we'll relax for six months, blow a hundred grand on liquor and prostitutes." He smiled. "When the time is right, the opportunity will present itself. When it does, you and I will be on a boat to the Cayman Islands, where we'll cash out the hundred and thirty million. Think of it as a new beginning."

Major Roberts's eyes darted around the cab. "General Syed scares me. We're of no use to him anymore. What does he gain by helping us?"

"I guess that depends on what he might gain from betraying us." Colonel Pitts noticed his pulse was increasing, his hands wet, suddenly sharing Major Roberts's unease. Instinct told him to shoot the driver in the back of the head and take control of the vehicle. Without warning, Colonel Pitts slammed into the seat in front of him as the driver stomped the Lada's brakes. The car nosedived as it slid to a dramatic stop, clouds of dirt rising through the headlights. "What's going on?" Colonel Pitts yelled. He rose up, looking out of the window. Click!

The doors locked. He yanked on the small metal handle and tried to force the door open, but it was rock-solid. He gripped the .45 to blow out the window, dropping it at the sight of multiple heavily armed men converging on the tiny Lada from every direction. They were disheveled, wearing no uniforms. They cried out in an excited mixture of Farsi and Arabic. He felt panic grip his being like an animal about to be slaughtered. "These are no soldiers!" He shoved the back of the driver's seat. "Back up! Move out of here now!" He punched the driver in the head, but the man was frozen, fixated on something outside the car, hands raised in terror. Four men stood at the front of the car. They held AK-47s pointing through the windshield. The largest of the four trained his weapon on the driver as the others opened the driver's door and pulled out the frightened chauffeur. They gave him a push, motioning for him to walk away. The Lada's rear doors unlocked, and the bandits threw open the back doors. Colonel Pitts and Major Roberts were dragged out. The wave of men pressed them against the side of the Lada. The men had bandanas covering all but their eyes. They acted like poor men who had found a huge satchel of cash. One of them held out a picture, studying the photograph then staring at Colonel Pitts. After several minutes he took out a cellphone, snapped a picture, and sent it. Soon he was having an animated discussion and, judging by the bandit's deference, he was talking to somebody powerful. The bandit ended the call and walked back to his men, now surrounding the Lada in a horseshoe shape.

Colonel Pitts held out his arms. "Wait, I'm a rich man. Whatever you are getting paid for this, I will double it— triple it!" The man who had strong-armed the driver walked over, holding his rifle by the barrel with both hands. He raised it in the air.

Colonel Pitts closed his eyes as the rifle butt struck him on the top of his head. Sparks of light and a deep ache filled his skull as he slipped into darkness.

***

One of the bandits led Major Roberts by the forearm around the vehicle, motioning for him to kneel. He did as he was told, watching as two others struggled with Colonel Pitts's squatty body. They wrangled him up to the edge, rolled him into the trunk and slammed the lid. The ass of the anemic vehicle sat low, the portly man's weight overcoming the twenty-year-old suspension. The man who had made him kneel came around behind him. Instinct told Major Roberts he would die where he knelt. There would be no reunion with Barbie, no days on the beach. He squinted at the sound of the rifle bolt being pulled back and the shell slamming into the breech. He closed his eyes and took a deep breath and waited for the explosion. Crunch, crunch. Was he leaving? A ray of hope emerged as the crunching grew fainter as if the bandit was walking away. He opened his eyes as car doors were slamming all around. The cars made a U-turn and accelerated, tires spinning, throwing dust and stinging bits of gravel into his face. He was alive, but for how long? He shuddered, gripping his shoulders as he stood in the cold darkness, watching the vehicle's tail lights until they disappeared into the coal-black night.

CHAPTER 37

Colonel Pitts winced at the throbs of pain emanating from his head and neck. His head hurt from the rifle butt, which had split the scalp over his right ear, and his neck hurt from his head hanging slack in the seated position. He raised his head from his chest, grimacing as he coaxed the sore muscles to elevate his head. The only complement to the agony was the mocking silence of the darkness. "Where am I? Who's here?" Colonel Pitts moved his head, rough fabric brushing the skin of his forehead, nose, and chin. It seemed to be an old burlap sack, pulled tight, stinking of mildew, dirt, and mouse droppings. He moved his cut and swollen tongue, his dry mouth tasting of copper. He was bound in a massive thronelike wooden chair. He moved from side to side, trying to fight free but the chair was wide-based, solid, and heavy. He struggled to raise his arms but couldn't because of the cruelly tight ropes. They were thick and abrasive, lashing his forearms to the flat wooden armrests. The ropes around his chest were unmercifully taut, restricting his breathing. His pulse quickened at the memory of the abduction. "Major Roberts? Roberts?" I'm alone. His mind labored to catalog his surroundings. There was a damp mustiness to the small space. He was underground, maybe a root cellar. Colonel Pitts strained his ears, the sepulchral silence tormenting his soul. The only sound was of blood pulsing through his ears. Who would dare do this? Was it a single captor? Were they Afghan or U.S.? Perhaps CIA? He swallowed hard, pushing back the panic. He fought to breathe through his nostrils, the tape over his mouth suffocating him. He had endured hardships, but he had never been so alone, so helpless. Time slowed down, the seconds becoming like minutes, the minutes like hours. His only companions were unwelcome. The cold sweat tickling his skin as it dribbled down his scalp, chest and back. The pulse in his ear and the stench of his own fear, wafting up from his armpits. I deserved better. How could this have happened?

Colonel Pitts froze at a noise nearby. He held the meager breath and listened. Footsteps! The sound of a single human being approached. A solid thump, ten to twenty feet away, was followed by shuffling of feet and another thump. It sounded like a heavy wooden bar had been lifted. Colonel Pitts sat as upright as possible, the abrasive ropes biting deeper. The heavy door swung open, hinges groaning as the man grunted against its weight. The sound of the man's shuffling feet was followed by more creaking and groaning as the door closed and the wooden bar dropped back into its slot with a thunk. The door's fit was tight, creating pressure he could feel in his eardrums as it shut. He readied himself, inhaling deeply as he drew his courage. "Who's there?" he mumbled against the tape.

Silence.

Colonel Pitts's lips and chin trembled as minutes of the cruel silence passed. Chk-fuuuuuuuuuuu. The sound of a propane torch filled the small space, the hissing noise decreasing as the gas was dialed down. The hissing was like a demon foretelling the agony to come. A hand was thrust under the burlap, its fingers grasping for the gag. Rip! The tape was torn off his mouth. Dink. The metal cylinder was set down on something solid. A telltale sensation of light and the flame's heat emanated from his left. Colonel Pitts instinctively faced his tormentor. "I'm Colonel James Pitts of the United States Marine Corps. What the hell do you think you're doing? I demand to know who you are and what's going on!"

A baritone laugh, sinister and amused, rolled from the darkness.

Colonel Pitts's muscles tightened, his body rigid. God help me, I'm in the hands of an Afghan. The swashbuckling bravado had departed. He was a child again, wanting to hide, whimpering through rapid breaths. "Whoever you are, I can make you a rich man. I have millions of dollars that I will split with you if you'll let me go." The shuffling feet grew close, a powerful hand grabbing his skull from behind. The fingertips raked his eye sockets as they gripped the burlap sack, slowly pulling it off his head. The room was pitch-black except for the dim illumination from the torch, propane hissing as it sat on a long table. The flame left the corners in blackness, concealing his nemesis.

Colonel Pitts strained his eyes at a ghastly shadow moving to face him. The tormentor was clothed like the grim reaper. He wore a heavy, dark flowing cloak with a large hood, his face hidden by its shadow. Only the eyes could be seen, glowing yellow through the pall cast by the dust and dim torchlight. The hate-filled eyes were familiar. The reaperlike figure turned to the table and reached for the torch, the hissing unbearable as it was turned up. The cloaked arm slid under a blue sheet that covered the table. His hand emerged, pulling out a sturdy six-inch wooden rod. Heavy-gauge fishing hooks swung from small eyelet screws turned deep into the timber. He was suffocating again, sweat running down his body as the cloaked figure moved behind him. Colonel Pitts gritted his teeth, clawing at the armrests as the hooks pierced the skin of his forehead. Thick fingers pushed the hooks into the scalp, setting them, one by one. The powerful hand then gripped the stick, yanking Colonel Pitts' head back, his face staring at the dirt ceiling of the subterranean tomb. The pain was there, but the pulling sensation felt as though the hooks would tear completely through his scalp.

FUUUUUUUUU. The torch hissed louder.

Colonel Pitts felt the heat approaching and thrashed in vain against the hooks. The torch, inches from his ear, sounded like a jet engine as the white-hot pain seared his neck. "AAAARRHH!" Colonel Pitts bucked against the excruciating pain. He kicked and thrashed like an animal caught in a snare, the hooks and rough ropes tightening. "Please! Please! Don't hurt me anymore. I'll do anything." The man's hand released the stick, leaving it dangling from his scalp. Colonel Pitts hung his head, gasping for air between sobs, tears streaming down his cheeks, warm urine emptying from his bladder.

The hooded man spoke for the first time. The deep voice and speech pattern were familiar, but Colonel Pitts could not place it. "Any pain you I cause will be nothing compared to what you have to my family done." The robed figure turned away, folding his arms as he paced methodically around the earthen crypt. "Colonel Pitts, familiar you are with Middle Eastern culture?"

Colonel Pitts spoke through panting respirations. "It's a rich, wonderful culture. I've always loved it."

The grim reaper chuckled. "Ahh, a student you are. Good. I guess then I no have to tell you of Hammurabi?"

Colonel Pitts stammered. "Who?"

"Hammurabi!" The voice boomed.

Colonel Pitts flinched.

"Hammurabi was ancient Babylonian. He powerful man, make many laws. He say, "Eye for eye, tooth for tooth." The tormentor used the torchlight, walking to the table. The Afghan appeared like a hooded demon as his large weathered hand grasped the edge of the dirty blue sheet covering the table. He looked at Colonel Pitts then at the table, yanking the blue sheet away like a magician. Colonel Pitts clenched his eyes shut, ignoring the burning curiosity to look. His reaction amused the captor, more mocking laughter filling the musty space as the Afghan walked to the other side. Colonel Pitts heard a sheet being pulled off another table. The suspense was too much, and his morbid curiosity triumphed over the fear. Colonel Pitts turned to the table on the left and opened his eyes. The crease between them deepened as his eyes adjusted. Medical supplies were laid out in neat, organized piles. Feeding tubes, endotracheal tubes, I.V. lines, sutures, and pills of various colors, sizes and shapes filled the small open compartments of wooden boxes. A defibrillator and a small respirator sat nearby. His eyes moved over the respirator, pausing in bewilderment at what sat in the center of the table. Colonel Pitts recognized the blue and white boxes. Ex-Lax. They were the old chocolatey doses no longer sold in the U.S. On top of the stack of boxes sat a huge pair of stainless-steel needle drivers on full display. The hemostats were loaded with a massive curved needle trailing feet of thick hemp thread. "Noooo! Please, God, nooo!" He sobbed and shook violently as he scanned the rest of the table, which was covered in picks, saws, and knives as well as an assortment of pliers.

The Grim Reaper snatched something from one of the tables that looked like a billiard ball with thick black leather straps around it. The hooded man's fingers touched Colonel Pitts's mouth. "Open!"

Colonel Pitts twisted away as the hooded figure tried to force the ball between his teeth. The figure stood back, staring at him in silence. Colonel Pitts watched in horror as the man picked up the torch and shook it in the air. "Open!"

The demon grabbed the stick impaled in his scalp and pulled his head back. Colonel Pitts opened his mouth. "Fuck you! You—"

The captor shoved the ball in, lodging it between his teeth. The unbearable pain in his jaw intensified as the demon cinched the straps around his head. The hooded figure dragged a small wooden stool across the dusty floor, positioning it in front of him. The terrorist sat down and faced him, saying nothing for several minutes. The eyes burned into him, growing as terrible as the silence foretelling his doom. "You not give me one second to answer before you kill my Adam. I promise you get more time. You live for years." The figure pulled back the cloak,

the hood falling to the shoulders of Hamasa of Nimroz,
father of Aamir and Adam.

CHAPTER 38

August 12, 2012, U.S.A.

A violent jar shook the jet as its tires scrubbed the concrete runway. Flynn pressed his fist into his belly, trying to quash the ache as the plane slowed. He hoped for nothing more than the strength to face Samuel Khan. The piece of paper his mother had given him came into his mind. He took out his wallet and, for the first time, unfolded it.

"A man who lies to himself, and believes his own

lies, becomes unable to recognize truth, in himself

or in anyone else, and he ends up losing respect for himself

and for others.

When he has no respect for anyone, he can

no longer love, and in him, he yields to his impulses, indulges

in the lowest form of pleasure, and behaves in the end like

an animal in satisfying his vices. And it all comes from

lying, to others and to yourself."

An excruciating loneliness filled him as he wrapped his arms around himself and cried.

**

Two military vehicles with flashing lights raced from behind until they were alongside the plane. A presence approached. Flynn turned as Rex Laster as the man plopped into the seat next to him.

Laster rubbed his hand through his unkempt red beard. "We're going to jail, sure as shit. They're going to blame every damned thing on us. We can't catch a fuckin' break, can we?" Laster's eyes narrowed. "Barnes told me he was sitting behind Agent Schillings, reading the emails he was sending back and forth to Afghanistan. General Smith's team from Camp Leatherneck found heroin in the jail and traces of it in most of the buildings and vehicles. They also discovered all kinds of links to a Pakistani general across the border."

"The Cobras and all those men—it all makes sense."

Laster put his hand out. "It gets worse. They found a mass grave right along Camp Rock's airstrip with hundreds of bodies in it."

"That son of a bitch. I'd love another shot at him."

Laster nodded. "Get in line. But from what Barnes said, it looks like he got away clean. They have no idea where he or that scar-faced son of a bitch are." Laster whistled gently. "Cobras, rockets, bombs, and hundreds of men—and he still couldn't root us out. We walked into and right back out of the mother of all hornets' nests. I'd say we gave a good showing of ourselves and ORION, being out there all on our own."

Flynn shook his head. "What about Izzy and Adam?" Adam's goofy smile came into his mind. Now he understood Hamasa's overprotectiveness, the man's coldness. "Don't kid yourself, Rex. Colonel Pitts whipped us out there. He had no help from Central Command. We wiped out his whole force, and he still managed to kill Izzy, and had it not been for Sher Dil, he would have finished off the rest of us. That man took everything."

Laster's eyes grew sober as he absorbed the comment. "God, I hate it about Sher Dil. I wish I could have done more for him. He deserved better."

A tsunami of emotion washed over Flynn. It was the proverbial straw that broke the camel's back. He tried not to cry again. Unable, he turned away, hiding his face as he looked out the small window. Two policemen in navy blue uniforms rolled a metal staircase toward the jet, disappearing under the wing.

Boom, boom, boom! Fists pounded on the outside of the door.

Flynn's heart accelerated. He held his breath as the plane's door burst open, blue uniforms visible. Two officers surged into the front of the airplane, scanning the seats.

"There he is!" said the lead officer, glaring as he pointed at Randall Gibbs. "Come with us peaceably and you won't get hurt."

Randall acknowledged the statement with a slight nod. The solemn man stood up and moped after them until he was out of the plane.

Flynn grabbed his bag, descending the stairs toward the runway. He stopped, leaning over the staircase, watching the MPs shove Gibbs into a white Chevy van. They slid the door shut and jumped in. The flashing red and blue lights were extinguished as the vehicle disappeared out of the terminal.

Laster came down the steps behind him. "That's the last thing I expected, but it's a good thing they got him out of here. That 9 mm he's been brandishing is the only reason he's still breathing."

"Maybe they are trying to make us feel better."

Laster spat on the ground. "It's insulting. They'll be laughing about it over beers and pizza before we get out of this airport."

CHAPTER 39

Samuel ushered Flynn into the foyer. His eyes were puffy though his voice remained steadfast. Samuel's hawkish eyes made Flynn shrink. "Follow me to my office," Samuel said then turned and walked away with uncharacteristic brusqueness. The weightiness in Flynn's chest returned as they marched across the marble floors, past the gilded masterpieces and tapestries, around the corner and through the cool granite corridor. The click of Samuel's heels grew louder, portending the inevitable. As the office door came into sight, sweat beaded on Flynn's brow and nausea roiled his abdomen. Samuel opened the door, switched on the light then walked to his desk. He motioned to one of the high-backed chairs parked in front of his desk. "Sit."

Flynn wiped his hands on his pants then sat.

Samuel's green eyes smoldered with intensity. "You were with him when he died?"

Flynn took a deep breath. "He died in my arms. I'm so sorry. I couldn't save him, Samuel."

"Tell me everything, front to back, all of it."

***

Samuel looked at the ceiling for what seemed like forever. Finally, he looked from the ceiling, his eyes as sharp as talons. "I can't believe he's gone. It just not real." Samuel leaned back into his chair, his brow furrowing. "For god's sake, why didn't you listen to Colonel Kelley? Why did you take Izzy back up that pass? You were covered by Colonel Kelley's radar. You had antiaircraft missiles! What were you thinking?"

Flynn shook his head and sighed. "I was scared of an airstrike coming out of nowhere like last time. I didn't know who I was up against, just that he was a maniac. We wiped out all but a few of his men, yet he still managed to take our scouts prisoner and counterambush us." The images returned. Izzy's cloudy eyes and blood-soaked hair, Adam's goofy grin, Hamasa's suspicious glare, and Sher Dil's trusting eyes. Tears welled. "It was an instinct," he croaked.

Samuel slammed his fist against the desk. "Damn you and your instincts! Ishmael was worth ten of you!" Samuel put his fist to his mouth, his body racking with grief.

"I'm so sorry, Samuel. I'll regret it for the rest of my life. If I could have died in his place, I would have."

Samuel's face changed to a mask of regret. "Bobby—forgive me. I didn't mean it. You are no more to blame than I am. You were led over thin ice. It's no more your fault than the ice that cracked. I had a premonition something terrible was going to happen. I felt it in the War Room, the first time Izzy and I saw you after Senator Ryan got you out of jail. I let him go along anyway." Samuel leaned back, staring at the ceiling. "All his life Ishmael had such ability, but his wildness was an issue. I shamed him for it since he was a child. When he was fifteen years old, he came to me. He knelt down and apologized for who he was, for being such a disappointment. 'I want to be a good son to you, Father,' he told me." Samuel's voice softened. "That's when it first hit me how much I misunderstood him. It was a tragedy, cruel and inhumane, for Ishmael to have to apologize for who he was." Tears rolled down his cheeks. "The fact is, he was better than me and I knew it. I tried to suppress it. Now I can never tell him those word he so desperately wanted to hear: 'I am proud of you and I love you.' I'll never forgive myself." He wiped his face with the back of his hand and sniffed. "All for a foolish dream that never had a chance of happening."

Flynn pushed the lump in his throat down as he peered into Samuel's eyes. "That's not how I heard it. I heard stories of a wise and gifted man with an abundance of patience for his son. Izzy felt like you understood him like no other. He always had your support and he knew it."

Samuel bit the back of his knuckles. "What father am I?"

"Samuel, I'm sorry."

"I know he believed he was making a difference, and he died proving it. That makes the latest development even more painful."

"Latest development?"

"Yes, Robert. The last several days, I have been speaking with someone unexpected. Do you remember you said something in the past about the CIA potentially being involved with the first team's bombing? Well, I recently got a series of calls from a Mr. Hoyt Green. He runs the whole CIA outfit in Afghanistan. He wants ORION, and he says he needs it yesterday. Honestly, I don't know what to think of this," Samuel said.

Flynn leaned forward. "That's Jay Black—excuse me, Randall Gibbs's boss from Bamyan."

Samuel's nostrils flared. "Yes. It infuriates me that Jay Black was Hoyt's righthand man all along. When I heard that Black was CIA and had materialized at Camp Rock, I was shocked but the more I thought about it, the more logical it became. We knew it was someone powerful after our eLORAN system." Samuel's expression tightened. "I don't like these people. I don't trust them, and I have no impetus to work with them. They've left us to die twice now." Samuel swallowed hard. "I've given it much thought. I'm pulling the plug on ORION."

Flynn put his hands together as if praying. "Samuel, please! We are so close to making this happen. This is our big break. I can feel it!"

"Twelve men died last spring. Izzy is dead and so is his dream. Let it go, Robert."

Flynn's face reddened. "It wasn't just his dream. It was OUR dream. And it's not dead! Colonel Pitts took everything but ORION. It's all that I have left. Please don't kill this, Samuel. Let me see this through."

"Bobby, forget about it. You're a wealthy man now. Your sentence has been commuted; you're free.

What about your mother? Why would you go back and help these people? Don't you know you're going to get yourself and anybody with you killed?"

Flynn's eyes became steely. "Samuel, I've spent my whole life never knowing what I wanted, never having a purpose—until now. If helping Hoyt Green is what it takes to get ORION in the hands of our boys, then I welcome the opportunity. If I don't do this, Izzy and all the rest of them have died in vain."

Samuel huffed. "You're too naive to realize what a damn fool you are!"

"No, Samuel, it was naive to think we could test ORION with a tiny team left out on their own. I need combat support, and now we have it. All we have to do is reach out and take it, to follow through. Samuel, don't you see? This is it—our last chance. We can't give up just to spite those bastards. We have to use them like they used us. Use them to get ORION onto the battlefield."

Samuel offered a bitter smile. "Bobby, you know you'll have to go in with them."

"I accept that, Samuel."

"You'll go in as a noncommanding officer. Who knows, maybe even Jay Black will be telling you what to do. I know what type of man you are, Robert. Can you live with that?" Samuel stroked his chin, studying him.

"If getting ORION the chance it needs means going out as a noncommanding officer, then, God help me, that's what I'll do."

A bemused expression came upon Samuel. "God? God has nothing to do with this. This Hoyt Green character—maybe he nullifies the agreement after the mission; maybe you all die in a plane crash on the way home?"

"Ah, so pessimistic, Samuel."

"Bobby, think long and hard about what you are contemplating. If Hoyt Green needs us that bad, can you imagine how terrible things must be in Bamyan? Do you think you'll be more than cannon fodder?"

"Please, Samuel, at least hear him out. That's all I ask."

☐

CHAPTER 40

"Here they come," Flynn said as the two visitors entered the War Room and strode toward them. The lead man was skinny with wispy, dyed hair. He wore a tailored gray suit and a white button-up with the collar open, carrying himself with an air of superiority. He was followed by a large-nosed man in uniform with upright posture and a military haircut.

Samuel motioned towards the chairs. "Good morning, gentleman. Please take a seat."

"Hoyt Green," the man said as he shook Samuel's hand. "This is General Malcom Stalig, my field commander." Malcom Stalig was career military, in his sixties with a full head of silver hair cropped close in a flattop. "As you may have gleaned from our intermediaries, we have a huge problem in Afghanistan that, if not resolved, could spell the end of U.S. hegemony in Asia. What I'm trying to say is Malcom and I are here to ask for your assistance. We are embroiled in a terrible situation at our headquarters in Bamyan Province."

Flynn fought the urge to throw Samuel's stapler at the man's head, shaking as he spoke. "You are in a terrible situation? You sent a spy to S&K to steal the eLORAN operating system and when you couldn't get it, you left us to our fate in an area you know is treacherous. Now you come here for assistance?" Flynn pointed at the pale, skinny man. "Samuel's son, my best friend, died over there, and you could have warned us. That is, if you gave a damn. Were you protecting Colonel Pitts since you thought you could just steal the technology?"

Hoyt Green straightened his tie and cleared his throat. "Look, Colonel Pitts was the best operator on that side of Afghanistan. I've relied on him for years to control that border, and he's done it well with few resources." Hoyt's brows rose. "After the airstrike killed your first team, I did do something. I sent an agent to Nimroz to investigate the colonel. The agent interviewed him and checked his inventory of planes and bombs but didn't find anything incriminating."

Flynn jabbed his finger at Hoyt. "You knew about ORION and you knew in real time we were testing it in Nimroz. Didn't you?"

Hoyt chose his words carefully, eyes roaming over Flynn's face. "I know you need me to be honest with you, so I will. I first heard of ORION two years ago from a procurement agent who observed it at a weapons bazaar. My analysts concluded its multiple redundancies made it a superior battle system. One of the problems was we didn't have rights to the technology. I sent my agent to be on your first team but that didn't work out, so we tried to develop our own eLORAN."

Samuel pounded his fist on his desk. "Why won't you give a straight answer? You knew they were in danger with Colonel Pitts, and you left us in the dark. Why didn't you just ask? I would have worked with you."

Hoyt hung his head. "Collaboration would be seen by inside interests at the Pentagon as an endorsement. The dirty truth is ORION threatens too many of our big-dollar programs. It's too goddamn effective and far too cheap, but more than that, I don't want it in our enemies' hands—not before we know how to counter it." His eyes tightened. "Those quadcopters can be made invisible to radar. Do you realize what a hundred of those equipped with thermite grenades could do to an armored column?"

Samuel Khan's jaw clenched as his eyes bored into Hoyt. "You said you tried to come up with an alternative?"

Hoyt Green squirmed in the Queen Anne's chair. "A gifted but troubled electronics officer created it."

Flynn turned and locked eyes with Samuel. "Jay Black," he said.

Hoyt nodded. "His real name is Randall Gibbs. He developed a suicidal drone—"

"Switchblade," Samuel and Flynn said in unison.

Hoyt's eyes narrowed. "Yes, Switchblade." He shot a suspicious glance at his counterpart.

"Now you're backed into a corner and will say anything to get eLORAN. How can I trust a man that sees Colonel Pitts as a top operator?" Samuel asked.

Hoyt let out a long sigh. "War does funny things to men. It can drive a good man over the edge. You have to understand, I coordinate hundreds of thousands of men in hundreds of different theaters. In that process, I have to make decisions that affect the collective. In hindsight I got this one wrong. I should have been more suspicious of Colonel Pitts and not so quick to write off blame to the Pakistanis. As far as ORION, I admit, I saw the genius of the system, but I suppressed it. I'm here to rectify that mistake."

"Go on," Flynn said.

"Our engineers are convinced eLORAN is the silver bullet we've been praying for. My problem is training my men with an operational system in time to save our asses in Bamyan." Hoyt swallowed hard. "If you help, I promise I'll do everything in my power to facilitate ORION finding its way into production."

"What's going on?" Flynn asked.

"Nothing I say leaves this room. Our forces are in Afghanistan for two reasons. Afghanistan is the richest geological find of this century, possibly ever. Trillions upon trillions of dollars' worth of recoverable assets lie in the hills of Bamyan and Wardak provinces alone." Hoyt looked like a kid in the candy store. "Diamonds, rare earth elements, precious metals, lithium, uranium—you name it. The assets are up for grabs because there is no protective central power authority in Afghanistan. The U.N. has tried to ensure the resources are developed responsibly and equitably among the regional players including India, the U.S., China, and Pakistan."

Flynn scratched his chin. "What's the second reason?"

"It involves China directly. The Chinese have rewritten the rules, exploiting our investment and hard work, and we have been powerless to stop them. The problems began two years ago with the assassinations of multiple international geological survey teams. Roving Chinese special forces have been killing not only the survey teams but anyone else trying to establish footholds, including my men." Hoyt stared at the floor, silent for a moment. "The minerals aren't all of it though. You see, China sits on huge reserves of oil and gas, but they don't have the expertise to develop it; therefore, they are reliant on ocean-borne tankers and overland pipelines, many of which run through Afghanistan and the surrounding area. If we can control the area vis-à-vis contracts then we can control the Chinese militancy via access to overland fuel. We must run them out of Bamyan if we are to establish a regional presence into the future. That way when the war begins, we will be in position to turn off the overland Chinese pipelines while the U.S. and Indian Navies blockades the Strait of Hormuz and disrupt their tankers. Within weeks, China's military machine would be without energy. That's the real reason we've been in Afghanistan for the last eleven years." Hoyt pulled out a white handkerchief and waved it in the air like surrender then dabbed his brow. "I was sent to stop them, and I have nosedived. The Chinese are using some cryptic electronic fighting system that we can't understand or counter. I have sent hundreds of men to their death and to this day, I don't know exactly how they are commandeering our weapon's guidance systems."

Flynn's pulse quickened at the statements. "War with China? How could a weapons system designed for a foot soldier help you?"

"It's not the weapons; it's the eLORAN operating system."

"Is their capability offensive or defensive?" asked Samuel.

"Both," Hoyt said. "It's more than jamming, blip enhancement, and more sophisticated countermeasures that we've encountered. They have the ability to wirelessly black out or assume control of the navigation system of every one of our guided weapons systems."

"Even laser?" Flynn asked.

"Yes, even laser designators. My scientists suspect some type of microwave inserted malware hijacks the targeting and guidance systems, but even that is hypothetical. We have multibillion-dollar platforms they've rendered useless. They've found our Achilles' heel."

Flynn frowned. "What are the Chinese assets on the ground?"

"Not nearly as much as we have but that is changing. With their capability and our inability to challenge them, the Chinese ships are delivering complex heavy weapon systems into Pakistan's Gwadar deep sea port in the Arabian Sea. The weapons are then transported into Afghanistan on Pakistani railroads. The Chinese formally deny any involvement in derailing the mining operations while their military presence is growing in malignancy. If we could find a way to use eLORAN to counter them, we could delay war with China for years, possibly decades."

Flynn acknowledged with a nod. "How much time do you have?"

"A month, tops. A twenty-three-man mission launched last night resulted in the deaths of every one of the men in the squad." Hoyt held his arms out. "I can't fight back. If they go on the offensive, we are finished. There is no way I could fight them off, and I fear they know it. Time is short. It just depends on how aggressive the Chinese are."

Flynn turned to the military man. "General, could you tell us a little about what an encounter with the Chinese system is like?"

"I'd be happy to, sir. First, our sweepers fly electromagnetic detectors over the mountains that are effective in determining where the Chinese are but after that—" he made a slicing motion across his throat. "I send in the foot patrol, and my men are annihilated by rockets. They have some type of targeting system remote to their soldiers but instead of using mortars, rockets are the kill vehicle. A Chinese general named Wong controls what we believe to be around five hundred men of the Chinese special forces Arrow Brigade. They are a high-tech, razzle-dazzle unit established in the 1990s. They operate from the safety of mountain lairs scattered around Wardak and Bamyan provinces. Any guided bomb we use is directed off or back into my forces." Sweat dripped down the side of his head. "We've tried bombing runs with gravity bombs, but those didn't work. They hop from lair to lair like gophers, and to kill them you have to get the explosion into that specific den. Since we can't get close enough to find the ventilation shafts to target, we do better with pop shots from the mortar tubes and howitzers down on the flats than anything else. Two weeks ago, one of our 155-mm shells got a lucky hit."

Hoyt put both hands together, fingertips touching as a flush crept across his cheeks. "The fact of the matter is that if S&K sends a team to Bamyan, you will be part of my family, under my protection."

Flynn poked a backward thumb at Hoyt Green. "Check this guy out. He tells us his teams always get smoked, but we are under his protection, part of his family."

Samuel's eyes grew sharp. "Flynn, are you sure this is what you want?"

"Yes, Samuel, I'm certain."

Samuel's eyes held his for several seconds then he looked at Hoyt. "When my lawyers are happy and I am are satisfied that S&K's best interests are protected, then we can assemble."

Hoyt exhaled. "Thank you, Mr. Khan. I trust you will act expeditiously."

"Just a moment," Flynn said. "There is something else, something more personal. Your Agent Gibbs threw my service dog off the plane at Camp Rock. I demand that animal be ready to pick up at Camp Rock after this is all over."

"Jesus Christ, son, all of this and you're worried about a dog?"

"That's right, asshole. Your agent, Axl Herron, has seen it. Contact him and have him care for it. Two kilograms of rice and chicken per day should do."

Hoyt shook his head. "Okay, whatever."

The thought of getting Sher Dil back buoyed Flynn's spirits. He softened his voice. "Give me three hours and I will show what a single ORION-equipped platoon is capable of when supported by the full weight of the U.S. military." He rubbed his hands together. "It won't take long to obliterate the Chinese once they engage us."

Hoyt frowned. "I've lost many men on those mountains. Don't think you can just waltz in with your cock in your hand and take them out."

"Mr. Green, I assure you, if you provide the assets to support ORION, the mission will be accomplished."

Samuel pointed to the large doors at the entrance to the War Room as if dismissing Hoyt and Malcolm like children. "Meet us back here tomorrow. That should give the lawyers some time." Samuel lowered his head. "I'll warn you, it is not going to be cheap but if it looks like we can do business then you will be filled in."

Hoyt's face turned a deep shade of crimson. "Now, wait a damn minute. You don't dictate terms and walk out, not on me!"

"Meet us here in the morning, 7:00 sharp," Samuel said in a pleasant tone as he corralled them toward the main door. "Mr. Green, General Stalig, it was a pleasure." Samuel pushed them out of the War Room then closed the doors and locked them.

CHAPTER 41

"The money is no problem as long as S&K actually delivers on developmental expertise," Hoyt said.

Samuel crossed his arms. "S&K will deliver."

Flynn's eyes opened wide. "Outside of my combat dog, there is one other thing."

Hoyt emitted an exaggerated sigh. "What is it?"

"Before we'll agree to help, we want Randall Gibbs out of the picture for good not just some theatrical arrest. Prison would suffice."

Hoyt put his hands out. "Putting Randall Gibbs in prison at this time is out of the question. Nobody can coordinate a mission like Gibbs. He can squeeze more performance out of a fixed amount of assets than should be possible. Without him coordinating the assault, the attack could break down. If that happens, we fail."

Flynn's muscles stiffened as he glanced at Samuel. "After the mission, Randall Gibbs goes to jail."

"Done. Randall Gibbs has been out of control for some time now. Maybe a jail cell will do him good."

"That's not all," Samuel said. "I had an epiphany last night that it could be in the agency's best interest that my men not make it home. I want a hundred million dollars in an account administered by a third party in case of any accidents. If they get back home alive, your agency gets its money back. If the men are killed, the money is distributed amongst their heirs."

Hoyt's shoulders shook with laughter. "What? You think I'll just wave my imperial hand and your squad will disappear? If it'll make you feel better, we'll open the account." He tapped his foot on the ground. "I've given you everything you've asked for. How are we going to go about this?"

"First, we have to get the eLORAN transmitters in place to propagate the grid and maintain ground control," Flynn said. "The problem is the robotic snakes that house the transmitters can only move two miles per hour, which is too slow given the circumstances. Samuel's engineers figure we will have to deploy close to a hundred transmitters, about a half- mile apart, to cover five square miles. We can accomplish that if we modify the transmitters and distribute the them with the quadcopters but that will require a dramatic diversion to pull it off."

"How about a squadron of low-flying helicopters?" Hoyt asked.

"That should work," Flynn said. "Once we get the transmitters stationary, we can spring the trap. The eLORAN grid is the control system for ORION. Therefore, there is no central guidance system to insert malware into. When eLORAN is deployed, the Chinese will do everything they can to find an electronic countermeasure. When they figure out they cannot manipulate it, they will physically look for the transmitting source. This is one of eLORAN's best attributes." Flynn pointed to the dots on the board. "The gridlike nature of the transmitters provides an exact location of an attack. When they show their location, we'll see how their technology does against old-style gravity bombs from thirty thousand feet."

Hoyt clenched his fist. "If you can pinpoint them for my pilots, enough B-52s could annihilate them."

Flynn smiled. "They're going to be dug in within two miles of wherever those rockets originate. Just make sure the bombs are incendiary to suck the oxygen out of those caves and tunnels." Flynn regarded the ceiling mural of the Turks' boats being boarded by the Venetians. The charging Venetians reminded him of the Chinese, emboldened and on the cusp of victory. "Mr. Green, you say the Chinese are emboldened by their success. Use that hubris against them. Call them out publicly as saboteurs and killers. They'll mock you and claim you have no proof. When we kill their team and expose them in Bamyan, they will have lost face and considerable influence in the area."

Hoyt's eyes searched Flynn's face. "Every second counts. If possible I'd like your team to fly to Bamyan within two weeks. Last night, twelve contractors from Nice, France, were ambushed and killed."

"I'll do my best," Flynn said. His mind jumped to Colonel Pitts. "Mr. Green? Any news of Colonel Pitts?"

"None. My sources think he probably escaped into Pakistan."

CHAPTER 42

August 26th, 2012

"Hello?" Brian Bollick's voice said.

Flynn smiled. "I finally found you! A lot has happened in the two weeks we've been back. I have a lot to tell you about Hoyt Green and ORION."

"Hoyt Green, Randall Gibbs's boss?

"Uh-huh, him. Samuel and I received a visit last week. They want us to lead a mission in Bamyan."

"Bamyan?" Bollick was silent for a moment. "What do you think about it?"

"It's what we always coveted, an in-and-out job with tons of technical support. Pay is five million dollars up front. The problem is Hoyt wants to leave as soon as possible. I've been looking for a week, and you're the only one I've found. I need your help."

"Five million! Hell, yeah, I'm ready. Let's see, hmm … I know Laster and Barnes were heading for Las Vegas, but I don't have a clue where any of the others went."

"Bollick, you find Barnes and Laster and get them back to Pennsylvania. I'll keep trying to find the others."

***

Flynn pulled into the barn like restaurant and parked next to Bollick's new black Porsche 911 Turbo S, admiring the muscularity of the sculpted lines as he walked past.

Bollick was seated by himself along the east wall. Flynn walked over and sat down opposite. "Nice ride but it looks a bit small for you. Has the steering wheel taken your balls off yet?"

Bollick gave a half-smile then pointed to the cellphone in Flynn's hand. "Any luck?"

Flynn shook his head. "Mendez is out of the country, and Sobieski's not interested."

"Him? Not interested in five million dollars?" Bollick shrugged. "I'll take his cut."

Flynn offered a bemused smile. "Flat turned me down. Says he had an epiphany that he would rather live."

Bollick sighed. "I guess I was a little more fortunate. I found Laster and Barnes, but they're in jail in Reno."

"Shit! We need at least four of us, and those two are in jail? Can we get them out? Who do I need to talk to? What the hell did they do?"

Bollick held out a plate-sized hand. "Calm down. I've already made arrangements to spring the louses. They'll be on tomorrow's flight."

Flynn let out a gush of air. "What happened?"

Bollick sighed and slid down in his seat. "They were at a whorehouse in Reno and got into a brawl with a group of swingers. Laster ended up on the wrong end of a whiskey bottle."

"One of the girls?"

"Damn, you're good at this! It's as if you know these guys." Bollick chuckled. "I spent all morning convincing Sheriff Grithers to release them. One of the victims was the sheriff's friend. Apparently, Barnes did something inappropriate to the man."

"Barnes? Surely not." Flynn rolled his eyes. "His mother must be a saint."

"Or a whore," Bollick said with a sideways grin. His expression changed, his inner brows dropping. "How's that bullet wound? You're awfully spry for a man that took a high velocity rifle round to the shoulder less than a month ago."

Flynn stuck his lower lip out as he nodded his head. "It was nothing but shithouse luck. The round went right through my humeral head but didn't shatter the bone. Doc said he'd never seen anything like it. The bullet just went right through punching a pencil size hole through it." He shrugged. "No vascular injury and all the tendons and nerves are still intact. It's a bit sore but that's it."

Bollick's eyes roamed his face. He started to speak but stopped himself and let out a big sigh as he shook his head. The big man appeared to be wrestling with his emotions.

Flynn patted him on the forearm and took out his phone. "I'll call Hoyt and tell him we leave tomorrow. I'll leave it to you to make sure Barnes gets his shit together and gets to the plane. You know how he likes to piddle around."

Bollick frowned. "What I am I, his dad?"

CHAPTER 43

Flynn stood at the concourse, awaiting the others. He turned at the sound of approaching footsteps.

"Well, there he is in the flesh."

Rex Laster had large green plastic sunglasses on. He moved in a shuffle, his form sagging. "Just glad to be here. The last two days have been a little exhausting." His left eye was purple and grotesquely swollen, protruding far beyond the confines of the sunglasses. A long row of sutures ran across the worst of it. Laster glanced around. "Where's that asshole Barnes at?"

"He's not here yet." He tilted his head. "Laster, are you sure there's no broken bones in your face? That looks like more than just soft tissue."

"Nope, the ER doc did a CT scan. He said it was a busted artery." Laster broke into a grin. "One of the bouncers was tough. Best scuffle I've been in, I'd reckon." He rubbed his chin in thought as if ranking his previous mêlées. "Shit was flying everywhere. I must have hit those motherfuckers a hundred times." He rubbed his knee. "Both my knees are sore from bouncing their heads off them. I was cleaning house until—"

Flynn raised on his tiptoes, half listening as he glanced around for Barnes. "Until the woman?"

"Who squealed on me?"

Flynn chuckled. "We had some time to burn waiting for you assholes, so Bollick glossed over it, said you were in a fight."

"I owe him a debt of gratitude for dealing with that Sheriff Grithers dude. Just so you know, Barnes started the whole thing."

"And she finished it." Flynn crossed his arms, studying Laster. "Do I even want to know what happened?"

Laster smirked. "No, but it is an entertaining story. Barnes and I were playing on the pool table with several groups of swingers and girls in the establishment. One of the husbands got tired of Barnes rubbing his wife's ass. The guy disappears and returns with this bowl of hot sauce and some chips." Laster chuckled. "It wasn't five minutes and that little bastard was helping himself to that man's chips and salsa."

Laster turned and held his arms out, framing the situation. "Barnes got a couple of mouthfuls down his piehole then stops dead in his tracks." Laster stifled a laugh. "I mean, it's obvious something is wrong with Barnes. That's when this guy starts laughing and pointing his finger at him. I gotta give it to this dude. It was pure habanero."

"Ambushed Barnes with habanero dip. Classic," Flynn said as he gestured toward the aircraft. "On the plane, please." As Flynn watched Laster walk away, Barnes came walking down the concourse. He passed without saying a word, following Laster toward the plane.

Brian Bollock stared at Barnes as he walked by then walked over. "That's a quorum," he said.

Flynn looked at his watch. "Just in time. I guess we can pull the rug back and leave this joint." He noticed Bollick was looking at him strangely. "What is it, Brian?"

"Well, I've just been thinking and all, and I know most guys wouldn't or haven't given me chances in the past, but you saw through my issues and did give me a chance. I want you to know I appreciate it."

The sudden sentiment caught Flynn off guard. "Well, I'm glad I listened to Izzy and gave you another chance. After being between you and Jay Black, I thought you were a steroid-eating asshole."

Bollick looked hurt. "Thanks."

Flynn turned his head thoughtfully. "I was wrong though. I've never seen you take steroids." Bollick mockingly threatened to punch him, then dropped his fist and laughed.

CHAPTER 44

September 19th, 2012, Bamyan Province, Afghanistan

Flynn rubbed his arms against the chill of the late summer night, watching the gear being unloaded from the jet. As the men assembled on the concrete, he spotted a lone figure striding toward them along the runway. "Hello, men. My name is Sergeant Willie McCoy. I have the dubious distinction of guiding you guys in tomorrow."

Flynn had heard of the man, one of the last of the original team of commandos, spared death by a fluke illness that had kept him out of a large mission in which all sixteen Americans were killed. McCoy had brown hair and intense intelligent eyes. He looked to be about forty, with a grizzled beard and the typical hardened build of a career operative. Sergeant McCoy looked around at them. "You boys stick with me, do what I say, when I say, and there is a small chance that you may not go home in a body bag. I hear your eLORAN system is robust. It better be because everything we have tried so far has gotten us killed." He gestured to the mountains. "I've lost many good friends on those fucking rocks."

"So far it's been perfect," Flynn said. "We've tested them near powerful microwave towers, which had zero effect on the system."

McCoy conjured up a hacker from deep in his throat, launching it through the air. "I'll believe this cool-guy shit when I see it." He glared at them then spun on his heels and walked toward a large canvas tent fifty meters away.

"Forgive Sergeant McCoy," came a voice that Flynn recognized. "He has seen much horror." Hoyt Green motioned to follow.

Flynn followed him toward the circuslike shelter, entering through a large flap that fell shut behind him. The super-cold space had a floor of hard-packed gravel and smelled of electronics. Noisy fans cooled massive banks of hard drives, which sat in a depression in the middle of the space. Powerful air conditioners resonated outside. Hoyt led them to a white roll-out screen and a row of chairs. Please, sit." An image of the adjacent mountain range came onto the screen. A green laser dot circled the western face. "This is the area we have narrowed the search down to. Intelligence from previous engagements suggests the Chinese are within two miles of the rockets they use to kill with." Hoyt looked at Flynn as he spoke. "Unfortunately, we can't get close enough to engage them. Initially, we employed some digital subtraction technology with our satellites, but a few early successes just resulted in the Chinese adapting, burrowing into the protective caves and tunnels below." He circled a red "x" on the screen.

"Sergeant McCoy will get you to this point." He tossed the green laser pen to Flynn.

Flynn circled the area marked with a red "x" on the map. "First we must get the eLORAN transmitters in to establish a forward grid that the avatars can deliver fire from. Once the grid is operational, we'll sacrifice a few of the avatars by sending them in with their heat signatures turned on. We'll try to goad the Chinese into an attack to give us their relative position. When they do, the helicopters need to spring the diversion, at which time we will fly in the transmitters and complete the grid. I'll then direct my avatars to engage anything that looks suspicious. Those avatars will deliver pinpoint firepower the Chinese haven't experienced here. When that happens, they'll panic, which will force some of them outside to disable the threat. Wherever a transmitter is tampered with, that's a target for the bombers and their incendiaries."

Hoyt rubbed his hands together. "I have twelve B-52s ready to carpet-bomb those son of a bitches. Those bombs will suck all the oxygen from the caves and tunnels."

"All this hinges on Sergeant McCoy getting us close enough to the mountain to get into the eLORAN grid," Flynn said.

"Don't worry about Sergeant McCoy. He'll be working with Randall Gibbs to get you as close as possible."

Flynn glared at Randall, flipping him the bird. "I object to that large pile of dog shit having anything to do with our safety."

Hoyt glared, tapping his foot. "Flynn, we talked about this! He's an integral member of the team. We can't do this without him."

"Keep him on a tight leash."

"I will," Hoyt said. "I took your advice and went to the U.N. with formal accusations against the Chinese. Predictably, they have lambasted and mocked our embassy, but we do have the ear of India, which is concerned with the Chinese aggression on their doorstep. If we can expose the Chinese, it will set them back tremendously with the Indians. Sergeant McCoy will show you the thermal suits you will use tomorrow and brief you on other relevant information. If he feels you guys can handle it, we go in at 0600 tomorrow."

"There's still a member of the platoon left behind at Camp Rock. What of him?"

Hoyt sighed. "Yes, your precious dog. I made you a promise and I will keep it. My agent in Nimroz isn't man enough to get a leash on the beast, but it is around and it is healthy."

CHAPTER 45

Bamyan Province, 1800 hours

Flynn cataloged the surroundings, pangs of unease twisting his gut. Figures hurried about, shoulders drawn tight, faces down. He eyed Sergeant McCoy, who had exited the main tent. The soldier walked over, shaking his head, a grim look distorting his face. "I've got terrible news, worse than we thought."

The blood rushed from Flynn's face. He leaned toward Sergeant McCoy. "How bad is terrible?"

"We're fucked, that's how bad. Intelligence has been scrambling all night to decode a horde of Chinese transmissions. They're adamant the entire Chinese contingent is amassing for an attack on this base by tomorrow afternoon. Hoyt has moved the go time to 0500."

Flynn's eyes bugged as he glanced at the silver dial of his watch, his breath coming in short rasps. "Sergeant

McCoy?" He held his arms out, struggling against the weight of the cloaking suit. "We don't have the slightest clue how to use these damn things."

Sergeant McCoy threw his head back. "Pfft, those suits are the least of it. We've never seen this type of activity from them before. They're coming. I know it; I can feel it in my bones." His eyes narrowed. "We can wait for them and die here, which I assure you we will, or we can have a fighting chance on the mountain." Sergeant McCoy sighed. "If we can make it to the ledge."

"The ledge?"

McCoy nodded. "It's a safe spot with access to the face of the mountain. If we can get to it, it may provide enough cover to deploy the grid. We just have to get it operational before they kill us. It's how to that has me stumped."

Flynn put his face in his hands. Pandora's Box was about to be opened—upon all of them.

Sergeant McCoy spat a wad of Copenhagen on the ground then looked him over with concern. "I'm sorry it must be this way. Get familiar with these suits and I'll do what I can to help you. We don't sleep tonight. If you have anything to tell anyone back home, I suggest you write it down."

***

0500

Sergeant McCoy walked through the hint of the morning light. "The Big Top is humming, and Hoyt has called in our Humvee. We're going in!" An armored

Humvee rolled up in a cloud of dust, stopping in the makeshift parking strip next to the tent.

Flynn swallowed hard. "We were up all night, but we're still not ready."

"Haven't you been listening, Commander? The Chinese are coming. It's time for your crew to show what ORION can do." Sergeant McCoy spat on the ground. "Don't be so negative. What's the worst that could happen?"

Flynn and Barnes crawled into the truck, followed by Bollick, Laster and Sergeant McCoy, who grasped the handle and slammed the blast door, its edges forming an airtight seal against the shell of the vehicle. The Humvee lurched forward and in seconds they were speeding toward the mountain range. The approach was flat and sandy, eventually giving way to boulders and uneven terrain. They bounced and careened, continuing through acacia trees and small scrub bushes until they stopped at the foothill of a mountain.

Sergeant McCoy jammed an old cigar in his mouth then opened his door and hopped out. The Reconnaissance Marine burst forward, moving with catlike nimbleness as he led the group through the cover of the boulders and crevices up the rocky foothill of the small mountain. Flynn and the others followed, placing transmitters as they went. Sergeant McCoy scampered under a shelf of rock large enough to shelter twenty men. His eyes went to the avatar-loaded dollies that Barnes and Bollick were struggling to pull up. "I can't believe my ass depends on those tin cans. They better make it up this mountainside."

Flynn fought to slow his breathing. "Those tin cans won't go anywhere unless we get this grid built over that mountain."

Bollick sat cross-legged and pulled out the laptop. He typed furiously, his eyes widening as he glanced up from the screen. "ORION is up for a square mile. We can finish the grid with the quadcopters."

Hoyt Green's voice came through the helmet. "You men hurry up and be careful. Chinese radio chatter is increasing."

"Sergeant McCoy, how about that diversion?" Flynn said.

Sergeant McCoy spoke into his microphone. "Base, this is Team One. I've got them in position. We're ready to move to stage two."

"Ten-four," a voice Flynn recognized as Randall Gibbs's boomed through the eLORAN network.

Flynn put his hands on either side of the helmet and pulled it down, cinching the chinstrap. "Laster, you and Bollick turn your avatars' heat signature to cool. Move up and deploy as many transmitters as possible. They must know we are close. We'll stay put under this ledge and rely on the avatars until we get that diversion. Then we'll use the quadcopters to finish the grid." He wiped sweat from his eyes as the robots ducked under the ledge and headed up the path. "God, I hope this works."

Sergeant McCoy used ORION to mark a string of red dots on the image provided by Barnes's quadcopter. "Follow this line." Laster and Bollick's avatars deposited transmitters along the red line. Another two thousand feet and the grid would extend over the top of the mountain.

Hoyt Green's concerned voice blasted through the speaker. "Team One, be aware the Chinese are talking about you. They must know where you are!"

McCoy peered from under the ledge. "Where are you bastards?"

***

"Golden Dragon, this is Red Tiger," an earnest voice shouted through General Wong's headset.

"This is Golden Dragon. What is it?" he asked his top commander, Ying Zhao.

"Two men are moving up the eastern approach to the command center!"

General Wong's heart pounded. He hadn't expected another attack so soon. He examined the multiple screens projected by the various cameras scattered about the mountain. Indeed, two human forms were moving toward him. His forehead creased at the lack of heat emanating from the approaching men. "They must be disguising their heat signatures, the fools!" The Americans were so juvenile and foolish, always bulldozing ahead.

Zhao's impatient voice came through the intercom. "Awaiting commands, sir."

General Wong watched the two forms slink up the path. Too bad there were only two to kill this time. He keyed his microphone. "Fire!" The familiar tearing noise accompanied the plumes of the four rockets as the weapons streaked high into the atmosphere, turning around and descending at hypersonic velocity toward the hapless Americans.

***

"Incoming! Four rockets," Randall's voice roared.

"Get the avatars to cover!" Flynn screamed as two rockets streaked high, barely missing Laster's avatar as it ducked for cover. The next two crashed into Bollick's likeness. The acoustical blast through the headset was like an ice pick to the eardrum. Glowing bits of robot exploded high into the sky, raining back onto the rocks.

Bollick reached out and grabbed Flynn by the arm. "We still don't have a large enough grid. Where's that diversion?" A falling sensation enveloped Flynn. Without the grid finished, he couldn't find, much less fight, the Chinese. His senses reeled as the adrenaline invited panic, igniting every instinct to turn and flee.

CHAPTER 46

Flynn ignored Bollick's cursing, concentrating on Laster's avatar, which the Viking had already moved back out in the open as if to say, "You missed me!"

Gibbs's low voice rocked back into the helmet. "Four more rockets, a half-second out."

Laster's robot was too quick, squatting behind a boulder as the explosions deflected off the opposite side of the granite rock.

Randall Gibbs's voice blared back. "Sergeant McCoy, you guys are close! I've triangulated the rocket trajectories. We've got two distinct points of origin."

Randall left his microphone on. Flynn could hear his fingers typing at incredible speed, never stopping to correct an error. A map appeared on Flynn's HUD with multiple preprogrammed previous points of origin of Chinese rockets. The new points were in the same area of previous attacks. God, I hope this works. He cast his eyes on the screen of a camera at the command tent. The view was mainly the back of Randall Gibbs, but he could also see Hoyt Green in the background. "Send in the bombers," Hoyt's lips enunciated. Flynn cast his gaze back to Gibbs. For a moment, he admired the man. Randall's arms were a blur, moving over the electronic interfaces. Large electronic control boards, flat screens, and keyboards were arranged around him like a drum set, him in the middle, his massive ass swallowing a hapless swivel chair. Randall leaned forward. "Rogue One, this is base. Do you copy?"

A voice on a faraway-sounding radio came across the eLORAN system. "Copy, base. This is Rogue One."

"Rogue One, drop your pod on these coordinates. Over," Randall said.

The radio crackled back. "Copy, base. We have received and are verifying coordinates."

Flynn looked at the four men crouched under the slab next to him. "That's our cue!" he shouted. The four of them flew the quadcopters to the pile of transmitters, picking them up and flying off in different directions, building the grid up the mountain as they went. Flynn fastidiously hooked the transmitters one by one with the quadcopter, racing to the next location and setting it down. Over and over he returned for another. The pile of transmitters disappeared just as the B-52's bombs erupted in a string of explosions on the other side of the mountain. Flynn clenched his fist. "They bought it!" In the confusion of the approaching B-52s, the Chinese hadn't noticed the drones. "The eLORAN grid is online. ORION is active all around this side of the mountain!"

Hoyt Green's voice came through the helmets. "Commander Flynn, show me what your team can do."

Flynn nodded. "Everyone switch your avatars to thermo-neutral and march out!" As the new avatars moved out, Flynn's muscles relaxed as instinct flipped from prey to predator. "Get the avatars to hidden positions then take those UAVs and look in every nook and cranny for any possible targets. You men on those artillery pieces, be ready. We'll be sending you coordinates soon. Give these bastards a heavy dose."

"Ten-four, Commander," an unfamiliar voice said.

Flynn flew his own quadcopter through an area of palisading cliffs, peering through the camera for an entrance, a man, or anything else he could paint.

Barnes's boyish voice flashed through the microphone like he had just hooked an enormous fish. "I've got multiple heat signatures in that cave." Flynn focused on the red dot on Barnes's camera. Kaboom! Kaboom! The 120-mm mortar tubes of Barnes's avatar went off. The rounds came in on target. The immense explosions collapsed the entrance, the cave belching a solid plume of dust, angled acutely up into the atmosphere. Through the dark cloud of dust and smoke, the heat signatures of multiple men emerged, crawling on their hands and knees in opposite directions. Flynn slapped his leg. "Hoyt, they're taking the bait! They're searching for the transmitters!"

Laster's voice blared through the helmet next as red dots appeared on his screen. "I found another group!"

The ten 155-mm Howitzers lying in the flats, nine miles to the east, opened up on the targets. Everything was happening so fast that Flynn struggled to concentrate. The camera screen from Laster's avatar shook as two forty-pound rounds packed with CL-20 headed toward the exposed Chinese troops. The huge explosions of the eLORAN-guided artillery shells joined the fray, destroying the mouth of a cave in an impressive display of overkill, the overhanging roof collapsing even more dramatically than before.

"Dude," Bollick muttered.

"Hey! My screen is acting up!" Barnes yelled.

Flynn smiled, watching the screens on his visor flicker. "Hook, line, and sinker! They're out of their minds trying to stop this attack."

"Take it in the ass, motherfuckers!" Barnes screamed like a banshee.

"Hoyt, they're initiating high-power jamming signals and physically destroying our transmitters," Flynn said. "Bollick is mapping the attacks on ORION's database." In seconds a computer screen appeared, showing the extent of the Chinese counterattack. Flynn studied it intently. "We've got twelve distinct groups of disruptions." There was an obvious pattern that he recognized in the way the different units moved. "They are arranged in a phalanx, one supporting the other, disarming the transmitters as they go."

Randall's voice boomed through the headset. "Grim Reaper, this is base. Drop your JDAMs on these coordinates."

"Copy, base. This is Grim Reaper. We have the targets programmed, and ten of us are heading that way. Popcorn and Cokes are extra, folks." The ten Stratofortresses aligned on the computer screen, heading right for them.

A bolt of alarm ripped through Flynn. He keyed his microphone. "Negative, base. Team One is still in position. Repeat, we haven't fallen back. Give us a few minutes. Over."

Silence greeted him. He tried again. "Base, abort the attack. Over."

The alarm turned to dread. Flynn locked eyes with Sergeant McCoy. "What do those B-52s have on board?"

Sergeant McCoy blinked rapidly. "Each bomber has a hundred seven-hundred-and-fifty- pound Mark 77 incendiary bombs." Flynn did the math. "That's seven hundred and fifty thousand pounds of thermite about to come down on us."

McCoy shook his head in disbelief, his eyes huge as he keyed the eLORAN microphone. "Hoyt, you have to stop the attack. We missed the order to fall back. Over!" He tried again. "Randall Gibbs, you son of a bitch! Call off the attack! Repeat, abort the fucking airstrike!" Sergeant McCoy's eyes were like saucers. "Randall turned the eLORAN patch at the command center off. That fucker ditched our radios as well! He just killed us."

CHAPTER 47

Sergeant McCoy fumbled with the microphone. "Joe? For God's sake, can you hear me?"

"I can hear you, Sergeant. I've heard it all. I can't believe he did it," said the Humvee's driver.

"Contact Hoyt at the base. Help us—"

"Negative. Already tried, sir. No one's answering the satellite phone and the entire communication link into the Command Center has been severed. Gibbs must have turned the router off."

"Severed?" Sergeant McCoy swayed. "Those bombs could be in the air by now." His frame slumped. "I don't see what can be done. We're going to burn out here."

Flynn's hands trembled. Would Joe risk his own life? Would he be so foolish, so heroic to try? The driver's voice returned, resonating with anger and determination. "I'm almost there, Sergeant. I floored it as soon as I heard that son of a bitch authorize the airstrike. You guys get as close to the drop-off point as you can. It's going to be close." The Humvee's engine noise crackled through the receiver, and the transmission went dead.

Sergeant McCoy jumped up, a wild and harried look on his face as he stepped from under the ledge, tearing at the heavy suit with desperation. He shot a glance over his left shoulder. "What are you guys waiting for?" He turned and hopped on one leg as he extricated himself fully from the suit and left them, running for his life.

Flynn was next to extricate himself, putting his head down and running after Sergeant McCoy. He squinted and veered sideways several feet to emerge from the cloud of dust McCoy was kicking up. Seconds later a stampede of footsteps was closing on Flynn from behind. It was like he was in a nightmare, unable to move through the deep sand. He extended his legs and pumped his arms, finally gaining enough speed to run on top of the grit. Now I'm moving. He's still outrunning me! Despite his age, the graying vet had another gear, continuing to pull away at a frightening rate. Flynn's chest ached with urgency as panic gripped him. Everything in his life had come down to this one mad dash. His mother's angry voice echoed in his head. "Is this your inferno? Is this your inferno?" It mocked, the anger mutating to delight. He pushed away the thoughts of burning, concentrating on his running. With a single-minded focus, he shrank the gap with Sergeant McCoy, slowly reeling him in as the older man tired. Flynn's lungs burned and his legs ached, lactic acid igniting the pain receptors in the muscles. He ignored their howls of pain, pushing his body harder than he could remember ever doing. Without warning, he stumbled, his eyes widening as he stuck his arms out reflexively before catching his balance. His legs were spent. Like wet noodles, they were barely keeping him upright. Sergeant McCoy pointed to something out in the desert. "There he is!"

Flynn scanned the horizon, detecting the rooster tail of dirt. That's him! That's him! His mind cried out like a desperate child. In seconds the Humvee skidded with a grinding noise through the sand, grating to a halt fifty yards away. Joe whipped the vehicle around and stepped out into an enormous cloud of dust. Like an angel straight from heaven, Joe moved to the back doors, opening them wide before running back and jumping into the driver's seat. Flynn rode a burst of adrenaline, his legs rallying as he mimicked Sergeant McCoy, jumping into the Humvee like he was Superman. He pulled himself up and into a seat as the vehicle lurched forward. Barnes, Bollick, and Laster were running behind, struggling to grab onto to something, their eyes bugging with fear. Joe mercifully slowed the roll, letting them catch up and crawl in. Barnes barely struggled in, his legs hanging out as Joe stomped the gas pedal. He had a death grip on the steering wheel, bouncing up and down in his seat as if it would help get going.

Sergeant McCoy appeared to have lost it, cackling and pointing at Bollick. "You should have seen the look on your face! You thought we were leaving you!" He leaned in his seat, slapping his thigh and breaking into hysterical laughter.

Bollick recoiled. "What the—? Hey, fuck you, asshole!" he said feebly through panting breaths.

Sergeant McCoy rubbed his hands together, his eyes less than optimistic as he scanned out of the dirty back windows. "Goddamn, I hope we make it out of here."

Joe turned around, looking grim. "Batten down any open windows or loose doors where heat can find its way in. If you have any water, pour it over your exposed skin then grab your asses and kiss them goodbye because we've got a snowball's chance of making it out of this valley before those incendiaries go off."

McCoy blinked slowly at the statement, seeming to sober up. "Thank God for you, Joe. I hope you don't regret it in a few moments."

Joe clenched his jaw. "The thought did cross my mind. I have never been accused of being smart." His knuckles blanched as he gripped the steering wheel, pressing his foot farther, the floorboard flexing with an audible pop.

Flynn struggled with the small blast window near him. The mechanism was caked with grit, the window tilted wide open. "Joe! I can't get it to close." Flynn hit it again and again. "Dammit, what's the trick?"

Joe yelled back. "Hit it harder. Just get it closed!" The Humvee bounced violently, throwing them into the ceiling. Flynn grabbed the edge of his seat, watching Joe with concern as the man fought the terrain for control of the front suspension. Joe wrestled with the truck and leveled it out then glanced over his shoulder, offering an optimistic expression. "Thirty seconds and we'll be out of the valley."

Sergeant McCoy's terror-spiked voice filled the Humvee. "There they go!"

Flynn's heart skipped a beat. He flinched at the blinding flashes of light like hundreds of flashbulbs going off inside of the Humvee. "God, no!" a voice Flynn hardly recognized as his own bleated. He slammed the palm of his hand against the small window as he squinted out of the rear glass. The explosions coalesced until the whole mountain was engulfed in a daisy chain of fireballs. The explosions illuminated the massive shock wave traveling across the sand at supersonic speed. Flynn shut his eyes, his head snapping back as the wave slammed into the rear of the truck, thrusting it forward, thick sandy air spraying into the Humvee through the open window. Crack! The window shut as Flynn struck it one last time and turned the handle. Milliseconds later an immense wave of heat followed the shock wave through the valley. Flynn bounced around, looking out the back window. Hundreds of acacia trees and scrub bushes were bursting into flames less than a mile behind. Like a devil from the depths of hell, the burning bushes gained on the Humvee with terrifying speed. He turned and looked out of the windshield. The bushes ahead were igniting, the temperature in the Humvee rising. Flynn pulled his 9 mm and sat it on his lap. I'll kill myself before I'll burn. He took one last gulp of air and ducked, pushing his face into the pistol and sitting on his bare hands as the Humvee became like an oven.

"Please, God! Not like this!" Barnes begged.

Flynn's ears burned now, and it was too hot to inhale. Guttural, grizzly-bearlike roars, as much fear as pain, filled the cab as they began to burn. Flynn kept his eyes closed, concentrating on the only positive stimulus, the sound of the GM 6.5-liter turbo diesel screaming at its limit. He willed his energy into the engine, trying to ignore the building pain. Just as it felt he must inhale, the heat dissipated. He rose up, focusing on hundreds of huge dirt devils left spinning all around, some destroyed by the fast-moving Humvee as they drove through them. Flynn inhaled slowly at first then sucked in hot but breathable air. His jaw dropped at the sight of the driver. The exposed skin of Joe's neck was a mass of blisters, bubbles growing before his eyes. The brave man had stuck with it. Moaning in pain, Joe kept his right foot buried, never slowing until they slid into the safe zone around the headquarters.

As he climbed out of the Humvee, Flynn marveled at the courageous man. It was one of the bravest displays he had ever seen. As he stood, wondering how he was alive, his attention was drawn to people stampeding out of the tents into the open. They were everywhere, jumping and hugging in emotional outpours. Flynn looked over his shoulder one last time at the Humvee. All four tires were blazing rings of fire. He nudged Bollick, nodding toward the vehicle. "Look at that melted gun rack on the back." Bollick rubbed his hand over his head then took a run at Sergeant McCoy and bear-hugged the man before holding him out at arm's length. "I'm sorry I called you an asshole."

The salt-and-pepper-haired commando grinned as he wiped his eyes. "I'm sorry too. I suffer from nervous laughter." His eyes twinkled for a moment. "We did it! Thank you, all of you." Sergeant McCoy placed his hand on his chest and turned to the Humvee's driver. "Joe, I've never seen anything so brave in my life. I'll tell my children and grandchildren about you." Sergeant McCoy embraced the man then released him, turning around, his eyes locking onto Flynn. "I've never encountered a more adaptable group of operatives. You came in here green and did a helluva job, one that I've failed at for two years." His inner brows rose high. "It's a testament to you, and it's a testament to ORION."

Flynn grinned, warmth rushing through him. "I get to go home because of you guys." He alternated eye contact between Joe and Sergeant McCoy. "Thank you both for sticking by us." Flynn noticed Sergeant McCoy didn't seem to hear him, the man's countenance changing as if preoccupied with something. Sergeant McCoy took out his pistol, pulling back the breech a fraction and peering in before slamming it shut and holstering the gun. He turned and started toward the command tent. "Excuse me, gentlemen. I'm going to rid the world of that piece of human waste," he said matter-of-factly as he started toward the tent, rolling up his sleeves as he went.

***

Barnes put his arms around Laster and Bollick's shoulders. "I guess we did it!? We're done, right?" Barnes stared at them as if amazed they were still alive. "I thought we were fried chicken for sure." He released the two and turned to the driver. "Joe, outside of my crew here, you are the craziest, most heroic son of a bitch that I have ever met. Thank you."

The man offered a sigh of relief, mustering a twisted smile as he touched the blistered skin. "My neck isn't happy about it, but I'm just glad it worked out."

Bollick walked over, peering at Flynn with concern. "What's the matter? Are you hurt?"

Flynn managed a tight-lipped smile. It didn't matter what he told himself. He couldn't share in their triumph anymore. All he could see was their faces, the visions torturing him. Izzy's face, not the beautiful smiling Izzy but the empty shell, eyes opaque and hair matted with blood. The impressionable boy, cold and dead in his grave. The broken-hearted Hamasa. Sher Dil howling on the runway. "I want to get Sher Dil and get out of here. I'm never coming back."

Bollick looked to the west. "Rescuing Sher Dil will make us all feel better." He stared deeply at Flynn as if he understood every emotion he was experiencing. He put a hand on Flynn's shoulder. "Don't be too hard on yourself. I was in Nimroz too, and I say you did one helluva job."

Laster seemed to agree, grinning like he had won the lottery. "A good job indeed."

Flynn focused on the familiar form of Hoyt Green, dancing two steps forward then one step back, meandering toward them with a look of satisfaction. "Gentlemen, my deepest and warmest congratulations on a superb job!" He raised his half-full glass of scotch. "Down the hatch!" Hoyt turned up the glass, making a face and shuddering as he recovered. He looked at Flynn as if he had something to share. "I'm sending patrols out tonight if you want to go back and examine the mountain."

Flynn massaged his temples. "Mr. Green, if it's all the same to you, I'm anxious to get Sher Dil, and everyone's ready to head home. Too much excitement for us here in Bamyan." Flynn imagined Colonel Pitts's sneering face. "Any word on Colonel Pitts's whereabouts?"

Hoyt crossed his arms and frowned. "Hunh-uh. The slippery son of a bitch vanished into thin air. Rest assured, I won't stop searching until he is located."

"He beat me at every turn and took some precious things from me. I just wish someday I come face to face with that bastard."

Bang! A gunshot from inside the tent made Flynn freeze. The shot was followed by yelling.

Hoyt's eyes grew as he spun around. "Oh no, Sergeant McCoy!" Hoyt turned and sprinted toward the tent, vanishing under the flap entrance.

Bollick scratched his chin. "Damn, I thought he was just talking shit. Do you think he killed Randall?"

Flynn shrugged. "If he did, he just threw his life away for a—"

"There's Hoyt!" Bollick blurted, pointing to the tent.

Hoyt Green was grim-faced as he emerged. He walked toward Flynn, shaking his head. "I know I promised to fly you to Camp Rock, but I can't. There's been a change of plans."

A sinking feeling hit him. "Change of plans! What do you mean, change of plans? You promised me. It was part of the deal. We go to Camp Rock today!"

Hoyt glared, his upper lip quivering. "What is it with you and your bleeding-heart affinity for that damned animal?"

Flynn stepped into Hoyt. "My passion for that animal is something you couldn't understand. Maybe it's because he saved my team at a time when I couldn't do it myself. When he did, he became one of us. I owe him."

Laster stepped up. "We don't leave one of our own behind, including that 'damned' animal."

Hoyt put his palms out, taking a step back. "Okay, okay. I'll have my pilot fly to Camp Rock, but there's a condition. He pointed toward the Command Center. "I have six armed men guarding Randall Gibbs as we speak. Sergeant McCoy just took a shot at him."

"You should have let him kill the bastard!" Flynn said.

"I have too much respect for Sergeant McCoy. I wouldn't let him ruin his life over that sociopath." Hoyt shook his head in disgust. "I'm tired of negotiating with Randall Gibbs. The fact is, I don't need him anymore."

Flynn pointed to the tent. "Well, arrest him then. That son of a bitch tried to kill the whole team."

"Randall claims he forgot."

Flynn's face grew hot. "Forgot that he turned off the eLORAN patch? Forget he didn't give Joe an order to drive out? He even forgot that he turned off the satcom and the UHF radio? What the fuck, Hoyt?"

Hoyt recoiled. "I had nothing to do with this. I'm sending him back to the States on suspension of duty until a court-martial can be arranged." Hoyt reached out and touched Flynn's arm. "Commander, I see it's hard for you, but please understand I'm doing this on behalf of Sergeant McCoy. Randall Gibbs is going out on my 737 with you guys whether you like it or not." Hoyt pointed a finger at Flynn. "That's final, and you're lucky I'm doing that."

Flynn felt as if he had been kicked in the gut. He glowered at Hoyt. "I swear, Mr. Green, I'll kill that son of a bitch if you put him on that plane with me. Then I'll be in trouble again. Don't do that to ME. Don't put him on that plane, I'm warning you!"

Hoyt glanced around uneasily. "I have to put him on that plane, Commander. I don't have a choice. He'll be unarmed and cuffed, under the constant supervision of Agent Schillings."

Flynn scoffed. "Agent Schillings is Randall's personal bootlicker."

Hoyt shook his head. "No, Schillings is a good agent. He's just able to communicate with Randall." Hoyt held up his hands, palms out. "Mr. Flynn, please, I've made arrangements for Randall to be arrested at Frankfurt. The rest of the way home, you guys will have the jet for yourselves. I promise he won't be any trouble."

CHAPTER 48

Flynn fought to ignore the building knot in his stomach. "I've got a bad feeling about this, Brian."

Bollick's brows scrunched together. "Me too. We have to be ready for anything." He patted his waistband. "I have that little .380 Sergeant McCoy gave me last night. If they frisk us, it'll be hard to find. Let's hope we don't need it," said Bollick.

Flynn patted his own waist. "I have one as well."

A cloud of dust covered them as the Humvee rolled up to the tent. Laster and Barnes got in first, followed by Bollick and Flynn, who crawled to the back seat. They pulled onto the airstrip and rolled to the hangar. A small group of soldiers stood around Randall Gibbs, who was in handcuffs, standing next to Agent Schillings with his chin to his chest.

Flynn grabbed some gear, leading the others to the stairs under the plane's front entrance. As they gathered, three MPs stopped him. The largest of them, a

Neanderthal-looking man with a huge brow ridge, put a stiff arm into Flynn's chest. "Hold your horses. I gotta make sure you're unarmed."

Flynn grabbed the MP's hand as his pistol was discovered. "Hands off. You can't have it."

Agent Schillings had moved with Randall to the bottom of the wheeled staircase. His eyes tightened. "Hoyt doesn't want his jet shot up at thirty-five-thousand feet. Let him have the pistol and any other weapon on you."

"Hey, as long as that lout is in cuffs, what does it matter? I'm sure Gibbs has a couple of his own. Have you searched him?"

Agent Schillings glanced at Randall. "He's already been checked. Just give up the weapon and get on the damn plane."

Flynn's eyes bored into Randall then into Schillings as the MP confiscated the pistol.

"Ha, ha, ha, ha! What you scared of, boy?" Randall said, his bloodshot eyes huge. "You ain't got a pistol big enough to stop me!" He held up his cuffed hands. "When I get out of these, you're a dead man."

Let it go. Think about Sher Dil. Think about Mom. He fought the urge to punch Gibbs in the throat, forcing himself up the stairs.

"Oh, to hell with that!" boomed a deep voice from behind him.

Flynn looked over his shoulder. Brian Bollick stood like a leviathan in front of Randall. Bollick built force from the ground then threw his hips and shoulders as he spun into the blow. Crunch. Bollick's fist found its way through Randall's belly, striking the huge man's spine. Randall fell to the ground and curled into a ball as Bollick shoved Agent Schillings, the man cartwheeling back and falling onto his butt. Bollick knelt over Gibbs, rifling through his pockets and patting him down. Bollick's hand stopped on something. He reached under Randall's waistband and pulled out a small pistol. "Imagine my surprise," he said, holding a .45 Glock in the air and tossing it to Agent Schillings. Bollick then pulled a tiny .380 pistol from an ankle holster hidden in Randall's boot. He stood and walked to Agent Schillings, bumping the man with his chest. "Give me one reason not to shove this up your ass, you powderpuff motherfucker!" He took Agent Schillings's hand and slapped the pistol into it. "Either you take care of this psychopath or I will." Schillings shrank as Bollick turned and walked up the stairs, muttering something inaudible.

Flynn wandered to the back of the plane, collapsing into one of the rows of seats.

Bollick followed him to the back, pointing to the opposite row. "These seats taken?" he said as he dumped his gear and sat down. "One more leg and we're outta here."

"Fuck you! I'll kill you, motherfucker!" screamed someone at the front of the plane. Randall Gibbs was kicking at Barnes, who was laughing, staying just out of range.

"I wish he wouldn't torment that schizoid," Flynn said.

Bollick's nose wrinkled. "I'd like to think he's headed to Leavenworth after this is all said and done, but I'm less than optimistic."

"They should send him to Camp Rock to replace Colonel Pitts. God knows he has the temperament."

Bollick blinked. "I can't believe Hoyt let him on the plane with us. You'd think he would be afraid that we'd kill the bastard."

"Maybe that's what he's counting on, to kill two birds with one stone."

Bollick waved Gibbs away, turning back to Flynn. "Do they have Sher Dil at Camp Rock like they said they would?"

Flynn offered a slight shrug. "Who knows if the plane will even land there? We've been lied to so many times."

"Well, I think we're headed to Camp Rock," Bollick said.

"We got your back, Flynn," said Laster. "If I have to hijack this plane myself, I will. No way we leave without him."

"Thanks, guys. It's good to have you on my side."

Bollick pointed his finger at Flynn. "Remember you said that. You may feel differently after you get to know me better."

Flynn chuckled, warmth spreading through him. It felt good to laugh.

***

"Prepare for landing," a voice blared over the intercom. Flynn set his jaw as he focused, his muscles tightening. It's time to take back what belongs to you. "Bollick, keep a close eye on me and on Gibbs. I may get distracted and let my guard down."

"Don't worry. I won't let him out of my sight," he said, grinding his fist into his hand. "I just hope he does something stupid."

Flynn looked out of the small window, the desert floor rising toward him. The 737 bounced down hard then straightened out, reverse thrusters roaring. The plane rolled over the bumpy surface to one end of the airstrip then turned in a half-circle, coming to a stop near a small control tower. A skinny, boyish-looking pilot emerged from the cabin. He ambled down the aisle, stopping at the rear door. The slight man got his hips under him and powered up against the latch, tripping it with a loud thump and swinging the door open. He turned around and smiled at Flynn. "You're the guy everyone's talking about. Commander Flynn, right?"

"Yeah, don't tell anyone, kid."

"It is an honor to meet you sir. You have no idea what it's been like in Bamyan this year."

"I believe you! Just do me a favor and get us out of here in one piece."

"Yes, sir." The pilot smiled and strode to the opening, leaning down and securing the staircase to the jet.

Flynn made eye contact with Bollick and Laster, then ducked his head under the door frame and exited the plane. He trotted down the stairs, scanning the runway.

His heart pounded, his face beaming as he spotted two men with a large dog less than a quarter-mile away. He quickened his step and sprinted toward Sher Dil. Randall Gibbs was the furthest thing from his mind.

CHAPTER 49

Bollick feigned sleep, reclining with a sweat-stained canvas hat pulled down over his face. He peered from under the brim, cataloging Randall's movements at the front of the plane. He growled with anger as Agent Schillings took Randall's cuffs off. The psychopath's hands gesticulated with emotion, punctuating an intense monologue to Schillings, his obviously uninterested babysitter. Bollick removed the hollowed-out Bible from his bag, opening the cover and reaching in for the hidden .380 automatic. He grasped the cold metal barrel and pulled out the weapon. He surreptitiously slid the pistol under a jacket on his lap, the barrel pointing toward the aisle Gibbs would come down. Randall Gibbs telegraphed his intentions like a child. Socially, Randall Gibbs was no smooth operator, but the powerful man was resourceful, genuinely psychotic, and not to be underestimated. Bollick took a deep breath and readied himself. He must crush Randall before the man uncorked his homicidal rage. Bollick's eye twitched as he considered the predicament. He was finally in a position of success, and Randall Gibbs was about to take it away. His hand tightened on the sharply textured grip of the pistol.

***

Salar Khan stood next to Axl Herron, who was straining to hold a leash attached to Sher Dil. Sher Dil yanked wildly against it, rising up on his hind legs. Axl fell back on his butt, the leash snapping. Sher Dil tore away, his now nourished muscles straining against the bone and sinew of his frame, his thick red tongue flopping out of the side of his mouth. Sher Dil closed the distance like an incoming missile, leaping into the air and crashing chest to chest with Flynn. Oomph! The impact knocked the wind from Flynn's lungs, paralyzing his diaphragm. He curled up in a ball and covered up, Sher Dil licking the side of his face and pawing his shoulder. Through stilted inhalations, he got a small amount of air. "Off," he said feebly, shielding his head from the heavy claws. He coaxed his lungs to take fresh air. Sher Dil's wet tongue went inside of his mouth just as he was inhaling. "Sher Dil!" Flynn gave up, scrambling to his feet to escape the onslaught. Whimpering, Sher Dil jumped up and put his front paws on Flynn's shoulders. The animal stood face to face with him, licking his beard with the huge, slobbery tongue. "I'm glad to see you too but stop it!" Sher Dil pressed his massive head into Flynn's stomach as if embarrassed by his own outburst.

Someone approached from behind. Flynn spun his head around, looking over his shoulder. Salar was strutting toward him, his arms opened wide. The jolly Pashtun flashed his toothless grin, his chest rising and falling with laughter. He wrapped Flynn in a rib-breaking hug, slapping his back with bearlike power. "Salaam Alaikum." Salar stepped back, his hands still on Flynn's shoulders. "My dear friend, I see you are alive and that pleases me greatly!" He frowned for a moment. "I was sure that you would not return." He glanced over his shoulder warily before turning back to face Flynn. "I have something for you. Tell no one." Salar slipped a yellow note card into Flynn's hand, again glancing around.

Flynn's brow furrowed as he looked at the front and back of the yellow paper card. Rows of numbers were neatly printed on one side. He folded the paper, placing it in his pocket. "What is it?"

Salar leaned forward, speaking in a hushed tone. "Bank account numbers to Colonel Pitts's private account in the Caymans." Salar put a hand over his mouth. "An account containing one hundred and thirty-five million dollars." His face beamed, eyes growing as he nodded with affirmation. "I verified the accounts myself."

"Salar, I don't understand. How—"

An expression, together wicked and amused, rose on Salar's face. He lowered his head, looking up through his brow. "Colonel Pitts and Scarface were captured on the road to Islamabad. Colonel Pitts used those accounts to barter for his life."

Flynn gasped and stepped back. "You have Major Roberts and Colonel Pitts?"

Salar turned and spat on the ground. "The scar-faced man was left in the desert. Colonel Pitts wasn't so lucky. He has been Hamasa's most special houseguest."

Flynn's eyes widened, his body shuddering as he thought of Adam then of Hamasa's severe eyes.

Salar nudged him. "Lucky for you, an old criminal like myself can't get to the money," he laughed, his eyes heavy from hashish and opium. "Believe me, I tried."

Flynn slipped the paper into his pocket, unmoved by the thought of the money. He leaned toward Salar, speaking in his ear. "Colonel Pitts, is he dead?"

Salar sighed, his shoulders dropping. "Yes, much to Hamasa's disappointment. Colonel Pitts was strong, but an abdominal infection got out of Hamasa's control." Salar pinched his nose, a look of distaste coming upon his face. "It was terrible. I almost felt sorry for the devil at the end."

Flynn felt a sense of satisfaction. He shrugged. "He deserved no better." He fought to repress the morbid curiosity entering his mind. Colonel Pitts must have endured terrible things. "At least he won't hurt anyone now." Flynn's expression lightened. "Enough of that rat. What about you? Where will you go now, brother?"

Salar's beard blew in the wind as he pointed north. "Home to my wife and children where I belong. My sons and I can afford to live honestly for the rest of our lives." He held himself high.

Flynn smirked at the thought of the proud man's illegitimate gains. "I cracked up when the recovery team was so excited about the three tons of heroin they recovered from the pass and Camp Rock." He mocked seriousness, shaking his finger at Salar. "You are damn lucky. One of them was considering firing on your truck when you and Hamasa were headed out of the north gate, but I told them you were friendly before they fired the rocket."

Salar's eyes sparkled with mischief. "That's why you will always be my American brother and why the money is yours." Salar pointed at the jet. "I think they are waiting for you."

Flynn hugged Salar then held him at arm's length, clutching his shoulders. "I will never forget you. Thank you—for everything."

Salar's eyes glistened. "Go with Allah and be sheltered by his loving generosity." He bowed slightly then turned and walked away, singing in his native tongue.

Flynn's eyes welled with tears as Salar disappeared around the hangar. He wiped away the hot tears and looked down at Sher Dil, who was watching the Pashtun stroll away. Flynn turned and walked to Agent Herron, now standing by himself, the short end of a broken leash dangling from his right hand.

The agent shook his hand, an ear-to-ear grin on his face. "Axl Herron. We met here last month. You remember, right?"

Flynn flashed an embarrassed smile. "I sort of remember you."

Axl snickered. "Considering the circumstances, that's pretty respectable. You were trashed." Axl glanced down at Sher Dil. "That's one fine specimen you have there, Commander." Axl's eyes shone with affection. "I've been feeding him all the rice and chicken I can lay my hands on. He let me slip a leash on him two days ago, and last night he even slept in my room."

Flynn scowled at Sher Dil. "Already working the field, huh?" He scratched Sher Dil's head. "He's quick to figure out who's buttering his bread, isn't he?" Flynn put his clenched fist to his heart. "Mr. Herron, I don't know if you have any idea what this animal means to me but thank you for taking care of him."

"Don't mention it."

Flynn glanced at his wristwatch then looked back at the jet. "I hate to run, but the pilot is in a hurry." He shook Axl's hand with both of his. "You're a good man, Agent Herron. Salaam."

The agent nodded crisply. "You're welcome. And call me Axl."

Flynn nodded at Sher Dil. "Come on, Super Dog. Let's go home."

***

Randall Gibbs's skin burned as he observed them through the portal window. The accusations made by Sergeant McCoy and Flynn would end his career. *I have nothing, no future whatsoever, and now he's going to pay.* Randall's chest rose and fell rapidly as Flynn and the dog turned and started back toward the plane. He stood and stretched, beginning his walk to the back.

Agent Schillings cut his eyes at him. "Where the hell do you think you're going?"

Randall shrugged. "Coffee is in the back galley. Want some?" He asked in the most innocent voice he could muster.

Agent Schillings rubbed his bloodshot eyes. "Damn it, Randall!" He poked a finger at him. "I uncuffed you and now you're pushing it. Sit back down."

Randall put his hands out. "I'm just going for coffee, I swear."

"Randall, if you go back there and start shit with those guys—" Agent Schillings patted his pistol, sticking out from the belt holster. "You heard Hoyt. You know what I have to do if you misbehave."

Randall frowned at the rebuke from the usually docile Schillings, walking away anyway. "What a cunt. He doesn't have the stones," he said under his breath as he moved toward the rear galley. He focused on his physical nemesis, Brian Bollick. The ill-tempered man appeared to be asleep. He was reclined, a faded desert hat over his face and a small jacket stretched over his body. "Schillings, you want a cup?" he asked loudly, observing Brian Bollick for a reaction.

***

Bollick listened intently to the sounds of Randall making coffee. His hair stood on end when he heard the clang of Flynn's boots coming up the rickety metal staircase. Flynn would have to walk right past Randall Gibbs. Bollick tensed as he leaned into the aisle, peering from under the brim of the stale-smelling hat. His right hand tightened around the pistol grip as the other pulled off the hat and blanket. Sher Dil was the first on.

Upon seeing Randall, he lunged without warning, clamping onto Randall's right calf, shaking furiously.

"Arrgh!" Randall reached into his waistband, pulling out a small 9-mm pistol that Bollick must have missed.

Bollick leaped into the galley, kicking Randall's hand. The small pistol bounced off the plane's ceiling then fell to the floor with a clunk. Sher Dil released and scampered behind him as Bollick took a step back, bringing the .380 level to Randall's face. He bent and picked up the 9 mm, tossing it to Laster. Bollick looked through the gun sights at Randall Gibbs. "Give me a reason."

Randall raised his hands. "What? I was just getting coffee, and that dog attacked me for no reason. I—"

Flynn emerged from the dark. He crept in and bent over, pushing the stairs away from the rear door. He took a step forward, his fist a blur, slamming it crisply into the back of Randall's neck. Randall teetered backward, spinning to face the assault as Flynn struck again. Blood splattered the ceiling as Randall's head snapped back. His nose twitched with rage as he spat several teeth on the floor. He grinned, wiping the blood away with the back of his sleeve. Randall Gibbs glanced at Bollick then back to Flynn. "You don't hit any harder than that pussy."

Bollick was still crouched in combat stance, pointing the pistol at Randall's head. "Make a move and I'll kill you, Randall!"

Randall turned to Bollick, his red face swollen with rage. "Well, fuckin' do it!" Randall turned away and stepped toward Flynn.

Flynn reached over to the galley kitchen, wrapping his fingers around the handle of the heavy metal coffeepot. He ducked the clumsy punch, swinging the makeshift weapon like a right hook. The metal pot bent around Randall's jaw, the giant's eyes rolling back. Randall staggered back a step, almost falling out of the door before catching himself on the frame of the fuselage, his countenance already returning. Flynn chose his target, visualizing a point a foot behind Randall's chest. He leapt into the sidekick, snapping his lower leg into the strike, turning his heel at impact. Flynn's boot disappeared into Randall chest, breaking the giant's grip, sending him hurtling into the abyss. Flynn felt a lightness pulse through his body as he rushed forward, grabbing the door and slamming it shut. He turned the lever counterclockwise and latched the airlock. Flynn stood panting at the rear of the plane. He turned and grabbed the small blue phone, mounted on the wall. "This is Commander Flynn. The rear door is secure, and the passengers are ready for takeoff!"

The small team broke out in joyous yelling and whooping, almost a battle cry. Sher Dil joined in, yelping and howling as he sat in the seat next to Flynn. The pilot's boyish voice blared over the intercom. "Brace for full-power takeoff."

Flynn tightened his belt and put his left arm over Sher Dil, barely fitting in the seat next to him. The lightly loaded 737 rocketed down the runway with a thunderous rumble of vibration and noise, pressing Flynn into the seat as it lifted off and angled high into the sky.

***

Axl Herron gasped in horror. A large man hurtled into the air, striking with an audible slap as his body hit the concrete runway. Concern gripped him, his eyes widening as the incredible thrust of the engines blew the hapless man down the abrasive runway like a tumbleweed. "My God," he muttered as he began to run.

Ghost Platoon

ABOUT THE AUTHOR

John "Jay" C. Campbell is a practicing Radiologist at Titus Regional Medical Center in Mt. Pleasant Texas. He was born in Perryton, Texas.

Printed in Great Britain
by Amazon